A SNOWSTORM OF MAGIC

A HAUNTED LAW FIRM NOVEL

ROBERT L. ARRINGTON

Book Design by HMDpublishing

ISBN: 978-0-578-92124-2

DEDICATION

I have acknowledged the support of my sweet wife in both of my previous novels. But it's time to move her to the front of the book.

To Deborah Patrice Harvey Arrington

Sweetheart, this one's for you.

CONTENT

PROLOGUE

Rob Ashworth guided the Honda CR-V up the winding road from the state four-lane connector toward the Tompkins house. The road was good, but steep, with numerous switchbacks, and required concentration.

Samantha sat silent beside him while they drove. He glanced at her from time to time, and she at him, her expression apprehensive, even though in theory there was no reason to be. It was two days before Christmas, and they had been invited to celebrate the holiday at the castle-like retirement home of James Wilson Tompkins, a most important client of both Rob's law firm and her accounting firm. They had been promised a fabulous holiday.

They should be tingling with anticipation. But they weren't.

Samantha finally said, her voice a bit timid, "Honey, you're not saying anything. Are you all right?"

"Switchbacks," he replied.

His answer emboldened her to challenge him, although after hesitation, "Is that all? You've talked on roads like these before. Are...are you thinking about last Saturday?"

He didn't answer, and she prompted, "Rob? Did you hear me?"

Finally, he answered, "Yeah. Some."

Sweetsen, Melton & Associates, CPAs, PLLC, had spared no reasonable expense for its Christmas party. The event occupied the small ballroom at the Martintown Country Club. There was a long table with heavy hors d'oeuvres, and a live dance band. Holiday decorations were everywhere.

At the moment, despite the surroundings, Rob Ashworth – associate attorney with Norville, Melton & Jennings, PLLC, married to a young accountant who was the daughter of the Melton in Sweetsen, Melton and employed by the other Melton, her father – was not feeling particularly festive. He sat by himself at a small table at the back, nursing the remnants of a gin and tonic, sucking on ice cubes, and watching the room.

His wife of three years was on the dance floor at the front of the ballroom, directly in front of the band. She had been there most of the night, but not, for a long time, with Rob.

The evening had started well enough. Rob and Sam had a couple of dances, and then chatted amiably. Then Will Sweetsen had asked Samantha to dance. She'd explained in advance to Rob that Sweetsen felt obligated to ask all the young female accountants, so he'd expected that she'd dance with him. No problem.

And then Tom Carter, an associate accountant a couple of years senior to Samantha, had asked her to dance, explaining, "I can't get my wife to dance." Rob was a good sport, and had nodded. It was okay to sit one out, although he really wanted to dance with Sam again.

The problem was that Tom wouldn't let Samantha go. He kept her on the floor for set after set. Rob could see her now on the floor, her dark, shoulder-length tresses swaying to the music. After a while, Rob had gone to the bar for another gin and tonic, and moved to a table at the back, conscious of others' eyes on him.

Ever since their dating days, he had had to get used to Sam attracting a great deal of admiring male attention. Relatively tall and long-legged, curvy, dark wavy hair, and enormous brown eyes will do that with regularity. But tonight? This was getting ridiculous.

Rob's eyes roved over the room. He saw Tom's wife sitting at a table toward the front, quite pretty with short-bobbed blonde hair, watching her husband dance with Samantha, evidently unconcerned, and sometimes dropping a comment to an older couple, whom Rob didn't know, sitting at the same table. Against the wall to the right sat Sam's mother, Libby, and her husband, Jack, engrossed in conversation with Will Sweetsen and his wife, Barbara.

At least here, no one was paying him any attention. He had danced once with a staff accountant whose husband was engaged in serious drinking, and had tried, unsuccessfully, to catch Sam's eye. But mostly he sat alone, sucking on ice cubes, and from time to time pushing his coppery hair, which really had needed a cut, except that a brief that was due in Bankruptcy Court had kept him from it, out of his eyes.

The present song ended and the dancers applauded. The band announced a short break. Rob saw Samantha's eyes wander the room and finally see him. She wound her way to him. Finally.

When she sat, he said, keeping (he hoped) the irritation out of his voice, "Welcome back."

"You moved," she said. "Why?"

"Oh, I got tired of sitting in front," he lied. "Can I get you a drink?"

She asked for a white wine, and he obliged by going to the bar. The line was long, filled with thirsty dancers, and by the time he returned with her plastic cup of Pinot gris, the band was ready to resume. They struck up "Taking a Chance on Love."

"Would you like to dance?" he asked. "This is a nice song."

Samantha sipped from her cup and shook her head. "Honey, I am really tired right now. Maybe in a few minutes."

Rob nodded, disappointed. But he expected to take her out on the dance floor once she had rested. His eyes roved the room again.

And then he saw Tom Carter winding his way to them, a wide smile on his face. Surely, he wasn't coming back to Samantha. But Rob knew he was, and he did.

Carter bent over Sam's shoulder and said, "Would you like to dance?" This time, there were no apologies, no explanations.

"I'd love to," Samantha said without a glance at Rob, and rose immediately. Carter led her to the dance floor.

Rob watched them go. He hadn't expected what had just happened.

His looked around the room again. Thankfully, no one was looking at him. He glanced at his watch. The evening was well on, but not nearly at an end. He wasn't sure what to do with himself. Except for the Meltons, he really didn't know anyone. Four years into practice, he was still a relatively junior attorney. So not much of anyone knew him, either. He considered asking Carter's wife for a dance. Turnabout, after all, was fair play. But he didn't know her, and he hadn't seen her dance all evening. She'd doubtless turn him down.

So he sat and sucked on another ice cube. Then it hit him. He could leave. He could go home. And yes, he could turn off his cell phone. Let Samantha figure it out. If Carter wouldn't run her home, then surely her parents would.

There was a downside to this course. It would 'attract the attention of' Jack Melton, his boss, and not in a good way. But at the moment, he didn't know what else to do except to just sit there.

From where he sat, the coat check was only a few feet away. It would take only a moment to get there. He was not intoxicated. The drive to the apartment would be no problem. It seemed a better plan than sucking on more ice cubes.

"Rob?"

He looked up to see Jack Melton, frosty hair and square face and all, hovering over his right shoulder. His boss.

"Sir," Rob said, automatically.

"Come on," Melton said. "Let's get a drink." He motioned toward the bar.

Rob really didn't feel like a drink, but thought he'd better have one. He nodded and rose to his feet.

At the bar, Melton ordered two expensive single malt Scotches, and insisted on glass snifters and not plastic cups. The two said nothing until the drinks arrived, and Melton lifted one, saying, "Cheers."

Rob had to admit the whiskey was good, and said so, with his thanks.

"If you think I'm doing this to thank you for your work on the Tompkins case," Melton began, "you're right. The brief was first class."

"Thank you, sir," Rob said, his head bobbing.

"But, if you think that's all this drink is about," Melton continued, "you're wrong. Libby and I have noticed what's been going on tonight. You don't think we have, probably, but we have."

"Tonight?" Rob asked, pretending not to understand,

"Don't give me that, Rob. You know what I'm talking about. Libby is going to talk with Samantha about it. In fact, she probably is doing that right now."

Rob looked past Melton's shoulder to see his wife seated at the table with his mother-in-law, an older and a bit plumper version of herself, in what seemed to be intense conversation. To their left, Carter was back at the table with his wife, but letting his eyes dart toward Samantha and her mother – who was one of his bosses, too – with some apprehension.

Bob still said nothing, but regarded Melton with raised eyebrows.

Melton smiled. "I've seen this before, Rob. No, not with Lib. Certainly not with Sam. With Susan."

Rob let his brows lift again. Who was Susan?

"My first wife," Melton explained. "The difference is this: Susan really was preparing to be unfaithful, preparing to leave. With Sam...well, she just likes the attention.

"But she has embarrassed you, and she and Carter have embarrassed her mother's firm. We can't have that.

"All I'm asking you is to treat her gently. You have a lot of time ahead of you."

Rob nodded and said nothing. They finished their drinks and returned to their tables. Samantha rose from her parents' table a few minutes later. Wherever she'd been heading, Carter intercepted her and led her back to the dance floor, talking in her ear the whole way.

To hell with this, Rob decided. He was at the coat check in a few steps. He presented his ticket to a bored young woman, thankful that Samantha had her own ticket in her purse. Leaving a single ticket for her would have been...awkward.

"Leaving us?" she asked.

He improvised. "I may be back," he said. "A dose of the night air may solve the headache."

She handed him his coat with a wan smile and a wish for him to feel better.

He left, and, as near as he could figure out, no one noticed.

As soon as Rob was in his car, he realized he didn't really want to go home, and just sit and wait. But where else would he go?

Then he remembered there was supposed to be a torch singer whom everyone was talking about at the cocktail lounge of the new hotel. That might be worth checking out. He didn't have to drink a lot more, and maybe his return home would coincide more closely with Sam's more closely.

The hotel was closer to downtown than the club, so it took a few minutes to get there. When he arrived, he found several parking spaces. Evidently the place wasn't going to be packed tonight.

Inside, he found most of the tables occupied, but several spots remained open at the bar. He hung his overcoat on the rack provided, and found a seat at the far end, away from the few patrons seated there.

A cheerful bartender in a tuxedo shirt and bow tie brought him a generous pour of B&B, something he could sip slowly. After a tongue-wetting sip, he turned toward the stage. There was a piano and a pianist, but no band. There was also a standing microphone.

And then he saw, really saw, the singer to whom he had listened absently while walking in. She was tall for a woman, maybe as tall as his five-nine, and certainly taller in the heels she was wearing. She also wore a shimmery red gown, long but with a slit skirt, and low cut at the bosom, that hugged a figure to make men gawk and women envy.

Her hair was somewhere between dark auburn and Rob's own strawberry blond. It shimmered in the lights over the stage, competing with her gown. Her nose was long and straight, her cheekbones high, her mouth wide. At this distance, he couldn't tell the color of her eyes. She was, all in all, an arresting sight.

What was her name? It was on an easel billboard outside. Christine, no, Christina O'Donnell, it had said.

As he watched, she thanked the audience in a husky contralto and began another song.

I'll be around, no matter how you treat me now;

I'll be around when she's gone.

Your latest love will never last, and when it's passed...

Rob shifted uneasily on the hard bar stool. This song was a little too close to what was at the front of his mind this evening. He startled when a voice at his left ear said, "Well, hello, Rob. What are you doing here by yourself this evening?"

He turned and looked up to see Jimmy Tompkins, the older son of James Tompkins Sr. and now CEO of Jiffy Markets, the client in the recently resolved action in Bankruptcy Court. Tompkins was over six feet tall, thin and ascetic-looking like his father, long-nosed with thinning brown hair touched with gray. Tonight, he wore a holiday sweater and gray slacks.

Rob had expected to see someone he knew at the lounge, and had an answer ready. "Sam is with her folks this evening. She didn't want to come out with me."

Tompkins' brows arched, and he observed, "I see. Well, you're certainly dressed up."

Rob felt the flush rise on his cheeks. It was true his dark blue suit and rep tie were unusual in the casually dressed bar.

"I...uhh, had a meeting this afternoon and didn't bother to change," he explained. That sounded a little lame, but Tompkins evidently bought it, expressing sympathy for working late on Saturday during the holidays.

Meanwhile, Christina O'Donnell was finishing her song.

"She's quite something, isn't she?" Tompkins asked, nodding toward the stage.

"Yes," Rob agreed, "very talented. Quite a voice."

"You'll see her next week at the old man's," Tompkins said. "She's on the guest list."

Rob said he and Sam were looking forward to Christmas with the Tompkins, and then Tompkins excused himself to get back to his wife, who had been eyeing the two in evident impatience.

Rob sighed with relief and returned to his drink, as the singer announced a break and left the stage to applause.

Rob was still turned partially to the stage, and saw her walk to the bar, where she accepted a glass of white wine. Then, to his surprise, she turned and walked directly toward him.

She had been head-turning at a distance, but was spectacular up close. She smiled broadly and extended a hand. He took it, and felt a tingle, almost like an electric shock. If she felt it, too, she gave no sign.

"Christina O'Donnell," she said. "I hope you like the music." There was some Southern Appalachian in her accent, overlaying something else that might have been Irish or Scots.

"Very much," he said, "looking directly into her eyes, and not letting them stray downward to the beckoning cleavage. Her eyes were large and arresting. For some reason, he had been expecting green eyes, but they were electric blue.

"I noticed Jimmy speaking with you," she said, nodding toward the Tompkins' table, where Jimmy and his wife regarded them in appraisal. "Am I going to see you next Wednesday?"

"Y-yes," he gulped. "We'll be there."

She didn't ask who "we" would be, just nodded and said, "Well, see you then." She winked and leaned in to kiss his cheek, which he immediately felt flame.

He watched Christina sway over to speak to Jimmy and his wife – Linda, he thought her name was – and then return to the microphone.

Rob listened in a state of confusion to another song, this one, "Can't Help Loving That Man of Mine." Then he paid his tab and left for home, thinking he was headed for confrontation.

But there was none. When he arrived at their two-bedroom condo in East Martintown, Samantha had changed into her nightgown and was brushing her teeth. He announced his arrival without explanation, and dressed for bed himself. They said good-night and turned off the lights.

The next morning was little different. In fact, there had been little conversation since, and none about the elephant in the room.

Maybe that wasn't treating Samantha gently, but it had been the best he could manage. For now.

They rounded a final turn and entered a straightaway leading to the Tompkins' mansion. That was all you could call it. Gray granite. Huge. Two towers, one at each end. It would have been a Southern Mountain Downton Abby except for the solar panels barely visible to the rear.

Out of the trees, the sky was blue but with scudding wisps of clouds. The forecast predicted a white Christmas, and possibly even a blizzard.

It was December 23.

Chapter One:

THE MANSION

Samantha

Samantha Elizabeth Melton Ashworth was outwardly calm as they approached the Tompkins mansion that now loomed in front of them. That was something she had learned from her lawyer father rather than from her more demonstrative mother.

"Don't show emotion except when you really need to show it," he'd always said, talking of his approach to business meetings and court. "No matter what happens. People pick up on agitation, anger, fear. Keep your poker face."

But inside, she was seething. Ever since last Saturday night, her husband had been cold and distant. *He* had let his anger show. Not in harsh words. Not in any words. Just distance and silence, and she was tired of it.

He was being so unfair. She hadn't done anything wrong, not really. It wasn't as though she had slept with anybody. She had just been having a good time, dancing with a co-worker. That the co-worker was visibly attracted to her was beside the point. Well, it had made the experience more...spicy. Yes, that was the word. Spicy. But she hadn't done anything wrong. Had she?

But for now, she would show nothing, say nothing. They had people to meet.

The road led to a circular driveway in front of the house. An arrowed sign directed drivers to the right. Circling what would be a flower bed in warm weather, Rob pulled up in front of a large double doorway. They could see the drive forked just past the house, with the right fork leading to what appeared to be a large garage partially obscured by trees, and the left leading back to the road.

Before Rob could turn off the engine, one of the double doors opened and two men emerged. One appeared to be around 50, about six feet tall and burly with grizzled hair above blunt hazel-eyed features. The second appeared to be a younger version of the first, his dark hair a little shaggy. Both wore denim jackets, checked shirts, jeans, and work boots.

The two walked around to the driver's side. The older motioned for Rob to roll down the window.

"Mr. and Mrs. Ashworth? he asked when the window was down. The accent was clearly Western North Carolina, but he sounded educated. Rob nodded, and said, "That's us."

"I'm Dave Thomas, the groundskeeper. This is my son Darrel. He's helping this week."

The younger man, who looked about 20, smiled and said, "Hello. If you'll leave your engine running, I'll park your car for you after you've unloaded. I'll bring you your keys when I'm done."

By the time Samantha had unfastened her seat belt and buttoned her North Face jacket, Darrel had circled the car and opened the door for her. He extended a hand to help her out. Samantha smiled her thanks. She could get used to this.

Rob popped the hatchback, and he and Dave went around to remove the luggage, while Darrel shut the door behind Samantha and circled to the driver's side. The engine was still running, and Rob had left the keys in the console.

"I'll take you to your suite," Dave said, "and then down to the solar so you can meet everyone. Darrel will bring your keys to you there."

Samantha's brows raised at the word "suite." She had expected a nice bedroom, but a suite? Despite her suppressed anger at her husband, she got a thrill of anticipation. This really was going to be special.

If Rob lets it be, she couldn't help thinking.

Samantha took her makeup bag, slinging her purse over a shoulder, while Rob and Dave divided the other bags. The air was chill and a little damp, the overcast growing. She shivered a little.

Dave noticed and said, looking at the sky, "I guess we really are going to get it. Well, let's get you inside. Don't worry, we've got our own generator, and we have a Land Rover if anyone really needs to get out."

They watched Darrel pull away and turned toward the double doors. Dave opened them after setting down a suitcase to free a hand, and led them into an entrance hall filled with holiday decorations. Samantha thought it lovely and inhaled the scent of pine needles with pleasure.

At the end of the entrance hall was a staircase in front and an elevator to the right. Dave motioned them to the latter. One floor up, he led them down a hallway to the right, which intersected another hallway lined with closed doors. Dave walked up to one bearing a plaque that said "Guest Suite 2," and again setting down the suitcase, produced a key from a pocket, and unlocked the door.

They entered a large sitting room furnished in a colonial style. It held a love seat and two chairs, one a recliner. There was a wet bar flanked by a writing desk and chair on the side opposite a window and a large screen television on the wall to the left of the doorway, over a fireplace with gas logs. A small bookcase held several volumes. When he had deposited the luggage on the floor, Dave crossed to the window and pulled open the drapes.

Samantha would have clapped her hands if she were not still holding the makeup case. The view of mountains and valleys, although partially obscured by clouds, was something to see.

Dave opened a door to the right, revealing a bedroom holding a canopied king-sized bed, a dresser, a chest of drawers, and another large chair. An open door on one wall revealed a bathroom with a shower, a double vanity, and a jacuzzi.

There was also a large closet.

"Do you need any help unloading your luggage?" Dave asked.

Rob shook his head. "I think we'd prefer to do it ourselves. Just give us a minute."

"I thought you might. I'll wait in the sitting room."

When the older Thomas had shut the door behind him. Rob put an arm around Samantha's shoulder and gave her a quick hug.

"This is going to be fun," he whispered.

So, he was thawing a bit. Well, she wasn't ready to let her anger go quite yet. But she managed a quick smile and whispered back, "I hope."

Unpacking did not take long. When they were done, Dave gave each of them a key, and led them back down the hall to the elevator.

"I'm going to need a map, I'm afraid," Sam said.

"Not a problem," Dave grinned. "There's one in the desk. First drawer on the right."

"Wi-fi?" Rob asked as they entered the elevator.

"Yes. And cable. Of course, the mountains and the weather mess with the wi-fi sometimes."

When they reached the first floor, Darrel met them with their car keys, and then excused himself. Dave ~~Thomas~~ led them to a hallway. Almost immediately, they reached a double doorway opening onto a long room whose opposite wall was almost entirely a series of heavy glass windows. There was a patio beyond, and a glass paneled door that led to it.

From inside, they heard voices and music.

Samantha and Christina

They entered a room designed for casual dining, socializing, or just sitting. On the side of the room where they entered, there were overstuffed chairs with reading lamps next to them on small tables. On the opposite end, there were several small tables scattered around, with a sideboard against one wall that held platters of holiday cookies and snacks, as well as a silver coffee and tea service. Against the far wall, in front of a door that must lead to a kitchen, there was a bar. A young blonde woman dressed in a white shirt and bow tie stood behind it, while a still younger girl, African American, in the same uniform, stood to one side.

With the overcast, ceiling chandeliers helped light the room. Samantha could not see where the music, smooth jazz renditions of Christmas songs, was coming from. Piped in, she supposed.

They took all of this in, but focused on the people seated around two of the tables. Samantha didn't know any of them, but she'd seen photos of the Tompkins men in the papers and on television. The tall, angular gray-haired man of about 70 had to be James W. Tompkins. He was seated at a table with a tall, elegant slender woman whose mostly unlined face showed her to be a few years younger than Tompkins, despite her head of feathery-cut but really striking silver hair. That was the wife, and Sam remembered the name was Heather from the tax returns she'd worked on.

An open-faced, smiling woman wearing an apron, hair bobbed to a page-boy, sat next to them. Samantha had no idea who she was; from appearances, she was an employee, but with "family" privileges.

At the table beyond sat Tompkins' son, Jimmy Jr., a younger carbon copy of his father. He was about 45 and his wife, a pretty brunette although a trifle plump, whose name (again from tax returns) was Linda, sat next to him. And then there was...Samantha involuntarily stiffened.

She didn't know the other woman at the second table. But Sam's competitive hackles were raised immediately. The woman was a stunner, plain and simple. Long, slightly curled dark red hair, clear complexion, electric blue eyes, wide mouth, and gleaming teeth, above a swan neck that stretched down to a deep V in the fluffy purple sweater the woman wore in contrast to the others' tacky holiday sweaters.

Samantha herself had inherited her mother's long-legged, deep bosomed dark good looks, and was not used to being upstaged. She realized she was about to be this time, and she didn't like it.

Dave led them over to the first table, where Tompkins rose and extended a hand to Samantha, saying, "The lovely Mrs. Robert Ashworth, I presume." Samantha dimpled, and said in reply, "Samantha. You can call me Sam, though."

Tompkins nodded and turned to Rob. "Hey, Rob. We're really glad you two could join us, but we're sorry Jack and Libby had to miss." He glanced over to Samantha. "They're your parents, aren't they, Sam?"

She nodded.

"Well, let me introduce you to everyone else."

Everyone stood. Damn, Samantha noted. The red-head, on top of everything else, was taller than she, with legs up to her neck.

"My wife, Heather. Our housekeeper, Mrs. Thomas. Laura, to us."

Heather and Laura shook hands and exchanged greetings with the Ashworths while the others walked around to join them.

"You know our son Jimmy," Tompkins was continuing. "His wife, Linda."

Jimmy Tompkins greeted Rob warmly. They had worked together closely in the case, and still were, because it was now in the Court of Appeals.

"I'm sorry brother Ralph and his wife couldn't be here," Jimmy said. "I was hoping you two could meet them."

"And this," Tompkins concluded, "is our holiday song-bird. Or at least I hope she will be. Christina O'Donnell."

Christina shook hands with Samantha first. "So glad to meet you," she said; and Samantha said, "You, too."

And then the woman surprised Samantha by taking Rob's hands in both of hers, and murmuring, her voice silky, "And so good to see you again, Rob. I've been looking forward to it."

Samantha saw her husband's face flame, and heard him stammer, "Uh, yes, so have I." He turned red-faced to Samantha and said, "I met Christina Saturday, honey. At the lounge. Jimmy and Linda were there, too."

Sensing the discomfort, the younger Tompkins said quickly, "We sure were. We were glad Rob stopped by. Sorry you missed it. Rob said you didn't feel like going out with him that night?"

So that was what Rob had said. But she replied only, "I was...busy with other things."

The younger Tompkins looked surprised at her response, and opened his mouth to say something, but his father interrupted to offer drinks to Rob and Samantha and suggested everyone take their seats. Samantha asked the young black girl for a Pinot noir, and Rob requested a beer.

Jimmy said, "Hey, Rob, you and Sam can sit over here with us." He gestured to the second table.

Samantha found herself, to her chagrin, seated next to Christina O'Donnell. Stealing a narrow glance at her husband, she smiled as warmly as she could, and asked, "Now exactly how did you meet Rob?"

She was thinking she shouldn't be surprised that another woman would find her husband attractive. She certainly did. He wasn't so very tall, but he stayed fit. He had broad shoulders, a slight cleft to his chin, a pug nose, and adorable hazel eyes. But she didn't want anyone poaching.

"I saw him talking with Jimmy, and wanted to introduce myself," Christina said. "I thought he might be on the guest list for the holiday, and he was. But I'm sorry I didn't get to meet you, too."

"Well, like I told Mr. Tompkins – Jimmy – I was tied up doing something else," she said. "But why would you think we were invited here? Had anyone told you?"

"Just a lucky guess."

Yeah, I'll bet, Samantha thought. She noticed out of the corner of her eye that Rob was looking distinctly uncomfortable, and had to ask Linda Tompkins to repeat something. He'd evidently been following her exchange with the O'Donnell woman.

She decided to take another tack. "I see you don't have an escort here, Christina. Is someone coming?"

"You mean a man?" O'Donnell's lilt was teasing rather than demanding.

"Well, yes." Sam admitted.

"Oh, no one who was able to get here," Christina said with a wave of her hand that implied it was nothing important. That might be true, Samantha thought; but she suspected the woman was just playing with her.

By this time Rob was striving mightily to dive into his conversation with the Tompkins. They were discussing the predicted storm. But Samantha noticed Linda's sharp glance in her direction that said she had heard at least part of Sam's sparring with Christina, and didn't like it.

So maybe it would be better if we all switched to the weather, Samantha thought.

"We're ready for whatever comes," Jimmy was saying. "There is a generator downstairs if we lose power, and plenty of fuel in a tank outside. We also have an outside propane tank. And the parlor has a large wood fireplace, and we have lots of firewood. There's also a wood fireplace in the Thomas' cottage. It's the building out back you can see if you look to the right, and connects with the main house with an enclosed walkway.

"Dad has enough supplies for an army. Linda here is still a registered nurse and licensed nurse practitioner. And if push comes to shove, we can get out with the Land Rover.

"We can even defend ourselves. Hey, if you want, Rob, Dad and I can show you the gun room before dinner. Linda can give Sam a house tour while we're doing that."

Rob embraced that suggestion with enthusiasm. He probably wants to put off talking with me, Sam thought. Okay, I'll play along.

"That would be lovely," she said.

But her hackles raised again when O'Donnell said, "I had the house tour this morning, but the gun room was locked. Jimmy, is it okay if I tag along with the guys?"

Why, she's still messing with me, Samantha thought. Well, it won't work.

"I'll stick with the house tour, thanks," she said, making sure she said it with her broadest smile.

And she *was* curious about the house.

The Gun Room

The gun room, it turned out, was on the far side of the first floor, behind a massive door of polished oak. A stuffed elk head with a magnificent spread of antlers was mounted over the door, which otherwise gave no indication of what was behind it.

"I shot this beauty in Wyoming a few years ago," the older Tompkins said, as he produced a key and unlocked the door. "But elk are now being introduced into the Carolina mountains. Re-introduced, I should say. They were all over these parts in colonial times. Woods bison, too. And...other animals."

Tompkins Sr. opened the door, flipped on tracked overhead lights, and stood aside for the others to enter. The room was large, but not ostentatiously so, purely functional and not designed for show, but the glass enclosed gun racks that lined the wall to the left were wood and polished so that they fairly glowed in the electric lights.

The racks were filled with rifles and shotguns of several makes and models. Rob recognized most of them. There were three Winchester Model 70 rifles like the one that still hung on the wall in his parents' home over in Marion, and which he still borrowed from his dad on the rare times he found to go deer hunting. Two were scoped, and one was not.

"What's the difference?" Rob asked.

"One is in .270. That's the first one with the scope," Jimmy said.

"The other two are in .30'06 and .338 magnum. That's the one with 'iron' sights. Do you hunt?"

"More when I was in high school," Rob answered. "I don't have much time these days." He grinned. "You guys keep me too busy." He waited until the two Tompkins chuckled, and continued, "We have a client, Mitch McCaffrey, who took me last fall. But I didn't get a buck. Mitch did."

"What about you, Christina?" Tompkins Sr. asked.

Christina smiled and said, "My dad taught me to shoot when I was a kid. But the only thing I've hunted is grouse. With a shotgun. I'm more into archery."

"Well," said Jimmy, "I'll show you something in a minute."

The case also held three Remington Ranch Rifles, which Rob recognized because Mitch had one he used for deer. One was scoped and the other two not.

"Different calibers again?" he asked.

Jimmy nodded. "Yes. One is .223. That's the one with the scope. The other two are .308."

Beyond the rifles was a case with several shotguns, some pump, some automatic, which Jimmy explained were in varying gauges.

"These will do for grouse or dove," Tompkins told Christina.

"So I see," she answered.

Beyond the shotguns was a case with the antiques. Rob's eyes lit up when they reached it. There was a rifled musket that had to be a Civil War Springfield, flanked by a Sharps carbine, followed by a Krag-Jorgensen and then an unaltered Springfield '03. Last was a double-barreled English-made express rifle that must kick like a mule, and had to have cost serious money, not that the others didn't.

"Yes, they all shoot," said Tompkins Sr. "And we have ammo for all of them. You'll notice that all of the cases are separately locked, and the drawers below them that hold the ammunition are, too. We don't want anyone who doesn't know what he's doing to get hold of them." He turned his eyes on Rob and noted the enthusiasm. "You know what you're looking at, don't you?"

Rob nodded. "Yes, I do. My dad is an NRA member and I read the magazines growing up."

At the very end, in its own case, hung a fiberglass compound bow, unstrung, with its pulleys plain to see. There was also a crossbow. The case also held target and broad blade hunting arrows, and quarrels for the crossbow.

"Now this I like," Christina said, almost putting her nose to the case.

"I'm afraid the pull on that bow might be a little difficult for you." Jimmy said.

She arched her brows. "You might be surprised."

We might at that, Rob thought. This woman held a lot of surprises.

The opposite wall held a case with handguns. They included Glocks, Browning, Beretta and Sig Sauer, a 1911 Colt .45, and several types of revolvers made by Colt, Ruger, and Smith & Wesson, again in a variety of calibers. There were also a broom-handle Mauser, a Luger, and a Russian Nagant revolver.

"These are my two favorites," Jimmy said, pointing at the Nagant and then at a Colt revolver. "The Nagant, if you look closely, has the imperial double eagle. This one was made before 1900. Hard to find. The Colt is a 1909 New Service, the 'last of the great revolvers,' some say. It's in .45 long and not .45 ACP like the later models. Some officers and non-coms still carried them in World War II. Again, the ammo is in the locked drawers, and all of them, antiques included, shoot."

Christina nodded politely and Rob with enthusiasm. He had recognized practically everything. He noticed a metal cabinet against the far wall.

"What's in there?" he asked.

Tompkins Sr. walked over an unlocked the cabinet. It held a rack of AR-15s with magazines of varying sizes.

"We doubt we ever need these," he said. "But we have them, just in case."

"They do make good varmint rifles, though," Jimmy added.

"I suppose you gentlemen are fans of the Second Amendment?" Christina asked.

Everyone laughed.

"You could say so," Tompkins Sr. said, and added, "Well, there's still time for a house tour. What about it?"

"Sure," Rob said. "Sounds great."

"Well, I've had the tour," Christina said. "If it's okay, I'll go to my room and relax for a while."

"Can you find it?" Jimmy asked.

"Oh sure," she called over her shoulder, already walking toward the door.

All the men watched her backside sway as she left. Rob turned toward Jimmy.

"How..." he began, but Jimmy cut him off.

"Linda and I saw her perform at a festival in Blowing Rock in October. We introduced ourselves, liked her, and invited her here. She accepted. We were a little surprised when she did."

His father's eyes narrowed. "Linda isn't jealous?"

Jimmy shook his head. "Envious, I'm sure. Not jealous. No reason to be."

Tompkins Sr. grunted, "Good."

Rob was growing a little uncomfortable. They must have noticed Sam and Christina sparring, and he didn't want to be asked about it. But all they did was lead him out of the gun room and lock up.

He wondered if they would run into the women.

The House Tour

After the Tompkins men, Rob, and Christina had left, Mrs. Thomas stood and said, "Well, I'd best get back to the kitchen to see about dinner."

"We'll start the tour in the breakfast room, Laura, and then let Samantha have a peek at the kitchen before we show her anything else," Heather Tompkins said. "Now you and the family can plan on eating with us, as usual." She paused and explained to Samantha, "We don't stand much on ceremony here. Dave and Laura are like family, anyway."

"Dave and I will," said Laura Thomas. "I'm sure Darrel will eat downstairs with Meg and Sally." She nodded towards the two young women, who still stood behind the bar and to one side, respectively.

Heather and Linda led them to a door behind and to the left of the bar. The blonde girl opened it for them, and they entered another spacious room with a long table and another sideboard. Windows lined the wall to the left, sturdy but not almost floor to ceiling as in the solar. Through the windows there was more view of the stone patio, and a better view of the brick barbecue pit. The opposite wall was lined with paintings of mountain landscapes. There was another door at the end of the room.

"This is the breakfast room," Heather said, "although we frequently use it for lunch as well. I will show you the main dining room after you've seen the kitchen. The paintings were all done by local artists."

"Really?" Samantha asked rhetorically. "They're lovely."

The blonde opened the door again and they entered a huge and spotless kitchen, with a central counter, a large grill, and three ovens. Copper and stainless pots hung over the counter. There was a door to the left that appeared to lead to another part of the house.

"This is Laura's domain," Heather said. Dave helps with the outdoor cooking sometimes, though. That door" – she gestured to the left – "leads to an enclosed walkway to their cottage."

"I'm impressed," said Samantha.

The two young women, hardly older than girls, walked around the counter to stand beside Laura Thomas.

"These are Meg Jarvis and Sally DeRatt," Heather said, earning smiles from both. "They are with us through New Year's. Meg is a student at Appalachian State, and Sally goes to Carolina Highlands. Darrel, Laura and Dave's son, goes to App, too."

Sally's name rang a bell with Samantha.

"Are you related to Tiffany, Sally?" Samantha asked her.

The young woman's smile grew into a wide grin. "A first cousin. I'm going to be in her wedding. How do you know Tiff?"

"She works in Rob's law firm. I've met a lot of the people there."

Linda Tompkins looked at her wristwatch. "We'd better get going if we're going to give Sam any time to rest and freshen up before dinner."

Heather led them to another door at the far end of the room. The blonde girl, Meg, moved to open the door again, Heather stopped her with a smile and raised hand and said, "Linda and I can take it from here, Meg."

The door led to the main dining room, which held more wall paintings, still another sideboard, and a table that looked as though it would seat 20.

"We don't use it often," Heather said, and led them out into another hallway and beyond that to what she said was the ballroom.

"We use this room even less," she explained. "If it is necessary to expand it, like for a wedding reception, we can open the double doors to our left onto the main entry hall...But right now I'll show you the parlor and then the theater."

She led them out still another door into a hallway that led to another hallway at right angles. Turning to the left, she and Linda led Samantha into a sitting room that held a bookcase, wet bar and music system built into the nearer wall, while the other side of the room was walled with large windows with the drapes drawn. It was filled with comfortable chairs and sofas with low tables and reading lamps.

"The main library is upstairs," Heather explained, "but we have a few volumes here." She pulled the drapes to show a view of the drive and the woods beyond, and led them to another door at the far end of the room. Opening double doors, she revealed another big room, with comfortable chairs and love seats at the back and several rows of cushioned stadium seats in the front. There were draped windows, but these were small. The far wall was covered by a huge LED screen, with a bank of electronics on the wall to the left close to the screen.

"This doubles for both movies and television," Heather said. "Jim and Jimmy make sure we subscribe to *everything*." She giggled. "Jim said there's a football game on television tonight, so I guess the guys will spend some time in here this evening."

"Well," Linda protested, "not just the guys. This is App's game tonight."

Samantha remembered Rob saying Appalachian was playing somebody sometime, but had forgotten when. Now she knew. She noticed a coffee and beverage station against the rear wall. Evidently, refreshments were never far off in this place.

"We'll skip downstairs for now," Heather said. Except for the HVAC, the generator, and fuel and other storage, it doesn't have anything but the staff quarters, the exercise room, and the pool. Samantha, I'll have someone show them to you later. Now, we can go upstairs. You will want to see Jim's study and the library. And the guests' parlor."

Rob

The Tompkins men ended the tour in the hallway outside the guests' parlor and study, only a short walk to the connecting hallway with the guest suites and rooms. Rob assured them he could find his way to the right suite on his own, and he did.

When he entered, Samantha was lounging on the couch in the sitting room, thumbing through a book she had evidently plucked from the small bookcase in the suite. When she closed it, holding her place with a thumb, he saw the title was *Old North State Ghosts*.

"If that one isn't interesting enough," he said, while removing his down jacket and hanging it on a coat rack next to the door, where hers was already hanging, "you ought to visit the library down the hall."

"I saw the library," she answered, fully closing the book and setting it on the coffee table in front of the couch. "Also the guest parlor and the guest study, computer stations and all. And the theater and the ballroom. Pretty impressive."

Rob took a seat, not on the couch beside her, but in an easy chair at right angles to the couch and coffee table.

"Did you see the indoor pool? Or the gym?" he asked.

"No, we didn't go downstairs. They told me about them, though."

"Well, you really ought to see them," Rob said, leaning forward. "The pool is a big lap pool. The exercise room isn't the biggest in the world, but it's fully equipped. I'm going to try it out in the morning."

"What else did you see?"

"The generator room and the fuel storage. We skipped the other storage. Jimmy was right. They're ready for just about anything. The weather won't bother us.

"They didn't show me the staff quarters, but I saw their kitchen, lounge, and dining room. That's not counting the Thomas' cottage, of course. All very nice. They don't have staff year-round. But Dave and Laura Thomas are here all the time, except for their vacations.

"I also saw the observation deck over the master suite. Did you see that?"

Samantha shook her head. "What did the O'Donnell woman think of all of this?" she asked, narrowing her eyes as she said it.

Rob, who had been about to relax into the chair, felt himself stiffen. "I don't know. She went to her room after the gun room...Why don't you go ask her? Her room's somewhere on this hallway."

Sam ignored the suggestion. "What did she think of the gun room?"

Rob spread his arms, palms out. "I don't know. She seemed interested."

"I'll just bet she was," Samantha said. Her mouth wasn't as pretty with a sneer. "She's just the type to want to shoot a trophy."

"What's that supposed to mean?" Rob demanded.

"The trophy never knows until too late," she countered.

Rob laughed in spite of himself. "I'm a trophy?"

"Well, there's something between you," Samantha said. "I've seen the way you look at each other."

"And how is that?" he demanded.

"You look at her the way a rabbit looks at a snake," Samantha said without hesitation. She had evidently been thinking about this subject. "And she looks at you like you're the rabbit. You're what's for dinner."

"Oh, come on, Samantha. I've only met the woman twice. I doubt I've said three sentences to her. You — you're just deflecting."

Samantha's brown eyes were flashing now. "What's that supposed to mean?"

Now Rob's dander was up. It was all going to come out. "You know exactly what I mean. You're the one who ignored me for hours, dirty dancing with that guy Carter —"

"We weren't dirty dancing! Don't you dare say that!"

Rob wasn't in the mood to back off. "Well, whatever it was, it was embarrassing to...to me." He had been about to say the same thing her dad had said, that it embarrassed his firm and her mother's, but bit the words before they escaped.

Samantha's tone turned bitter. "Now you sound like my mother," she accused.

"Do I?"

"I'm sure you know. I'm sure you've talked with Mom."

"I haven't." He didn't say he had talked with her father.

Samantha had been leaning forward, slightly flushed and breathing hard, but now she subsided into the coach. "Look," she said, "Tom is a friend at work. He's done me favors. We tell jokes at the office. He's very cute. He likes to dance and his wife doesn't. I couldn't leave him in the lurch."

"So instead you left me, your husband, by himself. And that was preferable? I suppose he's cuter than me, and that makes it all right."

"I-I wasn't thinking," Samantha said, a tear escaping her right eye. "And no, he's not cuter. And I didn't sleep with him, or anything. I haven't done that. I wouldn't. And he wouldn't sleep with me."

"How do you know? Has he turned you down?"

"You bastard! You know that's not true!"

Rob stopped and sighed. "I guess I do. But Samantha, you really hurt me, and you really made me angry. And I'm not hearing you say you're even sorry about it. Instead, you want to imagine something's happening with me and some woman I barely know."

He should have left it at that, because he saw her features harden. "You just can't stand competition. You can't take being upstaged."

If he had expected to hit a nerve, he was right.

"So she is competition. And you think I am a pale little shadow next to her. Is that it?" She was really flushed now, and shaking.

He almost suggested Samantha wait until she'd heard Christina sing, but caught himself this time.

"No, I don't think that," he said. "This whole thing is ridiculous. Here I am married to this beautiful woman who is yelling at me –"

"I'm not yelling!"

"Okay, arguing with me," he amended. "This woman who – well, I've never quite understood why this near-goddess picked me. Who has hurt my feelings badly. And I'm the one defending myself from...from nothing."

This time Samantha did appear to relax. For the first time in days, he saw the shadow of the playful smile he loved so much.

"So," she said. "I'm a near-goddess?"

"As near as any mortal woman can get."

He heard her deep sigh.

"All right, darling. Come here and kiss me, and I'll say I'm sorry. And I'll mean it."

But after the kiss, she said, "But that doesn't mean I won't be watching her – and you – this evening."

Chapter Two

LIGHTS AND LIONS

Christina

Dinner that night was in the breakfast room. Tomorrow's Christmas Eve dinner, Heather Tompkins announced, would be in the main dining room "even though it's so big."

But tonight's dinner was lavish enough, Christina thought. There was a venison roast from a deer Dave had shot in October, rare in the middle and more well done at the ends, with a tangy, slightly sweet gravy that contained currant jelly, Laura said. There were also slices of grilled halibut for anyone who didn't want red meat, a green salad with white balsamic vinaigrette, and oven-roasted Brussels sprouts and carrots. Laura had made the dinner rolls from scratch.

Guests could pick from red or white wine, decanted from bottles whose labels must have been pricey; and those who shunned alcohol could choose between pitchers of water and iced tea. By the time Meg and Sally had brought out carafes of coffee and a choice of pecan pie and peach cobbler, Christina was sure she could not eat another bite; but she managed a small slice of the pie.

"I am definitely hitting the lap pool in the morning," she said.

Samantha, who was seated two chairs down from her toward the end of the table, said, "Good idea. Someone with your build really needs to keep up their exercise."

Meoww! Christina thought, followed by you're pretty statuesque yourself, honey. But she didn't say it. She sensed Rob squirm in the chair beside her and noted Linda Tompkins' raised brows, so she changed the subject.

"Anyway, Laura, the dinner was absolutely delicious. The dinner tomorrow night will have to go some to beat it."

There were murmurs of agreement from around the table, and Jim Tompkins said, "Don't be surprised if it does. Tomorrow night, we'll get charcoal-roasted turkey with oyster stuffing. Of course, Christmas Day will be very informal, and you'll get leftovers from tonight and tomorrow night."

"They'll be good leftovers," Rob observed. "But what if it snows?"

"You mean when and not if," Tompkins said. "But not to worry. If you peek out the window, you'll see that the barbecue is open but has a shed roof that extends out from the walkway. Dave and Laura won't have to stand in the snow, even if we have to sweep or shovel away anything that blows in."

"You mean Dave won't," Laura corrected. "He's the outdoor chef. I'll only come out and check it every once in a while."

"Well, anyway," Tompkins said, "suppose we retire into the solar for more coffee and brandy, if anyone wants.

We can turn on the lights and watch for snow. There's a little time before the ball game comes on. Anyone like me who wants a quick smoke can grab a coat and step out on the patio."

"No smoking room?" asked Rob.

"Well, in my study upstairs. It has separate ventilation. But I don't want to go up there right now."

While Meg and Sally, with Darrel's help cleared the table, the others returned to the solar. There they found brandy, a fresh carafe of coffee, and cordials on the sideboard, along with cups, glasses and snifters, and sugar and cream. Darrel evidently had been busy. He would now help Meg and Sally clear up and wash, and then go downstairs for their own meal. It would be leftovers, but there were plenty.

Christina watched Jim Tompkins and Dave Thomas shrug on coats and exit onto the patio (Heather called it "the terrace") through a door at the far end of the room. Outside, she saw Jim pull a briar pipe and Dave a pack of cigarettes from pockets and light up, ignoring their wives' disapproving frowns. As they smoked and chatted, the first snowflakes drifted down, slow and lazy.

Heather walked to a wall and fiddled with a panel, and soft Christmas instrumentals began to play. She gestured to the sideboard.

"Please help yourself," she said. "We don't stand on ceremony, and the youngsters have the evening off."

There were decanters of brandy, bourbon and scotch, carafes of wine left over from dinner, and a bottle of port, as well as the coffee service, both decaffeinated and not. Rob strode to the sideboard, and turned to Samantha.

"Want anything, honey?" he asked.

"Well, I'll take a small port," she said.

Rob's eyes roamed over the other women. "Anyone else? I'm happy to play bartender."

"I'll get my own coffee, dear," said Heather, "so I can doctor it myself."

Both Linda and Christina asked for more wine.

Rob poured the wine into glasses, the port into the tiny ones that were designed for port or sherry. Christina thought it interesting that he knew that. She also thought it interesting that Samantha had carefully monitored every word she and Rob had exchanged before dinner.

I guess I have a fence to mend, she thought.

Rob poured Scotch into a snifter and handed it to Jim, then did the same for himself. He took a sip, and smiled.

"Peaty," he said. "Smoky. I like it."

Jimmy followed suit, and said, "This is what Dad buys. He likes the Island Scotches. I prefer Lowland, but I admit this is pretty good. Lavagulin, I think."

Big Jim (as the family called him, Christina had learned) and Dave came in, shook show from their coats and removed them, and headed for the sideboard. Jim took scotch and Dave, bourbon. Everyone seated themselves where they could watch the snow, which was now falling faster and harder. It had almost covered the patio and the lawn beyond. Christina seated herself close to Rob and Samantha, but not next to them. She was a little wary of Sam's reaction; and sure enough, Sam didn't look in her direction.

While they watched, the clouds lit with a bright, almost purple glow that seemed to be inside the cloud and then disappeared over the slope on the other side of the trees and down the ridge. There was no noise.

Christina winced. There was something wrong in that light. Something...unfriendly. She glanced at Rob and Sam. The latter was wide-eyed, as was everyone. But Rob's eyes were narrow and his brow furrowed. He had picked up on whatever was coming from the light, too. She'd thought he might.

"What was that?" Linda asked. There was a slight tremor in her voice.

"Ball lightning?" Jimmy suggested.

"Maybe," Big Jim said, "but I don't think so. We would have felt something, and ball lightning is unusual in a snowstorm."

"Maybe it was one of the Johnson family ghosts," said Dave, his voice audible but soft.

"Ghosts?" Linda asked. "Here?"

"Some people say so," Big Jim said. "It's why I could get this property so cheap...You tell them, Dave."

Dave leaned back in his chair and said, "All right. I grew up not far from here, in a cove over the next ridge. Everyone knew the story, and the grown-ups scared the kids telling it. My Grandpa Thomas could really give you bad dreams.

"When I got out of the Marine Corps, and came back here, and saw this job was available, I knew exactly where this place was. I remembered the stories."

"Well, don't keep us in suspense," Linda begged. "What is it?"

"Back before the Civil War, a man named Lemuel Johnson made a pile of money, for the time, running a chain of general stores. He liked his privacy, because he wasn't popular with everyone. Not the politicians who ran the state then, anyway.

"Johnson didn't hold with slavery, and refused to use his money to buy slaves. He was an outspoken Whig, and there were a bunch of people who agreed with him, especially in this part of the state and down on the coast. But the state was pretty much run by the tobacco plantation owners back then.

"Anyway, Johnson decided to build a house somewhere out of the way, where folks would leave him alone. When he was down in Martintown tending to one of his stores, he heard this property could be bought. This was about 1850 or so. He built a big house right here. It took a couple of years to put in a decent road and build the house."

Everyone was listening with rapt attention, and looking at Dave, whose voice remained quiet and matter of fact, and not at the snowstorm outside. Samantha nudged Rob to pour her some more port. He got up to do so, while continuing to listen.

"The house was big for its time, wood frame, but not nearly as big as the one we're sitting in now. There was room for a vegetable garden, and an animal shed for horses and milk cows, and for a cottage out back. Johnson didn't improve his popularity with some people by hiring a black freedman named Surratt and moving him and his wife into the cottage to take care of the garden and livestock and watch the property when Johnson was gone. Black people weren't supposed to have access to firearms. Everyone thought the man Johnson brought in did, but no one could prove it.

"There were even rumors the big house was a way station on the Underground Railroad, but I doubt that. This place just wasn't on a good route north.

"Anyway, Johnson had a son named Caleb. The two of them didn't always see eye to eye. When the war broke out, Lem Johnson was outspoken for the Union, but Caleb joined the Confederate Army. His daddy had to stay up here almost all the time, with his wife and his two teenaged girls, Caleb's sisters. The stores had to be closed. They couldn't get merchandise, with no trade from the North and very little from overseas.

"Well, the war dragged on, and son Caleb became disillusioned with the Confederate cause. He, and two others from his company, deserted, and made their way here. Lem welcomed him like the prodigal son, which he was, in a way.

"The Regulators found out about them and surrounded the house. They wouldn't give themselves up, and a firefight broke out. Caleb and his friends had Henry repeaters they had taken from Union troops. The house was stoutly built. Four of the Regulators died trying to rush the front door. It was a standoff.

"That night, the Regulators decided to burn them out. They used coal oil to set the fire, and they shot anyone who came out. Women, too. The Johnsons, their black employee and his wife, and both of Caleb's buddies all died. The house burned to the ground.

"The ghost stories have been with us ever since. Deer hunters see Caleb or Lem. Campers sometimes see the women. Some people claim to have met the Surratts while walking in the woods."

There was a long silence when Dave ended the story, then Samantha said, "Why, I read about them this afternoon."

"*North State Ghosts*?" Jim asked.

She nodded.

"There's a copy in every guest bedroom or suite," the elder Tompkins said.

"Has anyone seen any ghosts?" Rob asked. Samantha had watched him stir uneasily, while Thomas was telling the story. She was sure she was right about him. He could feel things.

As for Christina, she had felt her neck hairs raise herself. There was something, but it seemed asleep. It wasn't like the feeling when the light had passed. That had been hostile and...unworldly. But there was definitely something, or someone, close by. Human, not...alien.

"We had some reports during construction. The grading contractor had a few people quit," Big Jim was saying. "But nothing since we've moved in."

Dave spoke again. "It was a long time ago. I was a teenager hunting deer not far down the ridge from here. I was lost. The game trail forked ahead of me. I saw a black man step out of the brush and point down the right fork. He had grizzled short hair and was wearing old-fashioned homespun baggy clothes. He pointed down the right fork again. I spoke to him, and he turned and disappeared. I tried to follow him, but there were no footprints. Nothing.

"I took the right fork and found my way out pretty soon."

Christina saw Jimmy Tompkins open his mouth to ask a question, but he didn't get to ask. From outside came a long high-pitched scream. It sounded like a frightened woman.

Everyone gasped. Most jumped in their seats, and Linda, Heather, and Samantha screamed. There was another scream from outside.

All eyes turned to the windows. The snow was falling hard now. There were already a couple of inches on the patio and covering the lawn beyond. At the edge of the patio stood a mountain lion, long tail twitching in the falling snow. It couldn't be anything else. It was too big to be a bobcat, and bobcats had no tails.

As they watched, the lion snarled, inaudible through the thick glass, and turned. It padded across the newly fallen snow and disappeared into the trees.

But just before it pushed its way through the brush into the woods, Christina was no longer watching a big cat. She saw the back of a woman dressed in buckskin, or something like it, shod in brown buskins, bare- headed, her mane of tawny dark blonde hair down to her shoulders.

Christina gasped and heard another gasp close by. The answering gasp came from Rob Ashworth. She and he exchanged a glance and she nodded, the merest duck of her chin. He had seen the woman, too. Samantha's frown said she had noticed the silent exchange and didn't like it.

"Was that a...lion?" asked Linda, who was still gaping like a fish.

Dave Thomas nodded. "Yes, a mountain lion. A catamount. There have been rumors for years that a few of them are still around in the deep woods high up. There have more reports recently. But this is the first I've ever seen."

Big Jim rose and went to get his jacket.

"Where are you going?" Heather demanded.

"Out. I want to see the prints before the snow covers them," Jim said.

"James Tompkins, you are not going out there with that animal, in a snowstorm, in the dark. Sit down."

Dave Thomas spoke up. "She's right, Jim. There won't be anything anyway. It's snowing too hard."

Tompkins replaced his jacket. His laugh was shaky.

"Well, all right," he said. "Okay, let's watch football. The game will be on by now."

"That's for me, too," said Linda. "But are we safe?" She looked back at the windows.

"Oh, sure," said her father-in-law. "A bull elephant might be able to break this glass, but not a cougar."

Heather rose. "I think I'll turn in early and read for a while," she said.

Laura Thomas excused herself, too.

All of the men said they'd take in some of the bowl game. It was App State against Western Michigan, so there was local interest.

"I want to visit the library, if that's all right," Christina said to Tompkins. She had an idea.

"Certainly, dear," said Heather.

"Samantha, come with me," Christina said. "There are a couple of books I want to show you."

Rob's eyes widened, but he said, "Sam, that's fine with me. You're not that much of a fan. You'd like the library better."

Christina mentally crossed her fingers. Sam's body language was sending a loud "no."

But then Samantha drew a deep breath and forced a smile.

"Sure. I'll come. For a while, anyway."

Samantha and Christina

Heather rode the elevator with Samantha and Christina, and walked with them to the hallway that fronted the master suite, as well as the library and Big Jim's study. She kept up a patter about how she'd never seen anything like "that mountain lion" and how it had frightened her. The two younger women politely agreed, but otherwise exchanged no words until after they reached the library.

But as soon as they entered and found the light switch, Samantha rounded on Christina, narrow eyed and clearly unfriendly.

"I want to know what you want with my husband," she demanded. "What is going on between you two?"

Christina didn't answer the question, but instead took a seat in one of the easy chairs closest to the door and asked her own. "You didn't see her, did you, Samantha?" She waved at the other chair that flanked the one she had taken.

Samantha ignored the invitation to sit. She stood in front of Christina, a little too close for polite discourse, and stared down at her.

"*What* are you talking about?" she demanded, her voice more shrill than she'd really intended. "See who?"

Christina was determined not to engage Samantha's hostility. She smiled and kept her voice level.

"Samantha, please sit down. I'll do my best to explain. You deserve it. I'm not after your husband."

Samantha bridled, but then sighed and sat. The chairs were angled so that they faced each other obliquely.

"All right," she said, her tone still truculent. "But I don't understand what you're talking about."

"That's understandable," Christina said. "Most people wouldn't. But I'll ask again: What did you see outside next to the patio?"

Samantha shook her head and released another exasperated sigh. "I saw what everyone else saw. A mountain lion."

Christina shook her head. "That's what you thought you saw. But that was an illusion. It was a woman. Oh, it was a good illusion. It fooled me, too, at first. And it fooled Rob. But we saw the woman clearly right before she disappeared into the woods."

Samantha stared at Christina, open-mouthed. Whatever else Christina O'Donnell was, she was clearly some kind of nut.

"Do you really expect me to believe that?" she asked, her voice under better control now.

"No, I don't." Christina's voice remained calm. "But you obviously think I have some...romantic interest in your husband. I do not." She paused and smiled, "But I certainly understand why *you* do."

Samantha was not quite mollified. "Well, you certainly have some kind of interest in him. What is it?"

"The two of us share a Talent. He is a Sensitive, although I don't think he knows it."

Samantha laughed, a short bark, and actually smiled for the first time.

"Listen, honey," she said. "I'm married to the man, and he certainly doesn't qualify as the world's most sensitive man." She paused, and amended, a little reluctantly, but deciding she wanted to be fair, "At least, not all the time."

Christina nodded along. "I'm sure that's true. But he has the Talent to see things others can't. It's not truly developed. It kind of flickers off and on, like a light with a short. I picked up on it last Saturday, which was why I introduced myself. He was flickering in and out, as though he was upset about something."

Samantha's eyes widened, and her mouth twisted into a frown.

She must know what was bothering him that night, Christina thought, *and she's still a little raw about it.*

Whatever it was, Samantha didn't offer an explanation. Instead, she asked another question.

"Okay, suppose I go along with this stuff, just for grins. Who was this mystery woman?"

"I honestly don't know," Christina confessed, and added, "But I know who sent her."

"Really? Who is that?"

"I think you've heard of her, considering where your husband works. Her name is Alyssa McCormick."

Now Samantha was genuinely interested. "Is that the same Alyssa McCormick that Rob's firm got off from federal charges?"

Christina nodded. "The very same. We've been friends for a while. You see, Jimmy and Linda invited me here for Christmas several weeks ago. I wanted to come, but I started having a premonition about it. I talked with Alyssa, and she had the same...feeling.

"She promised she would check on me, find a way for me to know she was checking, and that she'd find a way to help if anything happens. The 'mountain lion' was her message. She knew I'd see through it, but of course she didn't think anyone else here would be able to do it."

Samantha's thoughts were whirling. She knew about the McCormick case. Other clients, the McCaffreys, were involved, too. It had been in the news. Rob had told her that there were all kinds of office rumors running around about it, but no one would discuss it. Not even her dad.

"So," she said slowly, "This McCormick woman is a... Sensitive, too?"

"No, not just a Sensitive. Alyssa McCormick is a Witch."

Samantha placed her hands on her hips and stared open-mouthed.

"I hope you know how crazy this sounds," she said.

"Oh, I do." Christina told her. "And I don't expect you to believe it – yet. I just wanted you to let your husband off the hook. I'm sure he's even more confused than you are."

"I hope that's all it is," Samantha said. This time, her voice was almost pleading. "Look, I can't go along with everything you just said. But you need to understand, Rob and I have had ...issues, the last few days. And then when someone with your looks comes along and acts interested in him..." she trailed off.

"*My* looks?" Christina asked, laughing. "Honey, have you looked in the mirror lately?" She was sure Samantha and her mirror were in fact good friends, but wanted to ask it that way anyway.

For the first time, Samantha's smile was genuine.

"Okay," she said. "That part I'll buy. You're not a threat. But don't ask me to believe the rest of it."

"For now, no I won't. But I think you'll come around. You see, there's more."

"Which is?" Samantha demanded.

"I think you have the Talent, too. It's submerged, repressed somehow. But I sense it's there. And I can help, if you want. I can give you the Witch Sight if you want it."

"This is crazy!" Samantha responded.

"Well, think about it," Christina said, then added, "If you want to learn more, come swim with me tomorrow morning, after breakfast."

Samantha stood.

"I-I'll think about it," she promised. "Right now, I'm going to find Rob. Good night...Christina."

"Good night, Samantha."

Christina watched her leave.

Well, she thought, it was a start.

Chapter Three

THE BLIZZARD OF CHRISTMAS EVE

Alyssa and Friends

Diana Corcoran McCaffrey walked through mist into the downstairs den in her home, shivering and shaking snow from her honey-blonde tresses. Alyssa, Mitch, and Ben Corcoran were waiting, seated before the big flatscreen television, which was not on. Instead, holiday music played softly.

Diana's eyes sought Alyssa's.

"It's damned cold out there," she complained. "I hope you appreciate the things I do for you."

"Diana, of course I do," Alyssa assured her. "I promised Christina I would check on her. We both had premonitions."

Diana wasn't satisfied.

"I know, I know. You told us," she said. "But why did it have to be me? And why did I have to wear this getup?"

Alyssa sighed. She thought she had explained this before. But maybe she'd better do it again.

"Diana, it's like I said. The fringed buckskin and beaded buskins came from my friend over in Cherokee. There are fangs from a real catamount in the fringing. I had to have something Native American, and preferably something local, something Cherokee, so I could create the illusion.

"As for why you, I told you that, too. You may not be aSpellcaster, but you are easily the most Sensitive person here. You have to be, to have your spell-blocking ability. So thank you. Thank you so much. But I have to ask: Did you pick up on anything?"

Diana's features went from irritated to thoughtful. After a long moment, she replied, "Yes-s-s. I sensed your friend inside, and one other person, I think a man...And... and there was something else, too. But not close by. Maybe down the ridge behind the house. Something... bad. Unfriendly. Not exactly magic, but...powerful."

Her husband, Mitch, who had stepped over to put an arm around the shivering Diana's shoulder, said, "Uh-oh. That's not good."

That brought back Diana's irritation. "Damn it," she said, "it's Christmas. We have two boys upstairs who are excited about a white Christmas. Can't all this...stuff... leave us alone *at Christmas*?"

Alyssa stepped over and took her hand. "I know, honey, I know. But sometimes things happen when they happen. Look, this may turn out to be nothing. I'll need to check again tomorrow, but I'll do it myself. Now that I've sent Christina a message, I can use a scrying spell. I promise I won't involve you or Mitch unless I have to."

Diana smiled and squeezed her hand. "We'll help if we need to, Alyssa. You know that. You've been good to us, too. I was just venting...Now let me change clothes, and,

Mitch, get me some Campari, please. Let's enjoy the rest of the evening."

"Diana, are you sure you want us to stay the night?" asked Ben Callahan. He and Alyssa were still an item, practically engaged, in fact; but he always got nervous when the paranormal presented itself. In the courtroom, he was in his element. But when the subject became casting spells or sensing auras, he was a fish out of water.

Mitch answered, "Absolutely, Ben. The boys know you're here, and think we drove you. Driving is out of the question tonight. We couldn't explain your absence if you used a Portal to get out."

Diana, on her way to the stairs to go to their bedroom, and change, said over her shoulder, "That's absolutely right, Ben. We'll see what we can come up with tomorrow."

"I just hope that's the most concerning thing tomorrow," Alyssa whispered, low that Diana wouldn't hear.

Mitch bit his lip. "Yeah," he said. "Me, too." But he quickly added, "Okay, people, name your poison. Campari for Di, scotch for me. What's yours?"

Samantha

When Sam reached the theatre, she found everyone sitting in the big chairs at the end of the room farthest from the huge screen. The stadium seats were empty. Jimmy and Linda Tompkins occupied a love seat, and were whispering to one another and paying scant attention to the ball game. Big Jim, Dave Thomas, and Rob had seats close together, with Rob at one end, Tompkins in the middle, and Dave on his other side. They appeared to be watching more intently, making comments on the play on the field.

Sam walked around the room behind them, so she could get to Rob without blocking anyone's view, and noted that someone had opened the drapes on one window. The outside lights showed the hard snowfall continuing. She wondered how the Appalachian State team would be able to return home in the morning. Doubtless the Asheville, Tri-Cities, and Charlotte airports were closed.

Rob had turned to Tompkins to make some comment about the game, and didn't see her until she sat on the arm of his chair and leaned over to kiss his cheek. He turned toward her, and his face showed both pleasure and apprehension.

"Hello, darling," she whispered in his ear. "How's the game going?"

He cleared his throat and answered, "The Apps have it pretty well in hand. They're three touchdowns ahead."

She leaned down and whispered again. "Okay. Come upstairs as soon as you can. There's something I need to tell you. Can you give me the key?"

He nodded and handed her the key.

Samantha stood clutching the key and announced aloud, "Just checking on my hubby, gentlemen. Enjoy the game."

Then she left with a wave, noting the smiles the others tried to hide. She had learned the house by now and had no trouble finding their suite. She changed to her pajamas and brushed her teeth, and then sat on the couch in the sitting room to re-read the segment in the book about the Johnson ghosts. She hadn't finished when there was a knock at the door. As expected, it was Rob.

He hugged her and laughed. "You know what everyone thinks you summoned me for, don't you?"

She nodded and giggled. "I know. But first, I've got to talk with you."

She saw him raise his brows, and she nodded. He grinned and disappeared into the bedroom without a word, returning quickly in a tee shirt and lounging pants.

He joined her on the couch. She drew a deep breath and began.

"Your friend Christina O'Donnell may be beautiful, but she's a nut."

"My friend? I barely know her."

"Well, she says you two have something in common."

"What? You know I can't sing."

"She didn't say you could." Sam drew back, looked sharply at him, and said, "You know, your singing voice isn't half bad, at that."

"Yeah, maybe in the shower. But what am I supposed to have in common with her?"

"If I understood her correctly, some kind of paranormal ability to see or sense things that other people can't. She called it the Witch Sight. She said yours flickers on and off, but she can help you with it." She drew another deep breath and added, "She says she can give it to me, too. She wants me to meet her at the pool after breakfast tomorrow. Like I said, she's a nut."

To Sam's surprise, her husband's smile vanished, and he stirred uneasily next to her.

"What exactly did she tell you?" he asked, his voice almost a whisper.

"She said the mountain lion we saw was just an illusion. It was really a woman. She said you saw it, too. And...well, I noticed the look that passed between you two. You can guess what I thought then."

Rob sat still, staring ahead at nothing until the moment became uncomfortable.

"Rob?" Sam broke the silence. "Rob, talk to me. What's the matter?"

He blinked and turned to her, looking her directly in the eyes. "Sweetheart, she told you the truth. I did see a woman. I thought I was going crazy. That's what she nodded to me about. She was telling me I wasn't hallucinating – or at least that she had the same hallucination."

"What? You saw a woman?"

He nodded. "I really did. A blonde woman in an Indian – Native American – buckskin outfit. Or maybe a pioneer outfit. What did she say it was? A ghost?"

"She said it was a message from her friend Alyssa McCormick."

"Alyssa McCormick?" he asked. "Our client?"

"I guess it has to be. What do you know about her?"

"Not a lot," Rob confessed. "Most of it has been on the news. I know she moved to Martintown this past spring. She is friends with the McCaffreys, and they're clients as well. Your firm's clients, too.

"I know she was in some kind of trouble with the feds. Some kind of foreign agency and tax charges. She hired Ben Callahan from our office, and he got Kat Turner and Marc Washington involved. She spent a night in jail, and then there was a big negotiating session with the DOJ they did by Zoom or something in one of our conference rooms, and then the charges were dropped.

"She's supposed to be involved romantically with Ben. I'm pretty sure that's true. They don't really keep it a secret, but if it started while the case was going on, it was strictly against the rules.

"But the file is sealed up, and nobody will discuss the case. That's unusual. I think your dad knows what's going on, but he won't talk about it, either. Has he told you anything?"

"He hasn't said a word," Samantha said. "Mom hasn't either. And they tell each other everything. *Everything*."

Rob's brows knotted, then cleared. "You know, there's a lot of rumors bouncing around the office about the McCaffreys, too. Something about the case Kat and Marc handled for Mitch over at the community college last fall. Something strange happened at the hearing, but I don't know what. No one, paralegals included, and they yap all the time, will talk about that, either. That's another sealed file. Are you going to accept Christina's swimming invitation?"

Samantha hesitated, then nodded and said slowly, "Yes. I think I will." She cocked her head and giggled. "I hope I don't feel inadequate being with her wearing a bathing suit."

"You? Inadequate in a bikini? Not a chance?"

"Who said I would wear a bikini?"

"Well, I haven't seen you wear anything else."

Samantha smiled and took his hand. She cleared her throat and said, "Honey, there's one more thing I need to say."

"Which is..." he prompted.

She breathed deeply and said, "Now I know what it's like to be jealous, and I didn't like it. Now I know how you felt Saturday night, and I'm sorry."

He said nothing but moved closer and kissed her. It was a deep, lingering kiss and completely satisfying.

Samantha drew back with another giggle.

"You know, darling, we really shouldn't disappoint everyone you left watching the game, should we?"

"No," he said. "We shouldn't"

What followed in the bedroom was completely satisfying, too.

Outside, the winter storm continued.

Samantha Dreams

Sam fell asleep spooned with Rob; but when she awakened, she was lying on her side, her face turned away from him, and they were not touching.

What brought her awake was the touch of a cold hand on her neck; and her eyes blinked open to the memory of her cousin Margaret telling her about feeling a cold hand on her neck when she visited the battlefield at Culloden in Scotland.

But Margaret said she had turned and seen nothing. Clearly visible here and now in the soft glow of nightlight they had left burning was a young blonde woman, slender, not very tall, pretty with eyes that might have been blue if the light were bright enough to see, wearing a long homespun brown dress. Samantha gasped audibly; and the apparition put a finger to her lips and then pointed toward the other side of the bed, where Rob slept.

Then she motioned with both hands beckoning. She wanted Samantha to get up. Sam obeyed the summons, but looking back at the bed, saw her own sleeping body, still lying on her side, while Rob sprawled on his stomach on the other side of the king-sized bed. So this was a dream, after all. It had to be, didn't it?

As Sam watched, the girl (for she was hardly out of her teens) raised a hand, palm out, to forestall her, and then moved soundlessly to Rob's side of the bed and placed a gentle hand on his almost-auburn curls. He stirred but did not awaken, and the girl turned her face toward Sam and smiled.

Then, without a word, the young woman glided around to Samantha, took her hand, and tugged her toward the door. The hand was cool, but not uncomfortably or creepily so, and the grip firm. The girl's hands were calloused. They were hands that had seen work.

Samantha allowed herself to be pulled through the bedroom and across the sitting room to the door. When they reached it, the girl made no attempt to open it, but walked through the hardwood, pulling Samantha behind. Sam felt no resistance from the door, but emerged into the dimly lit hallway beside her visitor.

Was this the mountain lion woman? Sam didn't think so. The description was different. One of the Johnson girls burned in the old farmhouse? That was more likely.

But of course, this was a dream anyway. Sam would wake up any moment now.

But the girl tugged her down the hall to the left of their suite to the next door, and pulled Samantha through that one, too. They entered a bedroom and not a suite, although the room was large with a desk and overstuffed chairs, and another king-sized bed, which held a sleeping woman.

It was Christina O'Donnell, sleeping on her back with her dark red hair spread across her pillow.

The girl let go of Samantha's hand and moved to the sleeping Christina's side. She didn't touch Christina, but pointed to her and turned her pale face to Samantha while mouthing a word. Samantha thought she was saying "friend."

Then the girl glided back to Samantha, took her hand again and looked directly at her, but with head cocked to one side, as though asking something. She wants to know if I understand, Samantha thought. Sam nodded and the dream girl smiled.

The apparition led Samantha back through the door to Christina's room and back down the hallway in the direction from whence they'd come. They didn't stop at the Ashworth suite, but went all the way down the hallway past the door to the suite where Jimmy and Linda presumably slept, to a window at the end of the hall.

There was an electric light somewhere outside. Samantha could see that it was still snowing hard. The girl pointed outside and, face lifted to Sam's, mouthed two words. There was enough light this time to be sure of the words.

They were "danger" and "beware."

Then she took Sam's hand again and led her back to the Ashworth suite, through the door across the sitting room, and into the bedroom. There she let go of Sam's hand, pointed to the bed, and whispered, audibly this time, "Sleep well." She lifted a hand to Sam's face, and gently closed her eyes.

Samantha woke Christmas Eve morning lying in bed, cuddled once again with Rob, his arm draped around her. She didn't remember lying down or re-entering her body. But it had been only a dream, anyway.

Hadn't it?

A Breakfast Call

Breakfast in the McCaffrey home was not quite chaotic. It was served in the great room on the main floor, because of the number present; and because Paul and Steve, Diana's sons by her first marriage, were up and awake, Mitch couldn't use any magical shortcuts to help.

These two were sitting at one end of the table wolfing down waffles with oceans of maple syrup and bacon, and Diana wondered if the sugar rush from the syrup could possibly make them more excited than they already were. Mitch had opened the drapes over the windows so they could watch the blizzard, and both had already been clamoring to go outside.

And it was Christmas Eve. Eight-year-old Steve was anticipating an overnight visit from Santa Claus; and Paul, whose ten-year-old maturity no longer allowed him to believe in Santa (something he kept from his younger brother), was hardly less excited in anticipation of what he would get for Christmas. Diana knew he was frustrated because he hadn't been able to find where the gifts were hidden, not knowing his stepfather had ways of hiding things even from the most inquisitive of children.

Alyssa and Ben were seated, too, drinking coffee and orange juice, and watching the snow fall with almost as much fascination as the kids. Mitch and Diana finished the eggs, more bacon, and toast, as well as still more waffles, which they carried to the table, as Mitch said, "the old-fashioned way," meaning he couldn't use his Talent to float them in.

At length they were all seated and ready to eat.

"Honestly, Diana," Alyssa said around a mouthful of toast and marmalade, "I think you're trying to fatten me up."

"No," Diana said before taking her next mouthful of eggs, "I'm trying to fatten us *all* up."

Mitch and Ben winced; and then Mitch grinned and said, "It's Christmas."

"And January will be exercise and dietary hell," Alyssa rejoined. "Thank you, Diana."

"Don't mention it," Diana said. "Misery loves company."

Breakfast had concluded, and the four adults were finishing a last cup of coffee (Paul and Steve having left for their room to watch *The Santa Clause*, again, with a promise that Papa Mitch would let them outside "after while"), when Mitch's cell phone dinged, signaling he had an e-mail or a text message.

He read the message, and said, "Oh, Hell. Fred Hutton wants a video conference in ten minutes. He wants Alyssa and Diana, too. Ben can sit in with Alyssa. You probably got the same message, Alyssa."

Ben had signed the security pledge, too, given his relationship with Alyssa, which would soon be formalized with wedding bands. He wasn't entirely comfortable with it.

Fred Hutton was their "handler" at the Defense Intelligence Agency. Mitch and Alyssa had insisted that their liaison be with that agency, and not the FBI or CIA, because the DIA was charged with protecting the country from foreign threats. Even though the DIA would share anything it learned with the other agencies, Mitch and Alyssa felt better removing themselves as far as possible from the possibility of spying on American citizens.

And they had insisted their contact not be Natalia Bathori.

"That vamp gives me the creeps," was the way Alyssa had put it.

They assumed Hutton was Gifted, but really didn't know for sure. He knew the lingo of magic, so they assumed he had some Talent, but they had never met him in person. All communications were by secure (they assumed) and encrypted electronics.

With Paul and Steve safely back in their bedroom, Mitch, with some help from Alyssa, was able to clear the table and load the dishwater with spells, much to Diana's delight. They would do the conference on the computer in Mitch's study. Although it was close to the boys' room, they wouldn't be overheard because the room partitions were solid, and because Mitch would further secure it with spell craft.

They positioned chairs so that Hutton could see them all, and then Mitch opened the computer. It took a few minutes to log on to the secure DIA video conference software, and then they saw Sutton smiling at them. From the background, he was at home, too, in a similar home office. The winter storm was big and stretched north and east as far as Washington.

They saw an open-featured brown face, the head completely bald, above an open collar and a holiday sweater. Mitch's first thought when they met on a similar video conference, was, "he looks like Hubert Davis," referring to the UNC basketball coach. Diana had giggled and said, "It's true." Hutton was about 50, a few years older than Mitch, and always dressed in civilian clothes, although Mitch and Ben were sure he had a military background and probably held a reserve commission in one of the armed forces.

"Merry Christmas," he said, and after the others had returned the greeting, the smile left his face and he continued, "Unfortunately, something has come up that needs attention."

The four waited without saying anything, and Hutton plunged on.

"Yesterday our satellites picked up on a UAP entering the atmosphere over the Gulf of Mexico. We followed it with satellite and radar as it headed northeast. Unfortunately, the snowstorm moved in and we lost it. We had scrambled some Alabama Air National Guard planes to follow it, but they had to turn back."

"What's a 'UAP'?" Diana asked.

"That's the current term. It means 'Unidentified Aerial Phenomenon'," Hutton said.

"He means 'UFO'," Alyssa supplied.

Hutton nodded. "That's the old term. Anyway, it never came out of the storm. Our radar isn't really reliable through the clouds, and neither is our satellite imaging; but as best as we can determine, it landed somewhere on the north side of Johnson's Mountain, not too far from you."

"So, you think it's an alien spacecraft?" Ben asked.

Hutton's smile reappeared. "Cross-examining, counselor?" he asked.

Ben colored. "Sorry. Difficult to turn off."

"Don't worry about it," Sutton said. "We really don't know what it is; but yes, that's the working hypothesis. We need more information. We don't have a way of getting a team in through the blizzard until the storm breaks, and that might be too late." He paused and pointed a stubby finger at the screen. "But Alyssa and Mitch can."

"Mr. Hutton, it's Christmas," Diana fumed. "Don't you have anyone else?"

"I'm afraid not. We have some people who are training on Portal...spells, and so do the Bureau, the Company, and NSA; but they haven't mastered them the way Mitch and Alyssa have.

"We want you two to go in and take a peek. Today. But be careful and don't take any unnecessary risks. Go armed."

"Johnson's Mountain," Alyssa mused. "Isn't that where Tompkins built his big mansion?"

"Yes, that's another reason. There are innocent citizens there and some down the north slope, too. We want to be able to take what action we can, as soon as we can, if they're in any sort of danger."

The four exchanged glances, and Hutton picked up on it.

"You know something?" he asked.

The four were silent, and then Alyssa said with evident reluctance, "We have a contact who is visiting the Tompkins place for the holiday. I had a premonition, and promised to check up on her. We sent Diana through a Portal last night. She confirmed there's something bad in the vicinity. We were going to check again today."

"I want you and Mitch to go, and I want you closer to where it landed," Hutton said.

Mitch was frowning. "Just a minute, Fred. This is way outside the scope of our consulting agreement. You're wanting us to put ourselves at risk, and maybe leave our families here without protection."

Hutton was ready for the objection. "I checked your contracts. It says, 'and other services from time to time as may be required and agreed upon'."

Ben broke in. "You forgot the proviso. I remember working on it. It says that Mitch and Alyssa will not be required to engage in any activity that will involve personal risk, except with their informed consent."

"So, I'm informing them," Hutton said. And I suppose we could always re-activate Mitch's commission."

Ben shook his head. "Not without violating the agreement. It specifically says Mitch and Alyssa shall not be deemed employees or be subject to military command."

Hutton sighed like an old-fashioned locomotive. "All right," he said. "We can't require this. We can't order this. But I'm begging, if you want to call it that. Right now, we have a foreign intruder on American soil, and I don't have anyone else I can send. Not until late this evening at the earliest, and maybe not until in the morning. So, I need you to go – unless, Alyssa, you can scry it."

"I tried a few minutes ago. All I could see was a round hump, covered with snow, in a field."

"You couldn't see inside?" Hutton asked.

"No, I can't visualize it. I'm working on being able to do more, but I'm not there yet."

"Then you have to go."

"Major Hutton," Mitch put in, "we won't be able to see inside if we go there, either."

"Mitch," Alyssa broke in, "Fred's right. I...I think Christina and those people really are in danger...Don't you, Diana? You were there."

Diana was blinking back tears, but nodded miserably.

"Yes," she whispered.

"Then we need to check in person," Alyssa said.

"All right," said Mitch. "We'll do it. But Diana stays here. We have children in the house, and we need someone with Diana's spell blocking ability here anyway. And Ben here can use a gun. We want the boys protected."

While Sutton was nodding, Alyssa chimed in, "I'll use scrying spells first, and then Mitch and I can go in this afternoon. We'll be all right."

"Okay," Hutton said, "Report to me on a secure phone as soon as you know anything. Do what you need to do to protect yourselves and any other American you find endangered. But don't take any unnecessary risks.

"And...there's one more thing."

They waited, and he went on, "The Bureau wants in on this. They have responsibility for domestic security. As it happens, they have an asset at the resort not far from you." His smile was sly and a little sheepish this time. "I think you know her. Her name is Monica Gilbert."

"What?" Diana exploded. "Not her!"

"Yes, her. She's being contacted now. She's expecting a call from Alyssa. We know you'd prefer that to asking Mitch or Diana to do it." His face turned solemn. "She's to get the same report I do. And bring her in if you need help. I'm told she's capable.

"Good luck, and Godspeed."

The screen went blank.

Diana exploded again.

"Monica! I can't get rid of her," she sounded as though she were about to cry.

"Worse than aliens?" asked Ben.

"Oh yes," Diana almost sobbed. "Worse."

They walked back to the breakfast area and looked outside. The blizzard was raging harder than ever.

Monica and Barry

Monica Gilbert and Barry Feldman were at breakfast in the main dining room of the High Country Resort and Convention Center, watching the snow fall through the windows while they ate. Outside, the patio had been cleared of outdoor furniture, so the snow fell and accumulated on the flat surface, giving them a good idea of the extent of accumulation so far.

"There must be two feet already," Barry said. "And it's supposed to keep on into this evening. That will have to be some kind of record."

Monica didn't respond to the comment, but cut into her eggs Benedict. The conversation had taken an unexpectedly unpleasant turn right before Barry had interrupted it with his remark on the snowfall. She was sure he was trying to change the subject, and she wasn't going to let him. They had come here for the holiday for relaxation and fun, and she wanted to get back to both without irritation.

After a bite of the Benedict and a sip of mimosa, she refused to talk about the weather, but steered him back to the topic he had started.

"Barry, I'm having trouble believing I heard what you just said," she told him.

Barry was having oatmeal with brown sugar, walnuts, and raisins, with a small plate of bacon (he was Reform, not Orthodox) and wheat toast on the side. He lowered his spoon to his bowl and answered.

"That I'm starting to have doubts about some of the things we're doing?" he asked. "Why not? Surely you've seen it coming."

She *had* been surprised at some of the things he'd said in work meetings recently, but said instead, "But you always have been one of us."

She meant being a progressive.

This time, he swallowed oatmeal and sipped coffee before answering. As he did so, his brown eyes looked directly into her green orbs.

"I still am. I just think that recently, we may have gone too far. I'm afraid some things we're pushing may be counterproductive."

"Such as?" She allowed her tone to become acid. One thing she liked about Barry is that he wasn't afraid of her. Maybe, she thought, I've been too indulgent.

He didn't hesitate to answer. "Well, for example, I don't like canceling people. Some of the people we've helped run off are harmless."

"But they are not harmless," she countered. "They don't teach correct values."

"They're not peddling hate," Barry said.

By now, neither of them was eating. They'd kept their voices quiet, but some at adjoining tables had noticed. She didn't care.

"Yes, they are," she said. "If they're not teaching correctly, they're teaching incorrectly."

"Is that all it takes?" he asked, and before she could answer, asked a follow-up. "Do we all have to think exactly alike?"

She smiled, using her "I'm superior" smile. "Of course. It's essential."

This time, Barry allowed himself a bite of toast before responding. "Monica, you say that. But I wonder if you really believe it. You say it to get approval and to make yourself feel good. It's a mantra like the Hanukah prayers I will recite at the service this afternoon. Except... well, I really do believe those."

Monica and Barry had been an item, on and off, mostly on, for more than a year now. She had had some adventures he didn't need to know about during her FBI

Special Operations training, but it had gradually become more and more exclusive. Barry, she had to admit was... sweet, and a little surprising.

One of the things that had surprised her was learning he was a believing Reform Jew. Monica herself had never had much truck with religion. But she had to admit the more she mastered spell casting (something Barry didn't know anything about), the more she realized there really were higher powers. It was only a small step to conceding there was a single highest power.

The thought made her uncomfortable, so she said nothing, concentrating on her eggs and Canadian bacon.

Barry was on a roll, though.

"Anyway," he finished, "it's fine to advocate and debate this stuff, but I don't see the point of compelling agreement. I'm starting to find canceling people distasteful."

Monica shook her head and warned, "Barry, you start saying too much of what you just said, someone will want to cancel *you*."

"Larry and Megan won't," he said, referring to his superiors at legal affairs, Larry Kincaid and Megan Stennis. He took a sip of coffee and grimaced. He had let it get cool.

"There are those who will," she warned.

"Including you, sweetheart? He asked with a sly smile. "You *enjoy* canceling people."

It was true that she did, although she thought of it as eliminating dangerous and inferior people. But she said, surprised at her sincerity, "I wouldn't cancel you, Barry. But...I thought we cared about the same things."

"I care about you," he said, his voice barely above a whisper.

Monica sighed and smiled, this time her affectionate smile. "I know, Barry," she said. "You were the only person who was kind to me last year, after that awful hearing at the college. I'll never forget that."

To her surprise, she meant it.

Barry was at the point of saying that if Monica hadn't been so determined to cancel Mitch McCaffrey, she could have avoided her humiliation, but bit into a slice of bacon instead. Instead, after swallowing, he whispered, "I didn't think about doing anything else" – which was not entirely truthful, he thought, remembering the day, but would be completely true now, so he said it with feeling.

At that point, their server appeared, offered to warm up their coffee, which they gratefully accepted, asked if the food was satisfactory, and assured them that the power lines were holding up fine, and the backup generator working well. The Hanukah and Christmas services planned for late afternoon would be held as planned. So would tonight's Christmas Eve dance in the ballroom.

The server had just departed when a cell phone in Monica's purse began to ring. Opening her purse, she saw it was the secure phone the FBI had given her.

Putting the device to her ear, she said immediately, "I'm not in a private place. May I call you back in a few?"

When she had placed the phone back in her purse, she raised her head to Barry, and said, "I have to find a private space and call back right away."

"What can they possibly want now? In this?" Barry asked.

"I don't know. I'll tell you what I can in a bit."

"Which won't be much," he grumbled. Monica wouldn't talk about what she did with the Bureau. He knew she was a consultant, but didn't know what they consulted her about. They had plenty of HR specialists employed full time.

"I know," she sighed, and rose to leave.

"I'll slide into the lounge and get a bloody Mary," he said. "Join me there?"

"As soon as I can," she promised and swayed away toward the staircase. Their suite was the only place she could be sure of privacy.

Monica and Springfield

Monica reached their spacious room with a sitting area, wet bar, and second-story view of the river and immediately placed the return call to Dennis Springfield. It was a video call, and she found him sitting in what was clearly a home office, wearing a bathrobe and holding a steaming cup of coffee or tea.

Someone higher up had evidently found whatever this business was important enough to interrupt his Christmas (or was it "winter" in the Bureau?) holiday, and now he was interrupting hers. She had to work to keep the irritation off her face and out of her voice when they greeted.

But her irritation turned to amazement when she heard the same story Hutton had told the McCaffrey's and their guests. She knew exactly where the UAP had landed, or pretty close; her demented mother was from that area.

"So," Springfield finished. "You'll receive a call later on from one of them. I'm not sure which, but they've got your number. When you get their report, report to me.

"Hopefully, that's all you'll need to do. But your directive is to give them whatever support they need. If they need you, one of them will come and get you." He meant by using a spell Portal, she realized.

Monica couldn't help but make a face, and Springfield picked up on it.

"I know you have a history, and not a good one, with those people. But they have the same orders you do. If they can cooperate with you, you can do it with them."

"If they will." Monica's tone was acid.

Springfield's gray eyes narrowed on the tiny screen. "They'd better," he said, "and so had you...Now I assume you have outdoor gear. Coat, boots, and so on?"

Monica shook her head. "Some. But I didn't expect to be outdoors for extended periods."

"Well buy what you need at the resort shop. The Bureau will reimburse you...Are you there alone?"

"No, I have a friend with me, a staff lawyer with the college system."

"Well, tell him something. But not the truth. This is Above Top Secret. Look, I hate to do this, but you guys are it. We'll get other assets in eventually, when the storm breaks, but that might be too late.

"Good luck. We'll talk later."

The call terminated and Monica left to go shopping. When she reached the resort's outdoors store, she found everything she thought she would need. Knee-high boots, a coat with a parka, thin thermal gloves, and thermal underwear. It took more than one trip to carry them to the checkout counter. She realized she would have to explain the purchases to Barry, somehow.

She paid for her purchases with her personal credit card, and stashed the receipt in her purse. She'd send it directly to Springfield, who could expedite reimbursement. If she submitted the receipt through normal channels, some nitwit bureaucrat would hold up payment on some stupid bureaucratic rule or the other.

She had a moment's uneasiness when she realized her regular job was as a bureaucrat who wrote and enforced rules for others. She thought about what Barry had said at breakfast. Did she push stupid rules? Angry at herself for the thought, she pushed it away ruthlessly.

The salesclerk was asking her if she wanted him to summon a porter to assist her with carrying her purchases to her room. She shook herself from her reverie with an apology after he repeated the question, smiling the whole time, and accepted. She couldn't very well use a levitation spell here in front of everyone.

When she followed the bellhop out of the store into the lobby, her eyes turned toward the glass sliding doors.

The snow was still falling – hard.

Chapter Four

MORNING AT THE MANSION

Breakfast (Samantha)

The senior Tompkins had announced the night before that breakfast would be served beginning at 8:30 in the breakfast room, and would be served buffet style. The food would be available until 10:30, and a light lunch available in the same room from 12:30 until 2:00. Dinner would be at 8:00, in the main dining room. Of course, everyone was assured, if anyone needed anything at any time, they needed only to page Meg or Sally, who had pagers with them at all times. Samantha thought that for holiday guests, visiting the Tompkins' was like being on a cruise.

She and Rob woke naturally, without an alarm, about 8:00, and decided they'd better shower before breakfast, in light of their late evening activities, even thought they'd need to shower again after Rob's stint in the gym and Samantha's swim date with Christina. Samantha went first while Rob shaved, and he took the shower while she applied makeup and dried her hair.

She didn't tell him about her dream. She didn't know what to make of it herself.

When they reached the breakfast room, it was almost 9:00. They found both the senior and junior Tompkins and their wives, all of whom were busy demolishing plates of eggs, sausage, bacon, home fries, and biscuits, except for Linda, who was limiting herself to cereal with fruit. They had already decided they had better go light on breakfast themselves, so they aped Linda, except that Rob sheepishly added a small plate of bacon with toast and jam. Of course, they took coffee and juice.

"Where is everyone else?" Samantha asked, remembering she and Christina were supposed to meet at breakfast.

"All of the staff ate earlier," Heather explained. "Linda is busy stuffing the turkey, the girls are helping her, and Dave and Darrel are outside trying to clear the barbecue area."

Samantha looked out a window to see the Thomas men with a leaf blower and a snow shovel, industriously engaged in removing snow from around the brick grill. She noticed there was a rifle leaning against the brick barbecue pit. They hadn't forgotten the mountain lion.

Only it wasn't a lion, she thought, if Christina and Rob could be believed, which she mostly did, although a grain of doubt remained.

"I expect Christina will be along in a minute," Linda added; and sure enough, Linda had barely spoken when Christina entered dressed in sweater and jeans, her hair caught in a long ponytail. Calling a cheery, "Good morning, all," she headed straight for the sideboard, where she took a small helping of scrambled eggs, a single slice of bacon, and toast. She seated herself next to

Samantha, to the raised brows and relieved smiles of everyone.

"How much snowfall do we have?" Rob asked. "I don't think I've ever seen this much."

"Dave measured it on the patio early this morning," said Jimmy. "Just over two feet, he says. The weather report says this will keep on until sometime this evening, so I expect we'll get another foot, maybe more."

Rob whistled. "Three feet. Wow."

"You know, I'm not sure I've seen more than this, either," Big Jim said, "although the one in '93 comes close."

Samantha's eyes darted to Christina and Rob. They had all been babies or unborn in 1993. At least, she and Rob hadn't been born. She wasn't sure of Christina's age. They all exchanged a smile, provoking a bark of laughter from Big Jim.

"Yeah," he said, "I know some of us are ancient history. Well, after breakfast, I think I'm going to my study to read, or maybe watch television. What about the rest of you?"

Jimmy responded first. "Well, I wanted to grab a rifle and nose around for more signs of that lion," he said, "but Dave talked me out of it. So I think I'll retire upstairs and check my e-mails and the internet, if the connection holds, maybe watch some TV myself. But later on, I'll dress up warm and keep Dave and Darrel company, maybe give them a break, on the barbecue. That turkey will roast slow most of the day."

"I can help with that," Rob said. "But right now, I'm going to change and hit your gym for a while."

"Linda and I are going to watch Hallmark specials on the TV in the parlor," Heather said, adding, "Christina, you and Sam are welcome to join us."

"Maybe later, we will," Christina said. "Right now, Samantha and I are going to swim laps."

Sam just smiled and nodded.

"All right, dear," Heather said. "I wish I had the energy you young people do. You'll find bathrobes and towels in the ladies' room outside the pool. Page the girls if you want anything."

Samantha

Samantha, Christina, and Rob rode the elevator up to their rooms, where Rob could change into his workout clothes and the two women could pick up their swimsuits. Samantha and Christina took only a minute to retrieve what they needed, and were on their way out before Rob could follow.

The two were silent as they rode to the basement and walked to the women's locker room. Inside, they found, as expected, a fully equipped room with lockers, bins of towels and robes, lavatories with large mirrors, and showers. A sign on one wall asked visitors to shower before entering the pool.

Christina appeared completely unselfconscious as she disrobed and slipped into a bikini just about as skimpy as the one Samantha produced from a plastic bag for herself, talking about the snowfall and how she hoped the power lines would hold. Samantha tried to imitate her, but couldn't help comparing her figure to the other woman's. It wasn't fair, she thought as she pulled the Carolina sweatshirt over her head. She'd been working hard at the office, and had her winter body and not her summer bikini body.

But when she fastened her top and turned around, she found that Christina, too, had a small but definite cold-weather belly. Christina noticed her looking, smiled, and patted her stomach area.

"It's the most wonderful time of the year," she said, and they laughed together.

"Let's swim," said Christina, and walked into the shower. Samantha followed. After a thorough wetting, they grabbed robes and towels, and walked through the door to the pool.

The pool was a lap pool, but was bigger and deeper than most such. It was surrounded by cushioned plastic chairs with small tables adjacent. There was a full water cooler with little plastic cups, and a bin for towels. The ventilation system must be very good, because there was little musty chlorine smell.

"What? No beer taps?" Sam heard herself ask. "That's what I expect here."

They shared another laugh, and Christina said, "Well, tell Big Jim and he'll have them installed the next time we're here."

"Ten laps?" Christina asked. Sam nodded.

They threw their towels and robes on chairs, and took long racing dives into the water, which was...perfect, Samantha thought. Warmed to be cool and not cold, but not bathwater warm. Christina was a strong swimmer, easily moving from the crawl to a strong breaststroke to a side stroke. But Sam had been on the swim team in high school and matched her.

Neither of them was completely out of shape. But neither was in top condition, either, so both were puffing and blowing pretty hard by the time they finished the tenth lap and climbed out of the pool. They stood side by side, panting, until Christina finally found the wind to talk.

"Thank goodness we got some exercise in the middle of all of this food and alcohol," she said. "God knows I can use it."

"Me, too," Sam agreed as she walked to the cooler and poured cups of water for them both. They gulped the water, toweled off, and threw on their robes.

"Can we sit for a minute and talk?" Sam asked. "I need to tell you something. And probably ask you something."

Christina nodded while knotting a towel over her hair, and took a chair next to Samantha's. Sam wasn't ready for the towel wrap, but used hers to rub her hair vigorously.

"What did you want to say?" Christina asked.

Sam told her about the dream. Christina listened intently, cocking her head and nodding along with the narrative.

"I just can't shake the feeling it was real," Sam concluded. "But I know it was just a dream."

Christina shook her head vigorously, loosening the towel so that she lifted a hand to steady it on her head.

"I think it was more than that," she said, her voice soft but firm.

"You believe in ghosts?"

Christina laughed. "Of course. I told you I have the Witch Sight. And so do you, now. The spirit who visited last night brought it out in you."

Samantha gasped and put a hand to her mouth, saying in a small voice, "I was afraid you'd say that. Now I'm scared."

Christina placed a hand on Sam's shoulder. "So am I, Sam. I told you I had a premonition." She pursed her lips in thought. "But it could be worse. We have a powerful friend watching. And now we know you, and Rob, and I can find ways to help one another. The spirit told you that."

When they were back in the locker room finishing drying their hair with the dryers on the wall, Christina's phone rang. When she took the call, she ran back into the pool half clad. She returned smiling in just couple of minutes.

"Well," Samantha asked her, "what's got you so cheerful all of a sudden?"

"That was Roger," Christina said, adding, "my boyfriend. He said he's been trying to call me, but the cell service has been so bad with the storm. And the call dropped while we were talking. I guess the towers are icy. We'll try later.

"He was supposed to be here, but he got held up in surgery; and couldn't get out before the storm hit. He said he would find a way to make it tomorrow for Christmas. I told him not to push it."

"He's a surgeon?"

"An ophthalmic surgeon. He was fixing a detached retina."

"Where?"

"His practice is in Boone."

"How come we haven't heard about him before now?" Samantha demanded.

"I told Big Jim and Heather not to mention it. I didn't want it to spoil anyone's holiday feeling sorry for me. But I was anxious all evening, afraid his car might be stuck somewhere. I finally got a text about the time we went to bed."

Samantha grabbed Christina by the arm.

"Oh, Christina, now I feel awful about last night. I made such a spectacle of myself."

Christina removed Sam's hand, and said, "Well, that's over. Don't worry about it."

"I still feel awful." Samantha drew a breath and changed the subject. "But tell me more about this guy. Have you got a picture? How did you meet?"

Christina showed Samantha a photo on her cell phone. Roger was a big guy, maybe a little too heavy, broad shouldered, older than Christina, with gray at his temples and in his neatly trimmed and pointed dark beard. He had a wide, friendly smile and white, even teeth. They had met a year ago when Christina was per-forming in Blowing Rock.

"I wish he were here," Christina said.

"I know you do. And so do I. "For you, and --" she trailed off.

Christina was about to pull her sweater over her head, and stopped. "And?" she asked.

"I was going to say I'd feel better with a doctor here," Samantha whispered.

Christina understood. They both sensed that something bad was coming.

"But," Sam said, her voice brighter than she felt, "let's not invite trouble...Let's go watch a Hallmark special." Her voice grew serious again. "But let's find Rob and tell him everything first."

They walked wordlessly to the elevator, neither able to shake the foreboding.

Sally

Sally, Megan, and Darrel had, after their post-dinner chores were done, enjoyed what was left of the evening last night. They had gone to the employees' lounge on the basement floor and watched most of the football game. Meg and Darrel were App students, Meg studying restaurant management and Darrel, construction management; and Megan's boyfriend, Jared, was a reserve linebacker on the team.

Sally was in paralegal studies at Carolina Highlands, and had no plans for a degree beyond her associate's diploma; but App State was local and Megan and Darrel were friends, so she cheered along with them. Actually, Darrel was maybe going to become something more than a friend; but they tried not to show it.

Sally didn't think they were fooling Meg, though, especially when she offered to walk Darrel to the elevator after the game, and then rode up with him to walk him to the door to the enclosed walkway to his parents' home. She'd only smiled when Sally had returned after the torrid necking session in the dimly lit kitchen.

Despite everything, though, Sally had gone to bed feeling uneasy, and couldn't figure out why. The storm, maybe? When her alarm sounded this morning, summoning her to get ready for today's cooking and fetching, she felt even more uneasy. She still didn't fully understand, but had a better idea of the reason for her unease. She had to tell Meg and Darrel.

But the latter was already helping clear the outside kitchen of snow, and his mother already bustling about the kitchen, when she arrived upstairs. She didn't get a chance to talk to either until after breakfast had been laid, and Laura told both to take a break. Darrel was still outside, but maybe he could take a break, too; and she suggested she and Meg go "outside" into the walkway. It was enclosed, and not really outside; and there was a side entrance from it to the patio, so she could stick her head out and ask Darrel to join them.

"I've got something to tell you both," she whispered to Megan on their way out.

They found, when they opened the side door, that Darrel and his father had just lit the hardwood charcoal. Dave said that it would be a while before the coals would be ready to take the turkey, and it was okay for Darrel to take a break. He followed Meg and Sally back through the door to the walkway. Meg left the door cracked so she could light a cigarette, and let the smoke out. She really wasn't supposed to do that, but Dave Thomas smoked himself and wouldn't tell on her.

"Okay, Sally," Megan said when her cigarette was lit, "what exactly do you want to tell us?"

Sally hugged herself against the chill seeping through the cracked door, shivered, and answered, "I had this dream last night, except I think it might be real. You both were in it."

"You want to tell us about a dream? Is that all?" Meg asked.

"Well, let her tell us, Megan," Darrel insisted. "Let's hear what she has to say before we form any big opinions."

"Whatever," Megan shrugged, obviously skeptical. "Shoot, Sally."

Sally's teeth were chattering. The cold bothered her more than it bothered Megan, who had thrown on a sweater. Darrel removed his coat and draped it over Sally's shoulders. He wore a bulky hoodie underneath, and would be okay for a while.

Megan snorted. "Sir Galahad to the rescue."

Darrel turned toward her, "Meg, shut up and let Sally talk."

Sally pulled Darrel's coat tighter and thanked him before beginning.

"I guess this was early this morning. Maybe 3:00 or so. I didn't look at the alarm clock.

"Anyway, I came awake, or I thought I was awake, and saw this black woman standing by the bed. She was middle-aged, I guess, a big gal, with a long old-fashioned dress and a kerchief.

"I realized I had to be dreaming. Then she reached down and took me by a hand and pulled me up out of the bed, and then I was sure I was dreaming. She started whispering.

"'Child,' she said, 'You are in great danger. Something bad is coming. Coming soon. You need to hold on to Jesus, and hold on to your friends.'"

"I asked her, 'Who are my friends?' I thought she meant you two, but I didn't know. She still had me by the hand, and she tugged me toward the door. I looked back and saw myself still lying there in bed. Then she pulled me right through the door and down the hall. I calmed down, because I knew I was dreaming."

She paused to watch her friends' faces. Darrel was biting his lip. Megan looked thoughtful.

Encouraged by no one laughing at her, Sally continued, "We sailed right through Meg's door and she pushed me over beside your bed, Megan. I looked back at her, and she pointed at you there asleep, then she came over and took my hand again.

"We sailed back out the door and the next thing I know, we were standing by your bed, Darrel. She pointed at you, too. Then she took me back inside the big house and upstairs to the Ashworths' room, and then to Christina's. She did the same thing.

"Then she took me back to my room and pretty much tucked me in. I woke up this morning sure that it was a dream. Now I'm not sure.

"I think I saw a real ghost. I think it was an ancestor."

"Ancestor?" Darrel asked.

"You know the Johnson massacre story?" Sally asked.

They nodded. Everyone who worked here had heard it.

"There is a story that one of the Surratt girls, a teenager, got out before the Regulators showed up. Her momma had sent her to buy fruit from a neighbor." Sally said.

"My momma's family thinks we come down from that girl."

Sally paused again to study faces. Both Darrel and Megan looked solemn.

"You don't think I'm crazy, do you?" she finished.

Darrel spoke first, "No. You see, I had a dream too. You were standing by my bed. There was someone with you, but I couldn't see who it was."

Megan made a noise somewhere between a soft cry and a gasp.

"I had the same dream," she whispered, then added, "What is happening?"

But neither Sally nor Darrel had an answer.

Rob

After his workout, Rob showered in their suite upstairs and dressed in warm clothes and boots. He tried to take the elevator to the first floor to check on Dave and Darrel outside, but when it opened, Sam and Christina stepped out into the hallway.

"We need to tell you something," Sam said.

She immediately told him about her dream, and how she was convinced it was true.

"You need to believe Sam," Christina said when Sam had finished.

"I-I do," he said after biting his lip in thought. "For some reason, I've felt uneasy ever since we got here. I thought it was because Sam and I had...something to work out. But we got past that last night, and the feeling was still strong this morning."

Christina nodded. "Rob, you're a Sensitive. So am I. So is Sam. We can see things, feel things, most other people can't. We have the Witch Sight."

"Witch sight?" Rob asked.

"I need to bring you up to speed," Christina said.

They didn't bother to find a room or even one of the hallway benches to sit on. Christina and Sam covered everything while the three stood there. There was no one close to hear them.

"What now?" Rob asked when he had heard everything.

"Why don't you go on outside?" Christina said. "Sam and I will check out the Hallmark specials. I think we just have to wait."

"For how long?" Rob asked as he punched the button to reopen the elevator.

But no one had an answer.

Chapter Five

THE SCOUTING MISSION

Hutton

Fred Hutton sat in the study of his home outside Arlington, Virginia, and watched the snowfall out the window. According to the Weather Channel, the winter storm stretched across the Southeast and lower Midwest as far north as southern Pennsylvania, playing havoc with last-minute holiday travels over a wide swathe of the country. The front was moving slowly to the northeast; and the peak snowfall so far was, as luck would have it, in Western North Carolina and Northeastern Tennessee, right around where the object had come down. Here, there were only about eight inches. So far, he amended.

But it probably wasn't luck. If the Weather Service could predict the storm, and it had, then doubtless whoever was driving the spacecraft had the wherewithal to predict it, too. Maybe they could even anticipate where the most intense snowfall would occur. Who knew?

And that was the problem. Nobody knew. Hutton had access to data on UAP activity going back for decades. He knew much more than what had been released to the public, but he didn't know what they were dealing with. Contrary to the wild stories posted on the internet by the UFO loonies, the United States didn't have multiple crashed spaceships or alien bodies. Sure, the incident at Roswell way back when had been real, but all the Air Force really got was debris and body parts. These were intriguing, and research had been able to piece together a few things. But not much.

What the United States did know, with pretty fair confidence, was that this planet was being visited by piloted spacecraft of varying designs and probably with varying pilots, whether biological or automated. That was why someone in the DOD at a level way above his paygrade had changed the term from Unidentified Flying Objects to Unidentified Aerial Phenomena. They didn't want to concede that what was being observed were objects. A "phenomenon" could be anything.

Hutton smiled. He had been a major with Air Force Intelligence before retiring and taking his present job. He was well aware that a certain type of general officer believed that if they called a duck an eagle, people would believe that it was so. And some would, for a while, anyway.

He was a good fit for this job, he had to concede. He had been tested as a "Sensitive," meaning his superior officers had said he had "extraordinary intuition" or "good instincts," when he was coming up in the military. He could even manage a few simple spells, but nothing beyond the "open a door" or "light the fire" level. But he was able to speak the lingo, so he was a good liaison with people who really know what they were doing, like McCaffrey and the McCormick woman.

He supposed they were lucky to have those two so close to the scene of the landing, although with Alyssa McCormick's ability to use Portals, that might not have mattered so much. And McCaffrey wasn't far behind. Still, it helped that they were familiar with the area. The few people at the Pentagon he had been able to reach had been able to scry a little bit of the landing site, which was only a snow-covered lump on a hillside. But no one had yet been able to "Portal" much. No one could figure out why. After the holidays, he'd have to get Alyssa back in Washington for more training.

What he didn't know was the reason for that particular landing site. The only thing significant close-by was the Tompkins house. Sure, Tompkins was a multi-millionaire from what he'd made with his convenience stories. And he gave money to causes that some of Hutton's "woke" colleagues didn't like. But he hardly had Bezos or Gates money. And he had no high-tech space travel aspirations like Bezos or Darnell, or Musk. It was a mystery.

He'd been told that they could get a force on site after the storm broke, but not before. All of the armed service branches had assets fairly close by when they could use helicopters or do parachute drops. Right now, McCaffrey and McCormick were what they had. They would have to do.

He started to call them again. But no, he decided, he would only be a distraction. They had their orders, and would call when they had anything to tell him. Right now, he'd better get downstairs and join Melissa and the kids before they came looking for him. It was Christmas Eve, after all. His son Donnie, who was in his second year at George Mason law school, and Donnie's wife, Audrey, had made it in before the snowfall. He and Melissa had a daughter, too, but Kimberly had been stuck in her apartment in Santa Fe, where she was in local television news, when the flights were cancelled. They would do a call or Zoom with her later.

He closed his computer and rose from his desk. He'd better get in some family time while he could. No telling what would happen later. At least, he reflected as he walked to the door, he had been able to keep the Company out of this operation. Those loonies would probably want to do something stupid like send in a pack of werewolves.

Having to involve the Bureau was bad enough, but manageable, he thought. He didn't know much about their asset, though, this Gilbert woman, except that she had a day job with the North Carolina Community College System, and had an unpleasant history with the McCaffreys – which was unfortunate, but something he expected them to handle. Well, he corrected himself, he knew that Dennis Springfield liked her. But then, he thought with a chuckle, that probably meant Springfield and Gilbert had hooked up, as they said nowadays.

He expected Mitch and Alyssa to handle working with Gilbert professionally. But could Gilbert do the same? Springfield had said she could. But Hutton didn't know her.

Another worry. Maybe he should give Dennis another call.

But no, it was too late for that.

Monica and Barry

When Monica reached her room at the resort, accompanied by the bellhop carrying her purchases, she found Barry on the hotel phone. He watched with raised brows as she directed the bellman to place the bags on the couch and tipped him. From the young man's sour expression, Monica was a lousy tipper. But then, Barry thought, a lot of women were.

He wasn't going to tell her that, of course. Instead, he said, when he had terminated the call, "Monica, what in world have you been buying?"

"Just some things I might need," she told him. "I thought you'd be pleased that I bought cold weather outdoor gear. You told me a walk in the snow would be fun."

"And you told me you didn't want to do it," he reminded her. "What caused the change of heart?" Before she could answer, the probable reason occurred to him, and he added, "It was that call from Washington, wasn't it?"

She sighed and nodded.

"What do they want you to do?" he asked.

"Maybe nothing. They'll tell me later. But yeah, I bought the winter clothes just in case."

"Why would you need them?"

She walked over to where he sat at the desk that held the telephone, took his hand, squeezed it, and said, "You know I can't tell you."

"Maybe I could help," he suggested.

Monica shook her head. "You don't have the right security clearance. If I tell you anything else, and the Bureau finds out, I could lose my consulting agreement."

Barry sat silent. There was nothing he could say to that. He had tried to get her to tell him what she actually did for the FBI, but she always refused.

"Well, in the meantime, I just got word that they moved the Hanukkah service to 1:30 this afternoon. The Christmas service is being moved, too. I think the hotel is concerned that they might lose power later this evening, no matter how upbeat they try to be."

"Do you still want to go?"

"I do. This is one of the rare times Hanukkah more or less overlaps with Christmas, and they have a rabbi. It won't be a long service."

"Well, I'll go to the spa after lunch. I'll have both my cell phones with me. I can send you a text if I get a call while I'm there."

"Are you really expecting a call?"

"Yes, I am. But that doesn't mean I'll have anything to do, except to call Washington and report. As long as I keep my secure phone handy, we can go ahead with our plans for this evening."

"But who is supposed to call you?"

She hesitated, then shrugged and said, "Okay, I'll tell you one thing. It's Alyssa McCormick."

Barry gaped. "Her? Why?"

"Don't ask anything else. I only told you in case she shows up looking for me."

"Is she a guest of the resort?"

"No, not that I know of."

"But if she's not, how could she get here, in... that?" He waved at the window, which offered a good view of the snowstorm, but because of the storm, not much else.

"Barry, I'm not answering any more questions. Period. Now, what do you want to do right now?"

"Do you want to go for a walk in the snow, to break in that new gear?"

Monica sat on his lap and encircled his neck with her arms.

"I do not." She giggled into his ear. "I prefer indoor sports."

He didn't argue with that.

Mitch

They had decided that Diana would take Paul and Steve out to play in the snow. She could block spells better than either Mitch or Alyssa, in case anything paranormal showed up, and Mitch could always sense her when she was close-by, and could be there in an instant. They wouldn't go far, maybe just a short distance up the trail to the top of the ridge. The boys wanted to build a snowman, but Mitch suspected they'd soon get cold and want to come inside.

In the meantime, Mitch and Alyssa would prepare, out of the boys' sight, for their scouting mission. That would require some thought. They had to plan for the weather, and they had to plan for action, if necessary. Hutton had told them to go armed, and they would; but they would rely mostly on spell craft.

If spell craft worked against...whatever they would run into, he mused. He had no reason to believe it wouldn't, but they were going to scout...aliens. He had to admit there was no other word that would do.

They were going to have to stay warm, and they were going to have to wear something that allowed for free movement. They had no military issue gear. Maybe, he thought, if they were going to continue to get assignments like this, they should ask for some.

But then, he thought, I don't want any more assignments like this.

He talked it over with Ben and Alyssa. Ben was a big help, because he, too, had served in the Army; Alyssa not as much, but she knew what she needed to be effective, so she would have veto power over what they picked out for her.

Thankfully, it was not frigid outside. In this part of the country, most big snowfalls came with the temperatures in the mid-30s Fahrenheit, and this one was no exception. Much colder air was due to follow, if the front ever moved on, which it showed no signs of doing yet. (Alyssa was a pretty good weather mage, but her range was limited; so they wouldn't be able to hurry the front.)

Layering would be the key. They would start with long thermal underwear. Mitch and Diana both owned a set; and, thankfully, Diana and Alyssa were able to wear one another's clothes. Mitch had a pair of cargo pants, and Alysa had a pair of winter trousers that would work. Mitch and Diana both had thermal socks, and they both had adequate boots.

Covering for their torsos and heads required some thought. Mitch eventually settled on a flannel shirt, a sweater, and over that an L.L. Bean Primaloft jacket. The winter coat Alyssa had brought was too heavy and long, and she really didn't have anything at home she could get by Portal; but Diana had a winter coat from Amazon Essentials that would work if she wore a sweater beneath it. The coat had a hood, and Alyssa would wear earmuffs and a baseball cap, over which she could pull the hood when needed. Mitch would wear a knit cap over his ears, and a brimmed bush hat. Mitch and Diana had night-vision polarized glasses, which would help them see through the snowfall. Alyssa would borrow Diana's. Both would wear lightweight thermal gloves that left their fingers free, and take a heavier pair to wear over the lightweights as needed.

They piled all of the clothing on the bed in the guest bedroom downstairs, where Alyssa and Ben had stayed. They would dress and leave from the basement so Paul and Steve wouldn't see. Diana and Ben would have to come up with some story about Mitch being gone with Alyssa that the boys would swallow – at least for a while.

Now for armament. Mitch led Ben and Alyssa to the gun cabinet and unlocked it. Alyssa suggested they take revolvers, because these were less susceptible of being jammed by spell craft.

"Why, honey?" Ben asked. "You're scouting an alien spaceship, not ...wizards." He was still a little bewildered when the discussion turned to magic. Ben was a gifted lawyer, but had not a jot of the Talent.

Alyssa regarded her lover with sympathy. She knew he was apprehensive for her, and she knew he was still getting used to her abilities, not to mention the McCaffrey's.

"Ben," Mitch broke in, "Alyssa may be right. We don't know who they are, what they know, or where they're from. They could as easily be from another reality as from another planet. For all we know, their ship is powered by magic. It's a sensible precaution."

He would wear his Ruger .44 magnum holstered at his right hip, he decided; and he had a .38 Police Special and a holster for Alyssa. For a long gun, he thought about taking the bolt-action Winchester, for the same reason they would take revolvers and not an automatic. But it was slower to fire and load, and he decided to take a chance on a semi-auto. He loaded four five round clips. One would go in the Ranch Rifle, and he'd shove three in a belt pouch. He thought about using a fifteen-round clip, but he wasn't used to it; and he could change magazines fast.

"It's pretty steep over there, as I understand it," Ben said. "Are you going to get tired lugging that rifle around in the snow? And won't you have to take it in a case?"

"Let me show you what I'm going to do," Mitch said.

He shoved a clip into the rifle, held the gun in one hand, lifted his other hand and spoke a word. A swirling mist appeared before him, and he reached into it holding the rifle. Both it and his arms up to his elbows disappeared into the mist. He withdrew his arms and spoke another word. The mist vanished. He repeated the process.

"All I need to do is open the closed-end Portal to get it out, and close it when I've put it back," he explained.

"Pretty slick," Ben admitted. "Are you taking knives?"

Mitch snapped his fingers. "Knew I was forgetting something."

He selected a Marine Corps model K-bar with a 5 ¼ inch blade for himself, to wear on a sheath on his left hip, and a CRVT neck knife, also in a sheath, for Alyssa. He would also take a Swiss army knife in a pocket.

"Well, that's it," he said, looking at his watch. "We'll add a water bottle apiece and a couple of power bars. We'll need to stay hydrated, and we might get hungry. We'll need to get going soon.

"And there's one more thing."

He reached back into the gun case and handed Ben a twelve-gauge pump shotgun, and then removed a Beretta 9mm pistol in a holster, along with two nine-round clips. These he placed on a bookshelf.

He looked Ben straight in the eyes.

"Ben, watch out for Diana and the boys. She can't and won't leave them. She can block spells, but magic users may not be all that show up, if anyone shows up. Please."

Ben clapped Mitch on a shoulder.

"You got it, buddy."

Mitch and Diana

As they were finishing up on compiling their arms and gear, Mitch heard Diana bring Paul and Steve in from the snow. Alyssa excused herself to change and to check on Christina by scrying, and Ben went with her. Mitch understood why. The two would need some time alone. He and Diana would need the same thing.

He found her upstairs, hanging up coats on the wall rack in the foyer. She told him the boys were happy but tired, and now wanted to watch television. She would let them, but wanted them to bathe first.

"Why don't you let them get a bath later, honey? They're not old enough to smell, and I want to talk with you for a few minutes."

She drew a deep, sighing breath, and nodded, her features solemn.

Satisfied that the boys had fresh warm socks, they helped them find a suitable movie on Amazon Prime to watch on their bedroom television. Diana promised them cocoa in a little while, if they promised in turn to bathe without complaint after the movie. They agreed enthusiastically.

"We'll see how that holds up after a while," Diana said, closing the door to the boys' room. "But they'll at least be quiet for now."

She followed Mitch to the master bedroom. When he had closed the door behind them, he took Diana in his arms and kissed her. She kissed him back. It was a loving kiss, containing the promise of future passion but without immediate urgency. When they separated, Diana began to cry.

"I'm scared, Mitch," she said. "Scared for you, scared for Alyssa, scared for all of us. Ben is, too. He's practically beside himself."

"I know," Mitch said. "He told me. But I'm proud of him. He'll do his part. And so will you."

"Why did this have to happen now?" Diana demanded. First, it was right before our wedding. Now, it's *Christmas*."

"I don't know, sweetheart," he said. "But listen. I've got to go down and change in just a minute."

He told her the plan, including arming Ben. She nodded approval.

"The house is warded and you can block spells," Mitch said. "Ben is an Army vet. He knows how to use a gun. I don't think anything will happen here. But someone has to stay with the boys, and someone has to watch out for you. That's Ben.

"We'll be back as soon as possible. We'll make our report from here. You can tell Paul and Steve that the grown-ups are hanging out downstairs. With any luck, Alyssa and I will be back before they know we're gone."

"What if they do find out you two are missing?" Diana asked.

Mitch opened his hands, palms up. "Think of something."

Diana laughed in spite of her anxiety. "Thanks a lot."

"One more thing," Mitch said. "If anything goes wrong, think of me. Picture me. I'll feel you and I'll be here immediately, the government be damned. Promise me you'll do that."

"I promise," she whispered.

"Good," he said. "Now kiss me again and let me go change."

The Confrontation Mitch and Alyssa

Mitch and Alyssa had earlier reviewed on Google Earth the aerial photographs of the top of the ridge down to the other side where the craft had landed. The slope on that side was steep, with outcroppings of granite pushing up between the trees at irregular intervals. There was a bare knoll about three quarters of the way down, which looked as though it might be, or had been, pasture, and then the slope continued, a little more gently, to the valley, where there appeared to be a couple of small houses. The knoll was the most likely landing spot.

There appeared to be another, smaller, open area about halfway between the probable landing site and the top of the ridge. They decided they would Portal there. They didn't want to emerge on top of the spacecraft, but wanted some tree cover on their approach. They didn't have winter camouflage, and a glamour spell could only do so much. The online photographs were without snow, so the going would be treacherous. Mitch decided they should add hiking sticks to their gear; and, fortunately, he and Diana had picked up a couple earlier in the fall at a store in Boone.

Alyssa was better at scrying than Mitch, and she found the open area they were shooting for. It looked suitable, though snow covered. She also reported that Christina was safe and apparently watching television with other women at the Tompkins place. It was time to go.

Paul and Steve were still watching their movie, and the four adults gathered in the den downstairs. There were last-minute hugs and kisses, and then Mitch and Alyssa stepped through Portal mist into a snowstorm on the side of Johnson's Mountain.

The walk down the slope proved slow, as they knew it would be, and treacherous at times. The snow hid depressions filled with dead leaves, and there were almost a couple of nasty spills. The hiking sticks proved to have been a valuable addition, as they used them to test the ground in front of them. The snow eased at times, and then poured down again.

Mitch finally called at halt at a point about 50 yards from where the trees ended and the nearly level knoll began, at a spot where a large oak tree created some space and a granite outcropping offer some cover. He pulled binoculars from his belt, and Alyssa took out a smaller pair of field glasses Mitch sometimes took to ball games. They had to remove the night vision glasses to use them. Diana had helped Alyssa put her hair, which she had let grow longer in recent months to please Ben, in a bun; and a strand had escaped. There was a breeze that whipped it into her eyes, and she swore softly and pushed it back.

Through the falling snow, they saw a snow-covered dome in the middle of the clearing, about another 50 yards from where the knoll began. In the distance, they saw wispy plumes of smoke from the houses at the bottom of the ridge, but were too far away to smell the woodsmoke. Mitch hoped no one who lived down there had tried to investigate the landing site.

At first, nothing moved other than the falling snow. Then, at the center of the dome, snow seemed to fall away, and two figures emerged. They were bipedal, thin to the point they would have appeared emaciated if human, and tall, well over six feet, Mitch judged. Each turned its head to the other, as though to speak, and they saw the heads were elongated, like some of the skulls in Meso-American graves. Both wore something that looked like high-altitude respirators. They were dressed in solid black form-fitting belted jump suits, with attachments at either hip; and their helmet-like head coverings were black, too, making them stand out easily in the snowfall.

"Evidently," Mitch whispered, "they can breathe our atmosphere, but require filtration, or maybe enhancement."

"Do you think they know we're here?" Alyssa whispered back.

"I don't know. Let's see what they do."

Mitch was good at glamour spells. He had placed one on both him and Alyssa, and the snowfall had become heavy again. He didn't think the aliens – that's what they had to be; no use pretending anything else – could see them. But they both had their secure cell phones. Even though these had been turned off, the batteries were fully charged. It was possible the creatures could detect the phones.

Now the two aliens began to walk directly toward them. The snow was deep enough to assure they didn't approach rapidly, but their advance was steady. As they walked, the creatures touched something on their belts, and their black suits turned snow white, making them more difficult, but not impossible to see.

"Should we take a Portal out of here?" Alyssa asked, still whispering. They didn't know what these creatures could hear.

"Not quite yet," Mitch said. "I want to get a better look at them. But can you port us back to where we arrived in a hurry?"

She nodded, her eyes wide.

She's afraid, Mitch thought. And Alyssa McCormick is as cool a customer as he'd ever seen. But he didn't blame her. He was afraid, too.

Well, he'd experienced fear before. No one served a tour in Iraq without fear. He took a long, deep breath, and muttered a calming spell. Out of the corner of his eye, he saw Alyssa do the same. It helped.

By now the creatures were almost to the trees, and still advancing steadily. Mitch spoke a word, low but firm and mist swirled to his left. Reaching into it, he pulled out the Ranch Rifle. He jacked a round into the chamber and engaged the safety. He glanced at Alyssa and saw her smile and give him a thumbs-up.

They saw one of the aliens twist a knob on its belt. Without warning, both Mitch and Alyssa were all but paralyzed. The sudden headache was blinding. They were in the grip of what felt like a strong compulsion spell; but it was artificial, not magical. But it worked the same way, and Mitch tried a blocking spell. It was mostly effective. There was still pressure, but he could move, and the headache retreated, even if it didn't completely disappear. He turned his head to Alyssa. She was breathing hard, but her "okay" sign said she'd done the same.

The creatures evidently realized they were being thwarted, because they turned their heads toward one another and communicated somehow, although Mitch couldn't hear what they said, or even if they said anything. Then they resumed their advance. By now they were at the trees and starting to climb.

Mitch decided to try a warning shot. Maybe that would back them off. He thumbed off the safety, aimed well over their heads, and squeezed the trigger. Nothing happened. The rifle would not fire. Whatever field the aliens were creating with their belt devices was suppressing firearms.

Devices, Mitch thought as he watched them continue their advance. That thing on their belts was an electronic device of some kind. His Talent was always good at manipulating those. Subvocalizing a spell, he reached out, but felt the spell slip away. He tried again. There, he had it.

Mitch grinned through the snowfall. He didn't know what this was, and he couldn't use it. But he could turn it off, short it out. Not bothering to subvocalize, he continued to chant the spell.

Abruptly, the pressure inside his head ceased. The headache was gone. The aliens' white jumpsuits turned black again. He had, at least for now, disabled whatever it was they were using. Evidently, he had done a number on it, because he saw them twisting the knobs on their belts frantically.

He decided to try a shot again. It was a snap shot, not aimed, but the rifle cracked and the bullet whined toward the creatures and blew apart a branch on a tree near the one on the left. The two stopped abruptly, conferred again, then continued forward.

Later, Mitch realized that Hutton wouldn't have approved what he did next. For all he knew he might be starting an interplanetary war. He should have asked Alyssa to open a Portal. But now, full of adrenalin, and thoroughly pissed off, he didn't think of that.

But damn it, they had attacked him. And Alyssa. He took aim this time, and fired directly at an alien's chest.

The .30 caliber slug caught the creature directly in its torso, and knocked it straight backward, "ass over tea-kettle" as his dad used to say, on its back into the snow. But it began to stir immediately, and the other stumbled over through the snow to help its fallen comrade to its feet.

Good Lord! He thought. That jumpsuit can stop bullets.

But it couldn't take away the kinetic energy of the bullets, and Mitch quickly took aim and emptied the rest of the magazine into the aliens, two slugs each, all connecting, and sent them sprawling.

As he ejected the spent clip and reached for another, he took a quick look at Alyssa. She had not drawn her revolver, but was busy chanting a spell. Before her, fallen branches and rocks both large and small emerged from the fallen snow. They flew directly at the aliens, who were again getting to their feet, and knocked them sprawling again.

They tried to rise again, but two more shots from Mitch flattened them still another time.

"Let's see what they do now," Mitch said to Alyssa aloud. The time for whispering was over. "Maybe they've had enough."

Sure enough, this time, the two creatures, when they realized they'd been allowed to rise to their feet, turned back toward their vessel. Mitch started to yell something after them, but closed his mouth, choking back the shout. Best to leave well enough alone.

Instead, he turned Alyssa and grinned.

"First blood to us, I think," he said. "Or at least first bruises. If those things are organic, they're going to be plenty sore."

"Should we follow?" Alyssa asked, and immediately corrected herself. "No, that was a stupid question. We should stay put. But let's watch for a minute."

Mitch nodded and they watched in silence as the long-legged aliens made good progress back toward their ship.

That was almost a fatal mistake. They saw the snow slide away from the dome again, and two more black clad creatures emerged. One of them lifted a short rod, and a blinding blot of light, pencil-thin, emerged from it and struck the oak next to them with a crack and sizzle as sap boiled.

"Plasma bolt!" Mitch, who sometimes read science fiction, yelled. "Duck!"

They both dove behind the boulder, and felt it crack and shudder.

"Let's get out of here," Mitch said.

But Alyssa was already opening a Portal, this time at ground level, and they crawled through it back to the clearing where they'd started.

They got to their feet, brushing away snow from their clothes and Mitch's rifle, and stood panting until they could calm themselves. Mitch put the rifle back in the closed Portal he had created, and both pulled out their water bottles and drank deeply.

"That," Alyssa declared, "was close."

"Too close," Mitch agreed. "But now we know they're not friendly."

"Do we?"

"Yes. Think about it. First, both of us are Sensitive and we can feel the hostility. You can cut it with a knife. Second, if they'd just wanted to say hello, they wouldn't have tried to compel us with that gizmo they have. And finally, if it were all a misunderstanding, they wouldn't have tried to shoot us. Q.E.D."

Alyssa nodded, her features solemn. "Now what?" she asked.

"We report in," he said. "As instructed."

"First, let me check on Christina," Alyssa said. "We're close, if she needs anything."

"Sure, and –" he stopped abruptly. "Alyssa, can you feel it? At the top of the ridge?"

Alyssa stood still, her eyes closed in concentration. Finally, she said, "Yes. Something is up there, or close. More than one. Somehow, they're human and alien at the same time. And they don't mean well.

"Mitch, we've got to get up there! I...I think they came from down there." She pointed downslope.

Mitch thought for a minute, and then said, "No. Not both of us. I'll go up and scout it out. I can open a Portal to the top since I can see it.

"You've got to go back and report in. We don't dare call from here. Our phones might not be secure – from them. I'll zip back and tell you what I've found out as soon as I can."

"Why can't you be the one to report?" Alyssa demanded. "Christina is my friend."

"I know she is, and I'll come get you if I need help. But you have to do one more thing."

"What's that?"

"We're going to need all the Spellcasters we can get. You've got to come back and bring Monica with you."

"What?" Alyssa's mouth gaped so wide, snowflakes fell on her tongue, causing her to cough. "Why can't you go get her?"

"I'm the one with military experience for one thing. But the main thing is that our orders, and hers, are that you're her contact. She may not accept direction from me. And she doesn't report to Hutton. But I think the Bureau will confirm she's to come."

"Sometimes you're too damned military for your own good," Alyssa fumed.

Mitch allowed himself a grin. "So Diana has told me." His grin vanished. "And frankly, I'd like to have Diana here, too. If our ability to block compulsion can disrupt that device the aliens use, Diana's Talent might stop it cold.

"But she won't leave the kids, not even with Ben; and I won't, I can't make her. Her contract isn't as extensive as ours, and she is well aware of that."

"She won't be happy that you're at risk," Alyssa said.

"She's already unhappy. So is your fiancé. But what they're doing, taking care of the kids and keeping a secure place to retreat, is important."

"What rank did you reach in the Army?" Alyssa asked.

"Eh," he said, surprised. "Captain. But it was a brevet rank. My reserve rank was first lieutenant. Why do you ask?"

"Because you're a leader. People will follow you." This time she allowed a smile, and gave him a mocking salute. "All right, captain. Let's get going."

They each formed Portal mist, and disappeared into it.

The snow soon covered their prints.

Chapter Six

THE MANSION AND THE RESORT

Rob left Sam and Christina and walked down the hall, across the breakfast room, and through the door, which was unlocked, onto the patio. As soon as he was outside, he regretted not bringing a cap with ear flaps. The baseball cap he was wearing covered his head, but his ears were going to get very cold if he stayed outside for long. Otherwise, he was dressed warmly enough.

He waded through knee-deep snow across the patio to the covered area housing the brick barbecue pit, where Dave and Darrel were minding the turkey. Dave was just closing the lid over the pan with the ~~roasting~~ turkey and nursing a steaming mug of coffee. Rob's mouth erupted with saliva at the smell of the roasting bird stuffed with oyster stuffing that hit his nostrils immediately upon emerging from the house and grew stronger as he drew closer. The snowstorm was in one of its momentary lulls, still coming down but not as hard, so visibility was good. The snowfall was expected to continue into the evening. It had to be well over two feet deep already.

"I should have told you to go through the kitchen, into the walkway and through the door from there," Darrel called to him. "Sorry."

"Not to worry," Rob said, brushing snow from his pants and boots as he reached the cleared area. "I should have figured it out for myself."

"Want some coffee?" Dave asked. "We have a Thermos...Or, if you prefer, there's beer in the outdoor refrigerator." He pointed to a small refrigerator recessed into the back of the brickwork, well away from the charcoal pit. There was a bottle opener affixed next to it.

Rob swallowed, his mouth gone dry after the burst of saliva. "A beer sounds good for now," he said. "Thanks. I'll switch to coffee later."

He bent and opened the refrigerator door, and finding a Yuengling, removed and opened it. Straightening, he took a long swallow. The beer helped.

"What's going on?" he asked.

"Well," Dave said, "I just put a lid over the turkey in its pan and banked the charcoal just a little. And I reduced the air flow to the coals a bit. That will reduce the temperature on the inside of the grill, and now the bird will roast slowly for hours."

Rob allowed a short laugh. "I don't know if I can hold out that long after smelling it."

"The meat is hot now," Dave explained, "but it won't be fully cooked for a while. It's better if it roasts 'low and slow' for a long time. What you smell are the meat juices seeping from the turkey into the oysters, sausage and spices in the stuffing."

"Whatever it is, it smells wonderful," Rob said. "It makes me want to eat it right away."

"Welcome to the club," Darrel said. "I go through this every year."

"You poor, starved baby," his father teased, and then, his eyes moving from Darrel to Rob, added. "But don't worry, either one of you. Laura and the girls have done all of the food prep, and they won't start cooking the rest of the meal until late this afternoon, but –"

He stopped and pointed toward the breakfast room, where Megan and Sally were busy at the sideboard.

" – Sally and Meg are putting lunch out now. Sliced venison left over from last night, chicken salad, sandwich bread, lettuce, tomatoes, onions, pickles, and so on. Potato and macaroni salad. And white bean soup with smoked bacon. No one is about to starve.

"In fact," he concluded, "just as soon as I'm sure I've got the fire right, I'm going to go in and get a bite, and then keep Laura company for a while, if you'll keep Darrel company." When he saw Rob nod, he continued, "I can have Sally or Megan carry food out to you, or get young Jimmy to take a turn here. You won't get cold. We have a space heater here in the ceiling, as I guess you've noticed; and if you stand close, the fire pit puts out plenty of heat."

Rob had noticed the heater, and was gratefully standing as close to it as he could get without bumping into one of the others.

"Sounds good," Rob said. "I'm okay to stay out for a while. Really."

"Thanks," Darrel told him. "I could use the companionship.'

They stood without speaking for a few minutes while Rob finished his beer and the other two sipped coffee.

Rob couldn't shake the feeling of dread, the thought that something bad was going to happen, and soon. He saw that Darrel was fidgeting, and kept looking through the snow, which had resumed a heavy fall towards the woods and then glancing over to where the rifle leaned against the wall of the enclosed walkway. He noticed it was the Winchester Model 70 with iron sights, the .338 magnum. Maybe Darrel was feeling the same premonition that something bad was going to happen.

"I see y'all are ready if that catamount shows up again," Rob observed, pointing to the rifle.

"Yeah," Darrel said, his eyes darting back through the snow to the wood line, "that, or –" he trailed off.

"Or...what?" Rob asked, not quite able to keep apprehension out of his voice.

Dave laughed. "Son, there's a lot of critters out there. Lions maybe the least likely. A bear could wander over if it smells the turkey. That's most likely. But there could be a bobcat or two. Coyotes." He stopped for a sly smile.

"Or we could get a visit from a Boojum. You know what a Boojum is?"

"Sure," Rob said, talking to hide his apprehension. "That's what we called a bigfoot back in McDowell County. But I used to hunt pretty regularly, and I never saw or heard one. Or saw a print or anything." Whatever menace he was feeling, he was pretty sure it wasn't a bigfoot.

"That's what we call 'em around here, too," Dave said. "But" – he nodded toward the woods – "they're out there all right. They just don't show themselves much...

Well, I think I'll slide on in and get some lunch. I'll send one of the girls out to see what you want in a minute."

Dave strolled over to the door to the walkway and left them. In just a few minutes, Sally DeRatt emerged from the same door, and asked them what they wanted. Rob noticed the look that passed between the striking-looking black girl and Darrel, and wondered fleetingly if anyone else had picked up on what was going on.

Darrel wanted a venison sandwich with mustard and pickle, and potato salad. Rob asked for a sandwich, but with mayo, lettuce and tomato, and mug of the bean soup.

"Tell you what," Darrel said, "that soup sounds good to me, too. But it'll be too much for Sally to carry. I'll run in with her to get the food, if you'll watch the grill. Don't worry, it'll take just a minute. You won't have to do anything."

Rob really, really did not want to be left alone. But he also didn't want anyone to think he was crazy. So he said, "Sure."

They had barely disappeared indoors when he heard a voice calling, from a short distance back toward the trees, "Rob! Rob Ashworth!"

Rob started violently. He felt like he'd jumped out of his skin. He peered through the snow and saw nothing. Then he picked up the Winchester and eased around the grill for a better look, holding the gun both hands but not against his shoulder. Not yet.

At this point the wood line was interrupted by the Thomas cottage. The walkway extended from the house to the Tompkins mansion making a sort of capital "I." Walking along the side of the walkway from the far end of the "I" was a man in a heavy jacket and boots, and wearing a bush hat and night vision glasses to help him see through the snow.

The man slowed his advance for a moment when he saw the rifle Rob clutched, but resumed his tread through the snow when he saw the rifle wasn't aimed.

"W-who are you?" Rob stammered, trying not to squeak but not quite succeeding.

The man stopped a few feet from the covered area. Rob noticed he wore a pistol at his belt but made no move to draw it.

"My name is Mitch McCaffrey," the man said quietly. "We've met at your offices."

Rob's eyes widened in recognition. He had met the man who had become one of the firm's best-known clients, very briefly, about twice.

"Mr. McCaffrey," Rob said, "I do remember meeting you. But what are you doing here? And how did you get here?"

McCaffrey opened his mouth to answer, but just then the door to the walkway opened, and Darrel and Sally came out carrying trays. Sally stifled a shriek and almost dropped her tray. Darrel, a little more composed, asked, "Who is this? What's he doing here?"

Sally's eyes were as big as Rob's, but her face broke into a dazzling smile, and she said, "Hello, Mr. McCaffrey. Remember me from comp class? Sally DeRatt." She turned to Darrel and added, "Mr. McCaffrey taught me English comp.

"But," she added, turning back to McCaffrey, "How did you get here?"

"Sure, I remember you, Sally," McCaffrey answered. "Rob knows me, too. How I got here is going to have to wait for now. But I need to talk with someone in the house right away. You're all in danger."

Rob, Darrel, and Sally all exchanged a look.

"And," McCaffrey added, "Frankly, I need to get out of the cold for a few minutes. And — it wouldn't hurt if I got something to eat."

Without a word, Darrel turned and walked to the door from the covered outdoor kitchen to the walkway. He opened it and said, "In here."

Samantha

"What's wrong, Samantha? Christina?" Heather Tompkins asked, her expression showing curiosity more than concern.

"Why, uh, nothing," Samantha said, feeling her face flush. She realized she hadn't been paying much attention to the film. For the last little while, the feeling of dread she couldn't shake had been growing stronger.

"I-I'm fine," Christina said.

"Honestly," Heather said, her voice gentle and matronly, "you two haven't said a word in a long time, and both of you keep fidgeting. If you don't want to watch with us, it's okay to find something else to do. Really."

Samantha exchanged a look with Christina, who nodded. She felt it, too.

"Samantha, why don't we go check on how lunch is coming along?" Christina suggested. "I'm afraid we're just bothering Heather and Linda. I admit I'm not into the movie."

Samantha agreed immediately, relieved. She didn't feel like watching television. Despite Heather and Linda's assurances they were no bother, they excused themselves.

As soon as they were in the hallway, Christina took her by the arm, and pointed with her chin toward the main door.

"I think whatever it is, is coming from that way," she said, her voice just above a whisper.

Samantha stood still, eyes closed. "Yes-s-s," she whispered. "I think you are right."

They walked quickly through the main entry hall and peered through one of the windows flanking the double doors. The snow was again falling hard. Visibility was limited. But Samantha's apprehension was stronger than ever. They stood still, their eyes searching.

There. Movement in distance. There were three, no four, figures on the road, trudging through the snow toward the house. Their progress was slow but steady.

"Who are they?" Samantha asked. "Where did they come from?"

Christina's head shook vigorously. "I don't know, Sam. I wish I did."

"What should we do?" Sam knew her eyes were wide, and she felt herself trembling.

Christina grasped a hand, and said, "Sam, the first thing we do is compose ourselves. I feel the same thing you do. But those people are coming here, and we can't give away that we're on to them. So take a deep breath and pull yourself together."

Samantha realized Christina was right. She inhaled deeply as instructed. Her trembling didn't completely stop, but it got better.

"I'm going to go tell Heather and Linda that we're about to have guests, and ask them to tell Jim and Jimmy they'd better come down. Why don't you go tell Rob and everyone else? Dave Thomas needs to know for sure."

They walked rapidly, side by side, until Christina, at the door to the parlor, squeezed Sam's hand and said, "We're going to be fine." Samantha squeezed back, mumbled "I hope so," and hurried down the hallway toward the breakfast room, while Christina turned into the parlor to tell the Tompkins women.

Whatever it was they'd been dreading, it was almost here.

Mitch

Rob, Darrel, and Sally led Mitch through the door from the covered outdoor kitchen to an enclosed walkway that connected the main mansion to the cottage, which Mitch surmised must be where some of the staff lived. There were several recessed quartz heaters set at intervals along the wall, and it was much warmer there. Mitch removed his outer gloves and shoved them into a coat pocket, but kept his lightweight thermals on.

Rob took from Sally a tray holding a mug of some kind of steaming soup, a bit of which had sloshed over the brim, and a sandwich on a small plate, and handed it to Mitch.

"Here," he said, "you can take mine. I can get more inside. But I'm afraid there's no place for you to sit."

"Actually, there is," Darrel said, walking past Mitch down the walkway toward the cottage. Everyone followed until they reached an alcove on the opposite side of the walkway from the patio, which jutted out into the yard on that side. It held a small table attached to the wall, with cushioned built-in seating on either side, like a booth.

"Mom asked Big Jim to include this when they built this walkway," Darrel explained. "She thought it would have a better view than the windows on this side of their house."

Mitch took a seat and motioned to the opposite bench.

"Rob," he said, "sit with me for a minute. And take the sandwich. The soup will do me just fine. Sally and – " he looked a question at Darrel.

"I'm Darrel," Darrel said. "Darrel Thomas. Sally and I work here."

" – Darrel," Mitch continued, "better get back. You can fill them in later."

"It's all right," Rob told the others. "Mr. McCaffrey is trustworthy."

They nodded and walked back down the enclosed hallway. They stopped and whispered for a moment when they reached the door to the outdoors kitchen, then Sally continued on to the door to the mansion, while Darrel went back outside.

Mitch spooned soup into his mouth. It was still hot and very good. He took two more spoonful's, mostly to warm himself up. Then he looked up at Rob, who still had not touched the sandwich.

"Rob," Mitch began, "you all must trust me. You're about to have guests. I don't know who they are. I don't know anything about them, or what they want with anyone here. But they're working for...a foreign country, and they don't mean well."

"What country?" Rob asked.

Mitch hesitated. "I don't know. I...I can't tell you how we know this, but we know someone has been on the way here for several hours. They came from the other side of the ridge, and, as best I can sense them, they skirted the woods down the road, and now they're on their way back here.

"They're...dangerous. But I think I can help."

Somewhat to Mitch's surprise, Rob didn't look all that surprised. He didn't voice any objection, but asked instead, "Does this have anything to do with that light that passed over last night."

Mitch decided he had to answer that one. "Yes," he said, "it does."

Rob nodded and asked another question, "You said, 'we.' Who is 'we'?"

"You may as well know," Mitch told him, "'we' means Alyssa McCormick and I."

Rob didn't look surprised at that piece of information, either, Mitch noticed. Had Kathryn Turner or Marc Washington told him something? He didn't have time to go into that now.

Before Mitch could say anything else, Rob spoke again.

"Mr. McCaffrey – "

"'Mitch' is fine," Mitch broke in.

"Okay...Mitch," Rob said, "you need to know that ever since that light passed over, several of us have had this awful feeling that something bad is about to happen. I still feel it."

Mitch studied Rob's intent, boyish face and closed his eyes for a moment to better sense his aura. Why, he decided, this young man has a touch of the Talent. He could be taught to cast simple spells. He hadn't noticed that before on the few occasions they'd met.

"Who, besides you, are you talking about?"

"You just met two of them. Darrel and Sally. Samantha, my wife. Megan, another maid. And Christina O'Donnell – she's another guest. I don't think anyone else, but I'm not sure. Sally and Samantha had really vivid dreams. The rest of us have just been...uneasy."

Mitch considered. Six Sensitives. That was a bunch. And that could help, but it also might make them more vulnerable, if whoever was coming had any of those mind control gizmos.

"All right," Mitch said, "I don't think we have a lot of time. Your visitors are getting close. I can feel it. But I don't think they'll try anything right away. My guess is they'll tell some story and try to get everyone to drop their guard.

"I'm going to stay here. When something happens come and get me. Or if you can't, just think, "Help!" as hard as you can. I think I may be able to neutralize them.

"And you need to fill in your wife and friends when you get a chance. Give them the same instructions. Christina knows Alyssa. She'll back you up."

Rob nodded. He rose.

"Wait a minute," Mitch said, "I'm not quite finished. This is important: If you feel a headache coming on, and get the feeling someone or something is trying to get in your head to make you do something, say these two words."

He gave Rob the words to the blocking spell and made Rob repeat them. Once, twice, three times. Rob might be strong enough to use it. He hoped.

"And there's one more thing," Mitch said.

Rob looked at him quizzically. "Which is?" he asked.

Mitch made a pained face. "Can you show me where I can take a piss?"

Alyssa

Alyssa stepped out of mist in front of the main entrance to High Country Resort. As she'd thought, no one was outside, and the snowfall was heavy enough to obscure the mist. She waded through the snow to the covered area in front of the automatic sliding door. She spoke a word and the snow fell off her pants and the tail of her coat. The snow was that deep.

The doors parted for her, and she walked into the lobby. It wasn't busy, but there were people there. A few glanced at her, but didn't pay much attention. She decided the first order of business was to get warm. She walked to the huge central fireplace and opened her coat to let in the heat.

She looked around the lobby, and saw a kiosk with coffee, and headed straight for it. She bought a large cup, added cream, and sipped with appreciation. She noticed the hotel had a business center. She needed to call Fred Hutton, and maybe she could do it from there.

Sure enough, the center was empty. It was Christmas Eve, after all. No one was transacting business. She nonetheless made her way to a cubicle at the far end of the room. She turned on the computer workstation there, just as a diversion, and pulled out her secure phone. She inserted ear buds and placed the call.

The government phones used satellites and not towers, so she wasn't sure the call would go through. But it did.

She reported on what had happened as quickly as possible. He interrupted with questions a couple of times, just to clarify, but otherwise listened.

"And, so," she concluded, "Mitch wants me to pull Monica in, so we can get another Spellcaster. If he wants *her*, it shows how dangerous he thinks these creatures are.

"I agree with him."

"You say he's up at the Tompkins place?" Hutton asked.

"Yes," we both sensed...something approaching it. Something both human and alien. We think Christina and those people are at risk. But someone needs to keep an eye on that spaceship.

"I don't want to go back by myself."

There was a long pause, and a burst of static that made her think she might be losing the connection. But then he spoke.

"Okay," Hutton said. "I get it. Pull Gilbert in. But give me a few minutes to talk with her FBI handler. If I don't call you, you're cleared. But..." He spoke that last word with emphasis. "But the mission is still the same. You can protect yourself, but you are there to observe and report. Be sure Gilbert understands that. Brief her thoroughly before you go back. Understood?"

"Yes. Understood," Alyssa said.

"I'm still trying," Hutton said. "But there's no way we can get anyone in until late this evening. That storm front has to move first. If any of our Users here could use the Portal spells you and Mitch are so good at, we could do better."

Alyssa knew exactly why the Portal spells weren't working for the DIA or the Bureau, or anyone. But she said nothing.

Maybe Mitch and I will have to lift the hex, she thought, now that this stuff has come up.

But she allowed the call to terminate without comment.

She sat in the cubicle for a minute, finishing her cooling coffee. Now she needed to find Monica.

She walked to the concierge desk, and asked the person on duty, a young guy in hotel uniform with a name badge that said he was "Tommy," how to get in touch with Monica Gilbert. He obligingly rang her room, but there was no answer.

"Pardon me, ma'am," the young man (he couldn't be older than 22 or 23) asked, "are you a hotel guest?"

Alyssa smiled and said, "No. I'm just visiting."

His eyes widened. "How...how did you get here?" he asked.

Alyssa laughed and said, "With great difficulty." Before he could respond, she asked, "What's going on right now? I need to talk with her."

Consulting a schedule, Tommy said, "Well, there's a Hanukah service in Salon B, and in the main theater they're playing *It's a Wonderful Life*. They'll show *Miracle on 34th* Street after that. The Christmas Eve service will be at 3:30, also in Salon B.

"And," he finished, "our casual dining restaurant is still open for lunch. The lounge is open. And...let's see, the spa is open."

"Thank you," Alyssa said. "That's very helpful."

She walked away, aware of his eyes following her, and stopped in front of the fire to think. Monica would not be at the Hanukah service. She wouldn't yet be drinking, probably. She'd look in the restaurant and if Monica wasn't there, she'd try the spa. There was a resort map on a wall. She walked over to study it.

Monica

Monica allowed herself a contented sigh. She was lying on her back, wrapped in a towel, a facial mask covering most of her face, and cucumber slices over her eyes. The sauna and steam room had been more than satisfactory, and the massage heavenly. She felt ready for a nap.

"Ms. Gilbert?" The querulous voice was at her left side. "Ms. Gilbert, excuse me, but there's someone here who wants to see you. She says it's urgent."

Monica sighed again, but not with contentment, and lifted the cucumber slices from her eyes. She raised on an elbow, clutching the towel to her chest. The attendant, a young woman dressed all in white, standing next to her, wore a name badge that said she was "Missy." She managed to look both apprehensive and apologetic.

"Who is it?" Monica demanded.

"She says her name is Alyssa McCormick."

Monica sat up. McCormick here? Monica had been expecting a call, and had her secure phone with her, but Alyssa being here meant something was up. And not something good.

"Where is she?" she asked Missy.

"Out front, in the reception area. She...looks as though she's been outside. In the snow."

"Tell her I'll be out as soon as I've showered," Monica said.

Missy hurried off to pass the word along, and Monica rose and made her way to the dressing room. She showered quickly, knowing there likely was no time for attending to her makeup or doing more to her hair than washing, drying, and a few brush strokes. She wondered what was going on that McCormick would come here.

When she reached the reception area, clutching her purse and the travel bag with her cosmetics, she found Alyssa McCormick standing, dressed in winter gear and tugging the hem of her jacket down to cover something she suspected was a firearm. This was ominous, she thought, intrigued and at the same time irritated. She hadn't expected this.

"Ms. McCormick," she said, offering her hand.

"'Alyssa' will do," McCormick said. "We're going to be working together." Lowering her voice, she added, "Let's step out into the hall and find a place we can talk."

Monica nodded. There were several women waiting for admission to the facility, and some were staring at them. She followed Alyssa into the hallway. They found it empty, for the moment.

"We need you," Alyssa began immediately. "Do you have winter clothes?"

"Yeah, in our room," Monica said. "But what's going on?"

Alyssa told her about her scouting mission with Mitch, including the encounter with the aliens.

"Mitch went up to the Tompkins place," she concluded. "I need to go back to the area close to the spaceship. I need backup. You're it."

Monica thought quickly. This was alarming, but it was also an opportunity.

"I'll have to call Dennis Springfield," she said, "to be sure I'm authorized."

"Check your phone," Alyssa said. "You should have a message by now."

Monica did as she was asked. Even as the phone emerged from her pocket, she heard it chirp with a text message. It was, sure enough, from Special Agent Springfield.

She looked up at Alyssa. "All right. Do I have time to tell Barry?"

"Barry?" Alyssa asked.

"My...friend. He's here. He's at the Hanukah service."

"You can leave him a note," Alyssa said. "I'll have you back as soon as possible. You need to change clothes now...Do you have a gun?"

Monica's lips curled in a smirk.

"I'm a witch," she said. "I don't need guns."

Chapter Seven

UNINVITED GUESTS

Samantha

Samantha was almost running as she reached the solar, which was empty of people, but she made herself slow down and catch her breath before walking into the breakfast room. The level of her apprehension was higher than ever, but she didn't want to show it.

When she entered, she found only Dave Thomas sipping coffee over the remnants of a sandwich and potato salad on a small plate, and Megan and Sally standing in uniform next to the sideboard. Glancing to her left out the window, Sam saw Rob sitting with Darrel at the small table in the covered grilling area. Darrel was eating, but Rob was saying something. There was a plate with an untouched sandwich in front of him.

Sally was whispering something to Megan. Dave was looking at them, and didn't notice Samantha enter from the door to the solar.

"Hey," he called, "y'all want to tell me what's going on?"

The two turned at his voice, but saw Samantha approach down the right side of the table as they turned, and shifted their attention to her. So did Dave, who raised his brows at seeing her. Evidently her excitement was showing.

"Well, hello, Samantha," Dave said. "What has you so flustered?"

Samantha made herself breathe deeply once again, and answered, "Some – someone's coming. On the road."

Dave's brows raised, but his tone was calm. "What are they driving?" he asked.

"Nothing," Samantha said. "They're walking. Up the road to the house. The snow is so deep, it's taking them a while. But they'll be here soon."

Dave rose. "We're not expecting anyone," he said. "I'd better go see who they are...Megan, go up and tell Jim and Jimmy. They should be in Jim's study. Jimmy may be back in his suite. Sally, tell everyone else. But tell Darrel to stay put. Someone needs to stay with the fire. Tell Laura to stay put, too."

As soon as he spoke, Megan and Sally went flying from the room in opposite directions. Dave walked into the solar, and Samantha followed. Dave went to the wall pegs that held the coats, and retrieved a jacket. Sam watched him shrug it on. The coat had a deep side pocket, from which he removed a snub-nosed revolver. He checked the cylinder and shoved it back into the pocket.

"Samantha," he said, "I don't want you to panic. But we aren't supposed to have any more guests, and we're pretty isolated up here. I'm just being careful.

"When we get to the door, stand behind me and Big Jim. Keep the others with you. This is probably nothing except distressed motorists who somehow found us. But I want to be careful."

Samantha nodded, feeling a bit relieved. Just then, Rob hurried up, and Dave repeated his instructions. They left for the front door, Dave leading, and Rob and Samantha following. Sally caught up with them when they were about halfway down the hallway.

Samantha felt her husband grab her arm. He leaned toward her right ear and whispered, "I need to talk with you as soon as I can. Christina, too."

"What" – she began, but he cut her off.

"I have some important information," he said. "I can't tell you right now. For now, let's do as Dave told us."

She nodded and walked on, completely mystified. She supposed she'd find out. Her feeling of dread was as bad as ever.

No, it was worse.

Rob

They found Christina, Heather, and Linda waiting on them in the entrance hall, gathered at the window and peering out through the snow. Big Jim and Jimmy, both wearing coats and overshoes, joined them in a moment.

Dave asked Linda to step aside so he could see, and took her place at the window.

"They're close," he said. "Jim, why don't you and Jimmy and I step outside and see what they want." Rob noticed Dave briefly patted a pocket, and caught their quick nods. He assumed that meant they were all carrying, and felt better, a little. He decided to speak up.

"What about me?" he asked. "I'm wearing a coat, and that will give us four people."

Dave hesitated, and then gave a jerky nod. "Well... okay," he said. "But stand behind us."

Dave opened one of the double doors, and they all stepped outside. The flagstone walkway was covered for a short distance, so they weren't standing in the snow.

By now the four approaching figures had rounded the turn in the driveway and were nearing the front entrance. All wore heavy coats with parka-like hoods. They were knee-deep, actually a little above knee deep in snow for one shorter figure Rob thought might be a woman, and their advance was steady, but slow.

Whoever it was had seen them step outside. They stopped, and one of the taller visitors called a greeting.

"Hello, the house. May we come in? We're lost."

The Tompkins' and Dave exchanged looks and Big Jim nodded and shrugged, so Dave called back, "Yes. Come on."

Rob noticed that all three of his companions had their hands in their coat pockets, and he approved of the precaution; but while his feeling of apprehension hadn't subsided, and if anything was stronger, he felt no immediate danger. Whatever these people were planning, it would come later. He assumed Sally had done as asked and informed McCaffrey. Rob wasn't sure what Mitch could do, but thought they might need him.

Within a couple of minutes, the four newcomers reached the covered area and started stamping their feet to shake off snow, with little effect. Dave, the Tompkins and Rob edged back toward the door to give them some room.

"Who are you?" Big Jim asked, his right hand still in his pocket, a gesture that wasn't lost on the newcomers, judging from the eyes darting from within the parkas, which they now pulled back to reveal themselves.

The biggest of the three, tall with broad shoulders, dark close-cropped curly hair over a square face with a Roman nose, said, "I'm Andrew Sorrelli. You can call me Drew. This is my wife, Elena Alvarez, and our friends and colleagues, Tim Lassiter and his wife, Karen Miller. We were looking for the turn to the High Country Resort and got lost. We found this road and decided to try it. Our SUV got stuck a ways back. We've been walking for hours."

They looked as though it was true. All were red-faced, their hair stuck to their foreheads, with the sweat of exertion pouring down their faces. All were fine-looking people, Rob noticed. Elena Alvarez was shorter than the others, no more than 5-5 or 5-6, her clear, striking Latina features oddly contrasting with large greenish eyes. The other woman, Karen Miller, was a little taller, slender with a mop of shag-cut brown hair, pretty and brown-eyed. Her husband was as tall as Sorrelli, but not as powerfully built. His close-trimmed blonde hair was now dark with perspiration, but would be a lighter shade when dry. His eyes were a pale blue, and he was sharp-featured, vaguely foxy looking like many of the Scots-Irish who had settled the Southern Highlands.

Jim removed his hand from his pocket and offered it first to Sorrelli, and then to the others. He introduced Jimmy, Dave, and Rob. When the visitors spoke, Lassiter's voice, sure enough, held a dash of southern mountain twang. The others' accents were harder to place, but definitely not foreign.

"Dave," Jim said, "let's get the snow brushed off of our guests' clothes and boots, get them in out of the cold, and some hot food into them. I need some lunch, too, and we can get their whole story inside and not here with the snow blowing on us."

Dave, who had followed Jim's lead on removing his hand from his pocket, although Rob thought he had done so reluctantly, said, "Sure," and took a broom from a boot against the wall. Within minutes, everyone was inside and the newcomers were being introduced to Heather, Linda, Christina, and Samantha. He tried to catch Christina's eye, but couldn't. He wondered if Sam had managed to tell her anything.

"You poor folks are just in time for lunch," Heather said. "Let's get your coats off, and take you to a warm fire for a few minutes. After we get you some food, we can find you some clean clothes" –

"Thank you," interrupted Elena Alvarez, who coupled her remark with a dazzling smile. "All of our clothes are back in the SUV. I don't see any way to get them."

"You can't, dear," Heather told her. "I'm afraid you're snowed in here...Sally, be a dear and run ahead and tell Laura we will have more folks for lunch. Then you and Meg be sure the other guest rooms are prepared... We'll have to check on clothes. I think Jim has some stuff that Tim can wear. Maybe Rob and Darrel can help with Drew."

Sally practically ran out of the entrance hall toward the solar to do Heather's bidding. Then she and Linda led the new arrivals to the parlor, where a big wood fire was blazing. As they walked, Rob noticed that all four of the newcomers were wearing a rectangular box belted at the hip, with buttons and a dial on the side. Just looking at them, Rob's internal alarm throbbed. He had no idea why.

"Interesting cell phones," he observed, hoping for information.

"They're proprietary," Sorrelli said, "issued by our brokerage company. You see, we're all investment bankers taking a holiday trip."

Rob would have liked to ask more, but decided against it. Instead, he saw a chance to talk with Christina and Sam. And report to Mitch.

"Tell, y'all what," he said. "Why don't Sam and Christina and I go see if we can help with clothes while you all are warming up? We'll join you in a few minutes."

He thought the newcomers were looking at him oddly, but no one objected.

He left with Christina and Sam and immediately put a finger across his lips. They understood and followed him to the elevator. When they'd reached the second floor, they started talking as soon as they were off the elevator and into the hallway.

Samantha

Samantha was not happy, and wheeled on Rob immediately.

"What do you mean, I should share my clothes with those...women?" she demanded. It came out pretty much as a bark, which was stronger than she thought she'd intended.

Rob grabbed her by the arms, and said, his voice soothing but intense, "Calm down, honey. I don't care about the clothes, but I needed an excuse to talk with you two in private."

Samantha shook herself from her husband's grasp, but made her breathing slow.

"Okay," she said, realizing she sounded petulant. "But...I. Don't. Like. Those. Women."

"I think I know why," Christina said. They say they are married. But I don't think they really are couples. They don't act like they are."

"Why do you say that?" Rob asked. "I know the women didn't take their husband's last names, but that's not so unusual these days."

"That's not what I meant," Christina said. "These people are supposed to be just getting to safe space from a harrowing, scary experience. In circumstances like those, married couples hug one another, touch each other. These four didn't.

"And Sam, didn't you notice the way Sorrelli was checking you out? Right there in front of his wife?"

Samantha felt the heat on her cheeks as she flushed. "Well, yes," she admitted. "But I thought he was checking out you, too."

"Oh, he was," Christina said. "But he was really focused on you. I got more attention from the other guy, Lassiter."

"Well," Rob growled, "I sure as hell noticed what Sorrelli was doing. I can't say I care for him, either."

Christina laughed. Samantha thought she understood why, but Rob looked completely flustered.

"What's so funny?" He was still growling.

"Didn't you notice the way the women were looking at you?" Christina asked.

"I did," Samantha said, mimicking her husband's growl.

"I didn't," Rob said. "How was that?"

"Like you're what's for dinner," Samantha snapped at him. "You mean you didn't notice?"

"Well, no."

Christina laughed again. "That's a man for you. Clueless."

Rob opened his mouth to protest, but Christina cut him off.

"We may have to use that," she said. "We may have to...flirt with them." Her eyes moved from Sam to Rob. "You, too, Rob."

Oh, hell, Samantha thought. Rob and I just repaired our jealous snits last night. Now this? And...I'm still frightened. Those people scare me.

"What did you want to tell us, Rob?"

Rob told them that Mitch McCaffrey was hiding in the house, and was there to warn them. That was another shocker. Sam knew that Mitch McCaffrey and Alyssa Mc-Cormick had been local celebrities for a while, although that had died down, and that they were clients of both her firm and Rob's. But this was unexpected.

"He said to see what we could find out, and get word to him," Rob finished. "And that if anything bad happened, to close our eyes and think of him. He said he can sense us if we do that – I don't know how – and will come to help us."

"But how did he get here?" Samantha asked. This was getting weirder and weirder.

"I don't know that, either," her husband said. "But he's here."

Just then the elevator door opened and Sally DeRatt emerged. She told them Heather had sent her to get two more guest rooms ready.

"Did you talk with McCaffrey?" Rob asked.

"For just a minute," Sally said. "He said to find out as much as you can, and remember what he told you."

Sally excused herself to find the linen closet.

"Well," Christina said, "I guess we've pretended to look for clothes long enough. Shall we go down?"

Without a word, Samantha walked over and pushed the button to summon the elevator. The door slid open immediately.

Samantha really wanted to go to their suite and hide, but she entered the elevator with the others.

Rob squeezed her hand, and she squeezed back.

Jim Tompkins

Big Jim Tompkins excused himself from the group and headed to the breakfast room, saying there was something he wanted to check on in his study. He went up the back stairs, because he wanted to avoid walking with the group and being asked for details, so he missed the elevator ride with Samantha, Rob, and Christina; and, because the stairwell and his study were on the opposite side of the house from his study, he heard none of their conversation.

But he wanted to check on something.

Tompkins had not spent years building a successful business spread over a large region without developing what he called a "bullshit meter." The two couples who had just showed up out of the blue, or rather, out of the storm, seemed all right, but something about their story was just a little too convenient. It was almost, he thought, as though they had set out to come here.

When he reached his study, he shut the door, locked it, and hung his coat on the coat tree next to the door. He removed the pistol from his coat pocket and placed it in its customary desk drawer. Whatever the visitors were, they didn't appear dangerous; and if they were armed, nothing was visible. He hadn't seen any suspicious bulges in their clothes. He supposed they could be carrying knives or something, but that didn't seem likely. He seated himself at his desk and opened his laptop computer.

He and Heather had stayed at the High Country Resort several times, and he had the telephone number in his laptop. He lifted the receiver on the desktop telephone and dialed the number. There was some static on the line, and then a busy signal. He lit a pipe, waited a couple of minutes, and tried again, with the same result.

He supposed the lines might be down somewhere. It wouldn't be on the access road here; he had spent too much money earlier this year clearing the trees away from the utility poles for that. And the power was still working fine. But there was a lot of rugged country between the public road and the resort, so yeah, sure. A line could be down.

Cellular service was spotty with the storm, but he decided to try his cell phone. Still a busy signal. Maybe he could connect by e-mail. He tried to find the resort page on the web, but he got a message saying that he was not connected to the internet.

Jim bit down on the stem of his now unlit pipe. This was getting frustrating. And odd. The internet connection had worked fine earlier today. What had happened? He supposed it could be the storm, but...

He decided to try rebooting the computer. That didn't work, either. Same message. Sighing, he closed the laptop. If he didn't go down soon, someone would think something was wrong.

Placing his pipe in the ashtray and rising from his chair, he began his short trip downstairs.

Something *was* wrong, but he couldn't figure out what.

Mitch

Mitch McCaffrey was mentally kicking himself. He was going stir crazy just sitting here. But except to rise and stretch, he couldn't move around. He didn't want to be seen. Not yet, anyway.

What he called his "spidey-sense" was ringing four alarms. He should have tried to Ward the whole house, he realized; but it was too late now. The foxes were in the hen house. He had placed a Ward on Rob, Darrel, and Sally, but he really wasn't sure how much good it would do against whatever tech the aliens and their flunkies were using. It would have been nice to Ward Christina, too; but he didn't share Alyssa's connection with the O'Donnell woman.

He wanted to take a Portal home, check on Diana and the kids, and make sure they knew he was okay; but he was afraid to leave right now. He had the feeling he'd be needed here. Maybe Alyssa could get word to her and Ben that she and Mitch were all right. Yes, she could probably risk a text to them. He couldn't, from here. He was too close to the spacecraft.

Well, he did feel a connection to Diana. He always did, except when she was blocking. He wasn't getting any bad vibes from it. He supposed that was something. For now, it would have to be enough.

Rob

Rob, Sam, and Christina entered the breakfast room together. Big Jim was still upstairs, but everyone else was already eating. Looking around, he saw through the window that Dave was out at the barbecue "pit," talking with Darrel. Rob noticed the sandwich on the plate he'd left outside had disappeared. Darrel likely had claimed it. That was just as well. He didn't feel very hungry. He'd just get some soup.

As Rob, Sam, and Christina made their way to the sideboard, Sally walked in from the kitchen and whispered something to Megan, earning a rebuking stare from Laura.

Rob noticed there was another crockpot of soup on the sideboard, along with some fresh bowls and utensils. Laura explained that the bean soup was almost gone, but she'd heated homemade vegetable beef.

Rob noticed Samantha took soup only, too, although Christina made a half sandwich for herself. Sitting beside Sam and across from Christina at one end of the long table, he noticed Jimmy, Heather, and Linda were eating lightly, too.

Not their new guests, however. Sorrelli, Alvarez, and Lassiter had loaded their plates with sandwiches, potato salad, pickles, and olives, and taken large mugs of soup as well. They were all attacking their food with gusto, their eating interrupted only with grunts of appreciation and compliments to the cook. They must be starving, Rob thought. He didn't blame them. They couldn't have had much, if any, breakfast; and that had been a long, cold hike up the mountain road.

Rob spooned his beef-vegetable soup slowly. Samantha, he saw, was doing the same. Christina ate more rapidly. He supposed she could handle the anxiety better. But, come to think of it, he didn't feel so anxious now. In fact, he was feeling pretty good. He reached over and placed a hand over Samantha's. She smiled, and they both began to eat more normally.

He took stock of how he felt, and remembered Mitch McCaffrey's warning about feeling pressure inside his head, even a headache. There was no headache; and if there was any pressure, he didn't feel it. He remembered the words Mitch had made him memorize. He didn't think he needed them. Not yet. He hoped not at all. He looked at Christina again. She didn't appear nervous.

When lunch had concluded and Megan and Sally were clearing the dishes, Jimmy offered more coffee, tea, or "something stronger." Sorrelli and Lassiter accepted more coffee, but the two women asked for water only. Rob had had water with lunch, and decided to help himself to coffee. Samantha and Christina didn't want anything.

"Well, y'all," Jimmy said to their new guests, "tell us more about yourselves. Tell us about your brokerage firm, where you live, and so on."

"Now, Jimmy," Linda chided, "let these poor people get some rest, get a bath, before you make them talk about themselves."

"Thanks, ma'am," Lassiter said, "but we can talk for a few minutes.

"We've worked with one another for several years. For a long time, we were with Merrill Lynch; but then we decided to get married. The firm wouldn't let us work together, so we left and went to" – he gave a name Rob didn't recognize – "in Nashville. It's small, but we've been quite successful."

"Do you have children, dear?" Heather asked.

Karen Miller spoke up, her voice cheerful. "Not yet, she said. We haven't been married but a year or two. That's in our future, though."

Rob found himself looking at her as she spoke. She really was quite pretty, he thought, even with her hair plastered to her scalp. But Elena Alvarez was even more spectacular, he decided. He noticed her trying to make eye contact with him, and as he complied, she smiled as though they shared some secret. He returned the smile without thinking. Embarrassed, he tore his eyes from Elena's, and looked over at Samantha, feeling a little sheepish, but saw she'd made eye contact with Sorrelli and that the two were sharing a smile, too.

Well, hadn't Christina said it might be a good idea to get friendly with these people? That couldn't do any harm, could it? And speaking of Christina, she was practically batting her eyes at Lassiter. This might be a pleasant experience, he thought. Somewhere, submerged under his fascination with Elena Alvarez, his alarms were still sounding. But he ignored them.

By this time, Big Jim had joined the table, and was finishing a sandwich. He spoke for the first time, since he'd said he was sorry to be late.

"All right, y'all. I know you want to clean up. Sally has your rooms ready, and you surely want to rest. We'll find some clothes we'll send to you. Hopefully, something will fit."

"I think you have some old clothes Tim and Drew can wear, dear," said Heather, "and Linda says she has a few things for the ladies."

"Actually, Mr. Tompkins," Lassiter said, "we'd rather meet with you. And Jimmy," he added.

"Really?" Tompkins said, "Why? What about?"

Lassiter looked embarrassed, but said, "Well, in the interest of full disclosure, we were hoping to call on you right after the holiday anyway. Frankly, that's really how we got stuck. We took too long to find the turn up here before going on to the resort, and the storm caught us."

Tompkins' mouth tightened. "I'm afraid I didn't plan this holiday gathering to talk business," he said.

"Aw, Dad," Jimmy said. "Surely we can spare them a few minutes."

Big Jim rolled his eyes, but said, "All right. We can meet in my study."

Lassiter said, "Thank you. Look, we're not going to gang up on you. Karen and I can make our pitch...if Rob and Samantha – and Christina – can keep Drew and Elena company. Our firm...may have some interesting proposals for them, too."

Sorrelli and Alvarez nodded with enthusiasm. Rob exchanged eye contact with Samantha, who nodded, and said, "Sure. We can do that. We can meet them in the visitor's parlor upstairs."

Christina spoke for the first time, "Actually, if it's all right, I'd rather sit in with Jim and Jimmy."

Jimmy said, chuckling, "You're likely to be bored, but sure." He turned to his wife. "Linda, what about you?"

Linda looked a bit sour, but said, "Include me out. I'm going back to the Hallmark Channel."

"Me, too," said Heather. "No business talk for me, thank you very much."

Heather sent Sally to show the guests to their rooms.

"Well, interesting people," Jimmy said when their new guests had left the room.

"Maybe," his father said, "but just a bit too mysterious for me. But...we'll see what they have to say."

Rob saw Christina was trying to get his attention, and Sam's. The two had been staring at the door. He took Samantha by the shoulder and turned her toward Christina.

"You two be careful," Christina whispered. "I don't think they're going to try to sell you stocks and bonds."

Her words reached where the dread had been buried, and some of it returned. But he found himself looking forward to seeing...well, Elena, he admitted, again. Sam seemed upbeat, too.

But he hoped they wouldn't regret it.

Chapter Eight

STAYING ON MISSION

Christina

Christina wasn't sure she had got through to Rob and Samantha. She didn't like their body language.

She studied them a moment more, then said, "Y'all have a few minutes. I want you to come with me. She rose from the chair, and turned toward the door to the kitchen. They slowly got to their feet and followed her; she thought they did so reluctantly. But they came.

"Hey, where are you guys going?" Jimmy called after them.

"Oh, we want to see what Laura is up to," she called over her shoulder.

But when they were in the kitchen, she turned immediately toward the door to the enclosed walkway.

This time it was Laura who was curious. "Where are y'all headed?"

"Just for a walk," she said. "We don't want to go outside."

Laura evidently accepted the explanation, because she said, "Well, if you want to see our little house, feel free. It's clean, and the door is open."

"Oh, is it all right if I come, too?" Sally asked.

Laura smiled, "Just for a bit, dear. I'm going to need you here."

Christina opened the door and led everyone out. Rob and Samantha followed, but Sally almost had to push them ahead of her.

Christina would like to see the Thomas cottage, but that would have to wait. She had another mission.

She was taking them to Mitch.

Rob and Samantha picked up their pace as they walked, more so as they drew closer to the alcove where Rob had left McCaffrey. Christina herself felt a little easier as they went. Maybe whatever was influencing them was weaker with distance. Or maybe it was just fading with time.

They found Rob sitting in the alcove studying something on his cell phone.

"Tell me what happened," he said as soon as Christina had settled into the seat opposite him, and the others had gathered around.

Christina briefly summarized the four visitors' arrival and the lunch. She described all four in detail. Then she plunged into the key point.

"They are definitely up to something," she said. "They really tried to work on us, especially Rob and Sam, but me, too, and some on Jimmy. I think they are all wearing some kind of mind control device."

"Now wait a minute," Rob said. "I didn't get any of that...I actually thought they were pretty nice."

"So did I," Samantha said, then grinned widely and added, "I didn't see any devices. And – well, that Drew Sorrelli is *sooo cute.*"

"Did you really?" Rob growled.

Samantha glared at him, and said, "Well, don't tell me you weren't flirting with Elena Alvarez."

Rob looked at his boots and colored.

"Did you see any 'devices'?" Mitch asked Christina.

She nodded. "They had these rectangular boxes on their belts, like a big cell phones. That's what they said they were, company-issued specially built phones. They kept fiddling with them during lunch." Her eyes turned to Rob and Sam. "Didn't you notice?"

Neither had, but Sally spoke up.

"I did," she said. "I was standing where I could see real well, but I tried not to be obvious. They were keeping one hand in their laps, like they were holding their napkins; but there were these dials on the sides they kept twisting. Once or twice, it looked like they pushed a button, too.

"I got this uneasy feeling, a little; but I don't think they were focusing on me."

"They weren't," Christina said. "Sorrelli and Alvarez were focused on Sam and Rob. Miller was working on Jimmy. Lassiter gave me some attention, but he was really focused on Big Jim."

"You don't seem to have been affected as much as Rob and Samantha," Mitch said. "Is that why?"

Christina said, "I think so. And also, when I started feeling something, I tried to run song lyrics through my head. I think it helped."

She paused, thinking. "And...last week, when I told Alyssa I was getting premonitions, she said she had placed a Ward on me. Maybe that helped."

"Alyssa is really good at working spells from a distance," Mitch mused. "Better than I am. Yeah, maybe the Ward helped. But I put one on Rob and it didn't seem to have worked. Of course, I don't know him as well as Alyssa knows you. A Ward works better when there is already a bond."

"I don't understand," Rob said. "You told me to use that...formula you gave me if I started feeling any pressure, especially a headache. But I never felt anything like that, so I didn't use it."

Christina saw Mitch's features go blank and his eyes close in thought. Then he opened them, and turned toward Rob and Samantha.

"I think I have the answer," he said. "These people are from that ship that landed over the hill. They're working with what – whoever attacked me this morning. It – he had a box on his belt, too.

"But what I faced was a frontal assault. It was hostile from the beginning. Those devices work some kind of artificial compulsion spell, but not every compulsion spell is a direct assault. Some go at you from the back door, so to speak.

"You all felt some level of attraction to one or more of these people. Especially you, Samantha, but Rob, too, and even you, Christina. They were trying to build on that, set you at ease, set you up. The first step was to take that attraction and ratchet up your reaction."

"Makes sense," Christina said, looking around. She saw some resistance from Samantha and Rob, but finally they nodded.

"But now what?" she asked. "Are you going to intervene now?"

Mitch answered immediately, "I thought about that, but no. Not yet. I'd like to know what they're after. It's pretty clear they want something from Jim Tompkins, and I'd like to know what.

"So I'm going to ask you all to play along a little longer. So keep your appointments. I'm going to Ward all of you, except Christina. She's already Warded. I'll renew yours, Rob.

"What about the...blocking spell?" Rob asked.

"Do you still remember it?"

"Yes, but what about Sam...and Christina?"

"They're both Sensitives, but I don't sense any spell-casting Talent. I do in you. Don't hesitate to use it."

He stopped talking and moved his eyes from one of their little group to another.

"I'm asking a lot of you. I'm asking you to put yourselves at risk. It may be necessary for some of you to play along with that bunch for a while. Rob, Sam, Christina – can you do that?"

There was some hesitation from Samantha, but they all said they could.

"All right, then, people. Sally, send Darrel to me. I'll fill him in and Ward him, too. All of you study my face, my features, really hard. If you think things are getting out of hand, close your eyes and think of me. I'll come running."

His eyes roved them all again.

"Stay focused. Stay on mission," he concluded, and added, "Good luck and Godspeed. I'll be praying for you."

The promise made Christina feel better. Now was as good a time as any to call on the Divine.

"Thank you," she said. "I'll be praying, too."

Diana

Diana McCaffrey sat in the great room with Ben Callahan. *It's a Wonderful Life* was playing on the large-screen TV, but she'd seen it before and wasn't paying close attention. A glass of white wine, mostly untouched, was getting warm on a coaster in front of her. She was too worried about Mitch to watch television or enjoy wine.

She glanced at Ben, who sat on the opposite end of the leather-covered Arts and Crafts couch. He had paid a little more attention to his Scotch-rocks, but not much. The ice was melting in his glass, which rested on another coaster. He saw her look, and smiled, the tiniest curve of the lips. He must be worried, too.

They were upstairs because Paul and Steve were still occupied (she hoped) in their room, and she didn't want to be too far from them. They had wanted to go back outside, and she had declined, smoothing over their protests with promises of unlimited TV and video games. They had asked where Papa Mitch and Aunt Alyssa were, and she told them neither was feeling well and they were resting in bed, meaning everyone should be quiet.

That had worked so far. It wouldn't for much longer, and she had no idea what she'd say.

Ben had kept the shotgun and pistol close by, hidden from the boys behind the Christmas tree. That un-nerved her, too.

It wasn't turning out to be a nice Christmas Eve day.

She almost jumped out of her skin when she heard her cell phone ring. She composed herself and grabbed the phone, hoping it was Mitch.

But it was Alyssa.

"Diana, can you come downstairs? Right now? I need your help," Alyssa said without any other greeting. "Just you. Tell Ben to stay put for now."

"Are you all right?" Diana said. "Is Mitch?"

"Yes, we're both fine. Mitch isn't with me. Please come right now."

Diana gave Ben a quick explanation, and then practically ran downstairs.

She found Alyssa, still garbed in her outdoors gear, standing on the far side of the couch in the library. But the person with her, also in heavy winter clothes, made Diana gasp.

She said the first words that came to her.

"What is *she* doing here?"

The second person was Monica Gilbert.

Alyssa

Alyssa waited before the fire, standing back from it because she was warm by now, in fact becoming a little too warm, and hadn't removed her coat, waiting for Monica to change to her heavy clothes and come down to join her. She tapped a foot, impatient to get going. There was still plenty of daylight, but dark came early this time of year. She wanted to save as much daylight as possible, in case action was required.

She hadn't heard from Mitch, but she could sense both him and Christina. They felt close to danger, but not in immediate harm. She wanted to see what was going on down at the alien ship, and then Portal up to the Tompkins house in case they needed any help.

Finally, she saw Monica walking toward her from an elevator.

"I'm sorry," Monica said when she walked up. "I had to leave Barry a note. And I had some trouble figuring out these clothes. I finally said to hell with it and used a spell."

Alyssa regarded Monica and shook her head. "This won't do," she said. "This won't do at all."

"Why?" Monica demanded. "What's wrong?"

Monica was dressed for the weather, but her coat was a bright, garish orange with equally vivid green slashes on the sides under her arms. That was the problem.

"Your coat and parka," Alyssa said. "It will be visible from a mile away, even in the snow."

"It's all they had," Monica said, her tone defensive. "What was I supposed to get? The salesperson said the colors were designed so someone could be found if they got separated from their party, and so no hunters in the woods would mistake me for a deer or something."

"Well, it will make you a great target for anyone really trying to shoot you. Anyone who's looking will see you," Alyssa snapped. "Don't you have anything else?"

"I have a wool dress overcoat," Monica told her. "It's black."

Alyssa shook her head. "No, that won't do, either. It's not insulated enough...Are you sure the shop had nothing else?"

"They said they didn't."

Alyssa bit her lower lip, thinking. There wasn't time to die the fabric. They couldn't exactly go shopping. Not today. Not in this weather. But...maybe Diana McCaffrey can find something.

"I think I know where we get you something better," she said. "Let's go."

She led Monica through the sliding doors out into the snow, through Portal mist and into the McCaffrey downstairs den.

"Diana," Alyssa said, plunging right into why she and Monica were there, "we need your help. Monica needs a coat that won't be so visible from far off. We couldn't get one at the resort. I'm hoping you have something."

"Wait a minute!" Diana snapped. "Where is Mitch? Is he all right? Why isn't he here? Don't just jump into my house with no warning, bringing this woman with you, and start demanding something without any explanation."

Alyssa opened her mouth to snap back, but closed it. Diana was right. She took a deep breath and started over.

"Mitch is fine, Diana. I'll explain where he is in a minute. He's not here because he had to go elsewhere. But we're losing time, and I have to know right away if you can get Monica another coat. If you can't, I'll have to think of something else."

"Not until you tell me where Mitch is," Diana insisted.

This was exasperating, but Alyssa understood where Diana was coming from.

"Okay," she said. "Mitch was needed at the Tompkins house. That's where he is. I haven't talked with him because he can't use his phone that close to the ship.

"But I know he's all right. I can sense that he is. You can, too, if you slow down, calm yourself, and think of him. Try closing your eyes."

This time, it was Diana who caught herself before flying off the handle. She closed her mouth, breathed deeply, and closed her eyes. After a few seconds, her eyes flew open again.

"I keep forgetting I have this...sensitivity you talk about," she said, her voice barely above a whisper. "You're right. I can feel him. He's worried, but he's okay." She swallowed hard, and said in a firmer voice, "Nothing of mine will fit her." She jerked a chin at Monica, who had stood silently, her face impassive except for a half-smile. "But I think I can find something of Mitch's that will do. It's the outdoor coat he wore until he got the PrimaLoft. It's brown. We may need to pin the sleeves up."

Diana turned toward the stairwell. "I'll get it."

"If you can find some more lightweight thermal gloves, that would be good, too," Alyssa called after her. "And bring Ben down with you this time. I don't want to explain what's happening but once."

After Diana had disappeared, Alyssa turned back to Monica. "I'm sorry Diana didn't speak to you," she said.

Monica shrugged. "No problem. I didn't speak to her either. We don't speak."

"Monica, what were your instructions from the FBI?" Alyssa asked.

"I'm to report anything you tell me."

"And? -- "

Monica made a sour face and said, "Okay, I get you. If you ask for help, I am to give you complete cooperation."

"Well, you can't cooperate if you and anyone on our team don't speak. Diana is on the team. So is Ben. These – creatures are hostile. We have to work together no matter what happened in the past."

"You better tell Diana Corcoran that, too," Monica said.

"I will."

Just then, Diana returned with a bundle of clothes and Ben right behind her. Both she and Monica looked the other way while he and Alyssa hugged and exchanged a hurried kiss and whispers.

"Try on this coat," Diana said, handing it to Monica, who slipped it on over her sweater after removing the coat she'd bought this morning. Mitch wasn't all that much taller and longer-armed than Monica, so except for being a bit too big through the shoulders, the coat would do.

Diana handed Monica thermal gloves, a wool stocking cap, and a black baseball cap with "Apps" lettered in gold in front. "This coat doesn't have a hood or parka," she explained. "You'll need these to keep your ears warm."

Monica actually smiled. "Why, thank you, Diana. That's...thoughtful of you."

Diana simply nodded, and that gave Alyssa the opening to repeat the short lecture on putting aside past differences. She plunged on into a brief account of that had happened outside the ship this morning, and the reason for Mitch's visit to the Tompkins mansion.

"Monica and I must check out the ship again, first," she concluded. Then we'll jump up to the Tompkins place and check on Mitch. We'll get Monica back to where she's staying, and Mitch and I will return here as soon as we can.

"But that may be a while. I dare not open a Portal close to the ship. After what happened, they'll be watching that spot like hawks. We'll have to Portal over to the same clearing Mitch and I used this morning, and hike down."

She saw Ben's grimace. He said, "I feel useless. I wish I could do something."

Alyssa patted his arm. "You and Di holding the fort here is enough, darling. But don't invite trouble. If we need you, we'll come get you."

"I can't leave the boys," Diana said, her voice pained.

"I know," Alyssa said, then, more sharply, "Monica, let's go. But first let's get you a gun. I'm sure Mitch has something."

"No." Monica's voice was firm. "I cast spells. I don't need guns. Guns should be illegal anyway."

Ben spoke up. "Honey, if she's not used to using a firearm, she'll be better off without one. Frankly, so are you, if she doesn't bring a firearm. Maybe a knife."

Monica said she didn't want a knife either, but Alyssa finally forced a folding buck knife on her. It was better than nothing. They were ready.

She took Monica by a hand and led her through mist into a snowy clearing on Johnson's Mountain.

Monica

As Monica walked through the Portal Alyssa opened for them, she thought about their last conversation.

Cooperate? With that smug bastard McCaffrey and his little bitch wife? Or with the other snooty bitch, McCormick? She would, because she had to. She had to follow Springfield's instructions – or at least appear to do so, and make it look good.

But there might be an opportunity to show them up. To make this mission her success, and not theirs.

Or even to embarrass them. She'd see.

Chapter Nine

THE MASKS COME OFF

Christina

Christina walked with Samantha to the elevator. Rob had gone ahead of them because he wanted to wash and change clothes before the meeting in the guests' parlor with Sorrelli and Alvarez.

"I wonder," Christina mused aloud, "if we ought to change, too."

"What?" Sam sounded startled, and added, "I guess I was a little lost in thought."

Christina stopped, grasped Samantha gently by a shoulder, and turned her so they were looking at one another directly.

"Samantha, are you all right?" she asked. "Are you really up to this?"

"I — yes. I am," Samantha answered. "It's just that there's so much to absorb, you know? I didn't know I was being...influenced. Those people seemed so nice. And so..." She trailed off.

"Appealing?" Christina supplied. "Especially Sorrelli?"

"Yes," Samantha said in a small, contrite voice.

They resumed walking.

"That's why I think we ought to change clothes, too," Christina said. "If we're going to play along, make them think we're being controlled when we're not, maybe we should try to be more...distracting ourselves. These people may be being controlled by aliens, but they're human."

"You mean wear short skirts and low tops?" Samantha asked, her inflection and features incredulous.

"Something like that," Christina said. "I'm not sure we should be too obvious. But anything that might throw them off their game might help."

Samantha took several moments to ponder what Christina had said, and then replied, "I get you. I'll think about it."

When they entered the elevator, Sam turned to Christina and blurted, "'Tina, I'm scared. What if it happens again? What if I can't help it?

"What if I don't even know it's happening? I didn't before."

Christina pushed the button for the second floor, and said, "That's why we have Mitch. You can send for him."

Thirty minutes later, Christina walked down the hallway from her room to the other side of the house, where the master suite, Big Jim's study, and the library were located. She had been longer in her toilette than she'd thought. She decided she needed to repair her makeup and do a little more with her hair.

In selecting her clothing, she decided she would dress "business smart," but slightly provocative. Smiling when she thought about her conversation with Samantha, she selected a tight-fitting, short, cobalt-blue skirt, above which she wore a white button-up blouse with the top two buttons unbuttoned, emphasized by a chain with an opal pendant, and over that a mauve light-weight sweater, which she left completely unbuttoned.

Torn between flats and heels, she finally selected flats. If something violent happened, which she didn't really expect, she'd need to keep her balance.

When she passed the door to the guests' parlor on her left, she found it closed, and could hear conversation beyond, but could not make out the words. Rob and Samantha's visit with Sorrelli and Alvarez must already be in progress. She breathed another prayer, for them and for herself, and walked on.

The door to Big Jim's study was closed, but unlocked. She opened and walked into another meeting already in progress.

Jim Tompkins' study, as with everything else about this house, was anything but modest. The entire room was richly carpeted. Bookshelves and wooden file cabinets lined some walls. The others were filled with framed family photographs and paintings of wildlife. At the far end were armchairs with adjacent lamps, a wood fireplace, and still another wall-mounted television.

But the first thing someone saw upon entering was his big oak desk, with papers stacked neatly, a laptop computer centered in a blotter, a land-line telephone with multiple lines, a pipe rack and humidor, and a large ash tray that now held one of Jim's pipes. He must have smoked it recently, because she could smell a lingering aromatic, not unpleasant, aroma.

Jim was not at his desk. He was seated at the small rectangular conference table beyond it, his back to Christina as she approached. Jimmy sat next to him, and they both turned to greet her. Tim Lassiter and Karen Miller sat opposite them, and they stopped whatever spiel they'd been giving to speak to her also.

Christina gave Tim a dazzling smile, and Karen the barest nod and curve of the lips. Tim appeared pleased, but Karen less so. "I'm sorry," she said, "I wanted to be sure I dressed appropriately for a business meeting, but it appears I overdressed."

She really did upstage Karen in that department. Miller was freshly bathed, and someone had given or lent her makeup, so she looked quite pretty. But a pair of Linda's slacks and one of Linda's blouses could hardly compete with Christina's wardrobe selection; and besides, both were a little too big for her.

But the only response to Christina's apology was from Big Jim, who simply smiled and said, "You're fine, Christina. Nothing to fret about."

Tim said nothing, but he managed to make eye contact with Christina, so she could feel his approval and – something else. She didn't mind. He really was, she decided, an attractive man. Slender, fit, and well-muscled under one of Big Jim's pullover shirts, which in his case was a little small. She hadn't noticed that so much before.

She angled her chair and pushed it back so Tim would have a better view of her. Otherwise, Karen was between them. She didn't seem to notice, though. Her attention was focused on Jimmy, who sat looking at her with some sort of a goofy smile, interrupted only by a short comment injected into the conversation in which his father was engaged with Tim.

She listened to some of Tim's pitch, but didn't really understand it. It was for an investment in some start-up company that would distribute charging stations for electric vehicles. There was more to it, but the conversation quickly went over her head. Christina certainly didn't see herself as stupid, but she had been a music and folklore double major. Finance was not her strong suit. Her friend Alyssa handled all her investments.

She just continued to smile at Tim, and crossed and uncrossed her legs several times to get his attention. My, my, he is charming, she thought. And attractive. Somewhere in the back of her head, little warning bells were starting to chime, but what were they about? Something...someone named Mitch had said to her. Or was it Alyssa? It was all so confusing.

She noticed as the conversation went on that Jimmy became more attractive. He was sold on the investment, and trying to persuade Big Jim. Karen was now dividing her attention between son and father. Tim kept casting his eyes at Christina with evident appreciation, but he focused on Big Jim, too. Dimly, she thought she understood. Karen had focused on getting Jimmy under control, first; and when she had, she shifted to helping with Jim. Tim was now focusing more on Jim, too, because –

Because he must have finished with me, she thought.

Christina sat upright with a gasp, getting Tim and Karen's attention. But she relaxed again, unable to keep her mind on whatever had bothered her. This experience was so fascinating, so...nice.

Her eyes wandered to Karen, whose right hand was at her waist, fiddling with some sort of cell phone or something. The sight revived her troubling thoughts. These two were working together to – do something.

She wished she could focus, but her eyes kept returning to Tim's profile.

Just then Karen spoke, turning to Tim as she did. "Are we ready, Tim?"

"Yes, we are." He stood and withdrew some sort of tubular device from a pocket.

Christina did not react. She couldn't. Jimmy just sat still. His mouth moved a little, but that was it. But Big Jim didn't sit still. He pushed himself up from his chair, saying, "What in the hell are you doing?"

Tim didn't flinch. He just said, "Sit down, Jim." He didn't shout, or even raise his voice, but the command was evident.

Big Jim sat.

Christina watched Tim walk around, place the tube against the side of Jim's neck, and press a button. There was a low hissing sound. Jim didn't lift a hand to stop him. Jim's eyes closed, and his head drooped onto his chest. Tim walked past the father to the son to repeat whatever he had done.

Karen rose, produced a similar tube, and stepped toward Christina.

"Hold still, honey," she said, her voice dripping feigned sweetness. "This won't hurt a bit. Then we'll all be such good friends."

Christina's head cleared. She didn't know how long that would last. But she couldn't move, couldn't scream, couldn't...well, for the moment, anyway, she could think. She closed her eyes, and imagined a face she had studied only a short time ago.

Mitch. Mitch, come quickly. *MITCH*! Her mind was screaming, even if her lips were still.

She felt a cold pressure on her neck, a little prick following, and heard a soft hiss. Then...

Nothing.

Samantha

This wasn't so bad, Samantha thought.

She had decided to take Christina's recommendation and make herself at least somewhat distracting, to throw Elena and especially Drew off their game, whatever it was. So she wore a push-up bra under a tight purple sweater with a V-neck, and a pair of jeans that were almost uncomfortably tight. She told Rob what she was doing, and why. He had simply given her a sharp look and nodded. So she guessed he was okay with it.

As for Rob himself, he was a man, and would resist any suggestions in that regard; so, she didn't try. Still, she thought, he looked nice in his khaki trousers, blue button-down shirt and sweater vest, and tassel loafers. Preppy, but nice. They really didn't look out of place together.

They found Drew and Elena waiting on them in the guests' lounge as promised, seated in chairs facing a coffee table with two empty chairs opposite, a bottle of Prosecco on a towel, along with champagne flutes, all taken from the wet bar, on the table. The guests' parlor was not as opulent as the parlor on the first floor, but it was comfortably furnished and well-stocked, like every other common room in the Tompkins mansion.

"Hi," Drew said, "you two have a seat and we'll just share some wine and chat." He was more striking than ever, Sam decided. Big Jim's clothes fit him, but barely, and the flannel shirt was way too tight across the chest and shoulders, so he'd left a couple of buttons undone, exposing a hairy chest. Samantha liked chest hair on a man. She liked Rob's, although his was thinner and coppery rather than dark.

"Yes," Elena chimed in, her tone welcoming. "Please make yourselves comfortable. We don't want to hit you with a sales job, not right away, anyway. I'd like to hear about you. You know, how long you've been married, your jobs, kids, whatever."

Sam had to admit that Elena was provocative, too. Linda's pullover top was small for Elena's chest, and the results of her putting it on were, well, spectacular. Sam was sure Rob appreciated it, and felt just a twinge of jealousy. Irrational? Maybe. But still...

These thoughts soon vanished in the conversation, which was free and easy, lubricated by the sparkling wine. She found herself talking about her career, her ambitions. Rob did the same. Drew refilled their flutes twice and they didn't object.

She didn't see the cell phone-shaped things. Maybe they didn't have the devices with them. If they did, they didn't pull them out and touch them. Samantha found herself relaxing and asking them about themselves. She had come in with her guard up. But they weren't doing anything.

She was sitting opposite Drew, and found herself drawn more and more to his dark eyes. He really was a handsome man. There was no denying that. There was no harm in looking, surely, especially since Rob was doing the same with Elena. She wanted to blame him for that, but decided it didn't matter.

The conversation became just a buzz as she was drawn more and more into those magnificent eyes, eyes that seemed as though she could fall into them. Now she was looking up into them, as Drew was standing over her.

Up? When had he got to his feet? She didn't remember him doing that. She was vaguely aware that Elena had done the same, and was standing over Rob.

The she felt something cold on her neck, a quick sting, and then the world swam around and disappeared.

Chapter Ten

RESCUE AND LIBERATION

| Mitch |

Mitch had allowed himself a stretch break from sitting in the alcove. That required him to stand in the walkway, where he would be visible to anyone coming from the kitchen, but it couldn't be helped. He couldn't allow his muscles to stiffen. He might have to move at any time.

And, he thought, I'll have to reveal myself to everyone else soon enough, unless I'm badly mistaken.

Then he felt it, the jolt of someone asking for help. Asking urgently. Christina. He was sure it was her. Rob's aura, and Samantha's, were different.

The sending brought him instantly upright from his stretches. He had to get to her fast.

Mitch was still not as good at creating Portals as Alyssa; but he had improved a lot with practice, and had completely mastered creating a Portal between him and someone with whom he felt a connection. He spoke a quick spell, not bothering to lower his voice, and walked quickly through mist, drawing the Ruger at his hip as he went.

He found himself in a large room, lavishly furnished, which evidently doubled as an office and reading room. He found Christina and two men he assumed were Jim and Jimmy Tompkins, slumped in chairs, and just coming around into consciousness. Something was wrong with them, but he didn't have to figure out what, because standing over them were a man and woman.

They were nice-looking people wearing ill-fitting clothes. They started at his sudden presence, the woman gasping and the man uttering a startled wordless exclamation. But they quickly recovered, turned their eyes directly on him and began to fiddle with those alien devices on their belts, their smiles betraying their confidence.

He was immediately assailed with a compulsion... something. He didn't know what to call it. But he was ready for it and could block it, and did. Their auras were both human and alien, and he'd have to figure that out, later. Their smiles vanished into alarm, and they began twisting knobs on the gadgets at their waists.

He was glad he had experience at disabling those things. The two were close enough to him that a single spell worked. Their mouths widened into round O's, and the man muttered curse. Their twisting fingers became frantic.

Mitch's thumb drew back the revolver's hammer into full cock, and he held it two-handed before him, moving it from one to the other.

"You people better sit down," he said. "I assure you this gun will work."

They didn't move, and he punctuated the next command with his own compulsion spell, something he usually found distasteful but now gave him satisfaction.

"I said 'sit down'," he growled, and again, "Sit. Down."

They sat, glaring at him.

He realized the alien part of their auras were each centered in a node of tiny, microscopic electronic devices clustered at the base of the skull. Nanites, he thought. But they were electronic, and he could manipulate electronics.

He started with the woman, whose eyes widened in alarm as she felt the spell touch her, her hands flying to the back of her head. The man growled and tried to rise, but a renewed compulsion held him.

But that caused the spell he'd been using on the woman to slip. He moved the nose of the revolver to point directly at the man's chest, and tried again. This time the spell worked. He felt the cluster turn itself off and begin to disintegrate. The woman cried out and lost consciousness, her head lolling to one side.

The man cursed again and again tried to rise. Mitch raised the nose slightly to point just below the man's eyes. That met with another growl and another subsidence. There were no slips in the spell this time, and the man uttered a little gasp, as though something had shocked him, and lapsed into unconsciousness, too.

Mitch checked both pulses, which were regular, as was their breathing. If what he'd done hadn't put them in a coma, which he very much doubted, they'd wake up as soon as their nervous systems adjusted.

Sure enough, even as he watched, their eyelids fluttered. In a moment, they were sitting up, their eyes wide in disbelief, and ... something else. Was it gratitude?

The woman spoke first. "We...we're free." She whispered, and then, turning to the man. "Oh sweetheart, we're free." She leaned over and hugged him.

To Mitch's surprise, the man – he wasn't sure which of the four these two were, and then recalled that Lassiter and Miller were the ones meeting with Jim and Jimmy Tompkins, so it was Lassiter – started to cry, tears that quickly turned to sobs.

The woman – Karen Miller, he realized – started sobbing, too. They leaned into one another and cried together.

Lassiter looked over his – wife's, lover's? – shoulder and said to Mitch, "We've done such awful things. We were about to do more."

"But darling," Karen blubbered, "That's over. We don't have to anymore."

Mitch heard something move behind him, and quickly turned his attention to the others in the room. The older man, who had to be Big Jim Tompkins, the younger, who had to be Jimmy, and Christina were now all awake and glaring at them. Their auras were now part alien, too; and he sensed the nanite nodes in all three.

As he watched, Jimmy, who appeared more fully recovered, started to rise, his face twisted. Mitch stepped back, keeping the revolver pointed toward Lassiter and Miller, and hurled Jimmy back into his chair with a compulsion.

"You don't need the gun for us now," he heard Lassiter say, his voice now composed.

Mitch un-cocked the revolver but didn't holster it. Keeping his distance, he worked the disconnection spell on Jimmy first, and then the other two. The nodes must not have been fully formed, because the spells worked more quickly this time. The three were soon unconscious again.

But as with Lassiter, their unconscious state didn't last long, and the three were blinking themselves awake within moments.

They awoke to the tearful apologies of both Lassiter and Miller, to which the Tompkins listened with evident puzzlement, although Christina nodded along in understanding.

"Will someone please tell me what in the bloody ding-dong hell is going on?" Big Jim griped. No doubt he was used to being in charge, and didn't like being in the dark. Fixing his gaze on Mitch, he added, "Who the blazes are you?"

"Jim, he's a friend, and he just saved your life – or at least your freedom," Christina said. Mitch noticed Lassiter and Miller's solemn nods.

"Mr. Tompkins, I am a friend. I really am here to help. I promise you an explanation as soon as there's time. Right now there's not."

Tompkins was not much mollified.

"Well," he snapped, "would you at least put down that hand cannon, and tell me how you got here?"

Mitch holstered the revolver, and said, "I'm sorry, sir but that's a U.S. government secret."

"You're a federal agent?" Jimmy asked, startled.

"Yes." Mitch decided he'd better not elaborate. "And I am sorry, but explanations will have to wait."

"He's right, Mr. Tompkins," Lassiter said. "Other people are in danger."

Christina had closed her eyes, but now they flew open.

"Mitch," she said, fear tinging her voice. "They've got Rob and Samantha, just like they did us."

Mitch felt his brow furrow as he concentrated. Yes, he could feel it. Four alien nodes, all nearby.

"We need to act quickly," Karen Miller said. "You – we – have to get Sorrelli."

Mitch looked a question, and Lassiter said. "He doesn't have to be compelled. He's on their side."

Mitch wasted no time.

"Follow me," he said.

Rob

Rob came to his senses, lying on his back on a couch at the back of the guests' parlor. His pants were unbuckled. Elena Alvarez was lying across him, her blouse undone, and her bra unsnapped. Her breasts were practically in her face. As he watched, her eyes blinked awake, and she pushed herself up from him, fastening her clothing as she rose.

"I'm sorry," she said, her voice soft, and then, more firmly, "You can't begin to know how sorry."

Rob fastened his trousers and sat up. Everything was blurry. He remembered sitting and talking with Elena and Drew, gradually being more and more absorbed with

Elena. He remembered a sting on his neck, and waking up to watching Drew and Sam leave to go to their suite, thinking he should care but hearing Elena tell him not to worry, so he didn't.

He remembered everything being submerged by Elena's lips on his, and hearing her whispered urging – no, command – to find a more private place in back where "we can please each other" as she put it, and his thinking, driven by the urgency in his groin, that was a wonderful suggestion.

They were just getting started when he felt a shock where his neck met his skull, Elena's body spasm above him, and losing consciousness a second time. Now he was awake and not understanding anything that had happened.

"Rob, are you all right?" It was Christina's voice.

He looked up to see her concerned face a few feet away. Mitch McCaffrey stood beside her, and there were others behind them. Jimmy, Big Jim. And the other two. What were their names? He shook his head to clear it.

"He's fine," he heard Elena say beside him. "We're fine. But you better go after his wife. Sorrelli has her."

That brought Rob fully awake. He jumped up, pushed past everyone, and ran for the door. He ignored Mitch's call to wait.

Mitch caught him at the door to their suite, grabbed him by the shoulders before he could use the key, and said in his ear, "Rob, wait please. Let me fix them first."

"Please, Rob," he heard Christina say, "Listen to Mitch. Do as he asks."

Rob said, "Okay. But do it fast. Whatever it is you're going to do."

He watched for what seemed like minutes, but could have only been seconds, as Mitch closed his eyes, muttered something under his breath, waited only a moment, and then did it again.

Mitch stepped back from the door, and said, "It's done. Now we can go in."

Rob unlocked the door and rushed in, leaving the others to follow.

Samantha

Samantha moaned. She couldn't help herself. This was so thrilling, so...good.

She was lying across the love seat in the sitting room at the suite, her sweater off and cast to the floor. Drew was bent over her and was nuzzling her breasts, his own shirt unbuttoned to the waist, while her hands roamed his chest and shoulders. She gasped as he supported himself with one arm, while his other hand unsnapped her jeans, and urged him on with her hands.

She wasn't sure how this had come to pass. The four of them were talking, and then there was that sting, and then Drew was whispering to her to find some privacy for them and let Elena and Rob have theirs. The walk to the suite was a blur, and then everything dissolved into sensation.

Somewhere deep inside her head, someone, it had to be her, was screaming this was wrong, wrong, wrong. But that person wasn't in charge. Another Samantha was lost in the moment, lost in this man's embrace, which she wanted desperately.

She lifted a hand to the back of his head to pull his lips down to hers, again. Without warning, she felt a shock at the base of her spine and spasmed, feeling him do the same. She lost consciousness again.

She was out only a moment. Then she was herself. Really herself. Drew was coming around, too, and blinking in confusion. She shoved against him, but he was heavy.

Then someone grabbed and pulled him off her. It was Rob, his face twisted in hurt and rage.

"Get off my wife, you son of a bitch!"

She watched wide-eyed as Rob delivered a hard left to Sorrelli's groin, followed by a right cross to Sorrelli's chin that straightened him and sent him staggering back. She saw someone move to Rob's left and the air shattered with the roar of a handgun in the confined space. The gun roared again.

Two reddening holes appeared on Sorrelli's chest, and the wall behind him reddened still more with the splash of blood. Sorrelli opened his mouth to speak, but blood poured out. He reeled back into the wall and collapsed. Samantha gagged when she saw the ghastly exit wounds.

Elena Alvarez stood stony faced, holding a smoking revolver in both hands. Rob had gathered Samantha's sweater from the floor and come to her with it. Samantha took the sweater and burst into tears. Rob sat beside her and gathered her into his arms, his lips making comforting noises into her ear.

Samantha watched in mute bewilderment as Mitch McCaffrey walked up beside Elena and took the pistol from her. Elena didn't resist, but shook herself away from Mitch, walked to Sorrelli's still-twitching corpse and spat on it. She spat again.

"*Bastardo!*" she hissed, her voice savage and trembling, and repeated in English, "Bastard!"

Samantha was shaking, still bewildered, but managed to pull on her sweater and fastened her pants, realizing for the first time that others had crowded into the room. Despite the trembling in her legs, she pushed Rob away gently and rose to her feet.

Samantha knew what had happened now. This hadn't been seduction. This had been rape. Some crazy part of her mind gibbered that a lawyer like her husband might call it "attempted rape," but that didn't matter.

She walked to Elena's side, blinking through tears that still streamed wetly down her cheeks, and leaning forward, spat on the now still corpse herself.

Turning to Elena, she said, "I couldn't agree more."

Then she heard Big Jim Tompkins' voice from the door.

"*Now* will someone please tell me what the bloody hell is going on?"

Mitch

Mitch was embarrassed. He had meant to take Sorrelli prisoner. Instead, he had been caught flat-footed, like any recruit. He should have anticipated that Rob would be incensed and not have let him go for Sorrelli the way he did.

Not that he blamed Rob. Samantha was his wife. He wasn't sure he could blame Elena either. He suspected she could tell a frightful story about the man who had claimed to be her husband, but surely was not.

But he could kick himself for having been so intent on watching Rob's violent encounter with Sorrelli that he hadn't felt Elena pluck the Ruger from his holster, which he hadn't snapped when he'd holstered it. Now he had a bloody corpse on his hands and no one to interrogate.

He had to shrug it off. He wasn't a real government agent, after all, just an amateur pressed into duty. He hadn't been on active duty, or even to reserve camp, in years. And he'd better answer Big Jim's question.

"This man," he said, pointing to Drew Sorrelli's still bleeding dead body, "is – or was – the agent of a foreign power." He didn't dare say, yet, just how foreign. He didn't know himself. "The others who came with him, were under his control until I released them. I am a contractor working for the United States government." Well, that much was true. "I can't tell you anything else right now. I'm not sure how much I can ever tell you.

"I need to debrief Lassiter, Miller, and Alvarez. Right now. I'm going to let you and Christina, maybe others, listen in, because I'm going to need your help. I'm sure that will mean someone will be coming around with secrecy agreements in the near future. But that will have to wait."

"Do you have any identification on you?" asked Jimmy. His tone was not hostile.

Mitch chuckled. "I don't even have a driver's license," he said.

Christina spoke up. "Jimmy, you need to trust Mitch." Her eyes swept the room. "I want you all to understand. This man" – she cast her eyes on Sorrelli's body – "had you under his control. He had Big Jim. He had me, and Rob, and Samantha. He would have taken everyone else.

"We've been saved from slavery. Mind control of the worst sort."

"It's true," Elena said, and Lassiter and Miller nodded and voiced their agreements.

There was a flurry of excited whispers from the doorway and the hallway outside. The gunshots had brought everyone in the house running.

Jim Tompkins had not built his businesses by being indecisive.

"All right," he said. "I need Darrel and Dave to get a tarp and get this body outside in the shed outside the garage. It's cold enough there that the corpse won't smell.

"Someone, I guess Megan and Sally, needs to get this mess cleaned up. He pointed to the bloody carpet and wall. "As best you can, anyway. Wear masks so you don't gag."

The two young women exchanged a look and made disgusted faces, but nodded.

"We can meet in the parlor downstairs in – let's say ten minutes. Mr. – what did you say your name is?" He looked at Mitch.

"I didn't. But it's McCaffrey. Mitch McCaffrey."

Tompkins's brows lifted. "The one who was in the papers?"

"Yes."

"Well, it doesn't matter. Who do you want in the meeting? You're in charge." He paused and added, "For now, anyway."

Mitch hesitated, thinking. Finally, he said, "I want everyone who was under control. Lassiter, Miller, and Alvarez, of course. And...does anyone have military training?"

"I do." Dave's voice came from the hallway. Mitch couldn't see him.

"Army? Marines?" Mitch asked.

"Marine Corps."

"Iraq?"

"Yeah. Desert Storm and back again in '03. You?"

"Army. Iraq. 2005. Called up from reserve."

"What was your rank?"

"Captain. Brevet. Permanent rank was first lieutenant. Yours?"

"Gunnery sergeant."

Mitch grinned. "You outrank me, then."

Dave grinned back. "You're a good officer."

The others had watched this by-play like watching tennis. Mitch decided to simply pick up the thread and continue.

"And then both Misters Tompkins," he said. "That will do for now. Everyone else will be filled in later."

"Okay," Tompkins said. "It's settled. Ten minutes. Linda, can you organize some fresh coffee? Good...Oh, and someone needs to get Samantha a brandy. She looks like she needs it."

"She's not the only one," Christina said, causing a nervous laugh from the group.

Mitch made his way out the door and allowed Christina to lead him to the elevator. He thought of Diana. He wished he could spare a minute to go to her.

And he wondered how Alyssa was doing with Monica.

He looked at his watch. It was 3:15. Less than two hours of daylight left.

Chapter Eleven

THE KRAXX

Alyssa

Alyssa led Monica through the trees, rocks, and snowfall down the ridge toward the knoll where the alien craft rested. They had been able to spell a couple of young saplings into walking sticks, and these helped, but the going was still slow, making sure they didn't step into snow-covered depressions filled with leaves, or stumble over hidden rocks. The snowfall sometimes seemed to let up, but that was a tease. Within minutes, it was heavy again.

The trip was even slower than it had been when she and Mitch had made it earlier. Alyssa's watch said it was already pushing 4:00 o'clock. The sky was darkening, so they wouldn't have much observation time when they were in position.

But, she reminded herself, they still had to do it.

She already regretted bringing Monica. The woman had done nothing but complain the whole way, sometimes muttering under her breath, at others more loudly. Alyssa had had to warn her several times to move quietly and keep her voice down. They really didn't know the capacity of the alien technology to pick up sounds.

Of course, she reflected, the woods were hushed with the snowfall. There was no animal movement, and few bird calls. Any noise they made seemed magnified.

They stopped for a quick breather, and Monica's litany began again.

"I could be at the bar," she said. "I could be taking a nap. I could be getting laid."

Alyssa turned to her and placed a glove-covered finger over her lips. "How many times do I have to tell you to keep your voice down," she hissed. "And I don't what to hear what you're missing. We'd both rather be somewhere else.

"Besides," she continued, "haven't you already been laid? At the resort, I mean."

That brought a smile.

"I didn't know I had a quota," Monica sniffed. "Do you ration yourself?"

Alyssa wished Ben were here. He couldn't cast spells, but he at least would try to be helpful. And he could shoot. She'd heard him discuss hunting with Mitch. He could do something. And she just missed him.

"Oh, skip it," she whispered. "Look, we're almost in position. We're about to veer off to the left and find a spot away from where Mitch and I encountered them this morning. They're bound to be watching that spot closely. Let's get moving.

"And remember," she finished, "we aren't here to start anything. Our orders are to watch and report."

They resumed their journey down the ridge. Alyssa had to give Monica credit. She moved much more quietly now. Within minutes, they had reached a spot that would do. There was no large granite outcrop, as with the other space, but there were several large oaks and poplars that would offer some cover and protection. Ahead there were a few saplings and low rock outcroppings. But visibility was pretty good.

Monica touched her on a shoulder and pointed to an enormous round hump in the middle of the knoll. "Is that it?" she whispered.

"Yes," Alyssa whispered back. "Can't you feel it?" She meant the ominous aura that came from the craft, all the more disturbing for having human elements as well as alien.

Monica nodded, her features composed and solemn. Alyssa heard her gulp.

"We have maybe an hour, max, to observe, before it's too dark," Alyssa whispered.

"I hope not that long," Monica moaned. "It's frigging *cold* here just standing."

"Well, let's give it a few minutes," Alyssa said, keeping her voice low and trying to keep the irritation out. "If we see nothing after 30 minutes, we can go."

She removed the field glasses Mitch had loaned her from their case at her waist, and after taking off the night vision glasses, studied the spaceship. Only the regular shape of the dome revealed how the snow hid something artificial. The slight breeze lifted and stirred some of the recently fallen snow. Otherwise, nothing moved. The falling snow had completely covered the footprints of earlier this afternoon.

Without a word, she handed the field glasses to Monica, who studied the clearing before them for a minute or so, and then handed them back. They settled in to watch, every now and then slipping behind an oak to stamp their feet to stay warm.

Alyssa was almost ready to touch Monica's arm and whisper she was ready to leave when there was movement at the craft. Four black encased figures emerged. Two were un-naturally tall, like the ones she'd seen earlier, clearly alien. Two were shorter, bulkier but hardly rotund, their auras human but tinged with alien – something.

Alyssa crouched, motioning with her right arm for Monica to do the same.

"They may know we're here," she hissed.

Sure enough, the four put their heads together, and one of the aliens began a slow haul through the snow toward the tree line. The others stayed put. Alyssa watched them with the field glasses to see if they would pull those plasma wands from their belts, but none did.

It didn't take long for the alien's path to be determined. Alyssa didn't want another confrontation, so she grabbed Monica by a shoulder and said, low but urgently into her ear, "Let's go. I'm going to open a Portal."

She rose and turned to face the ridge, and opened a Portal to the clearing they'd been using as a staging area. From there they could Portal to the Tompkins mansion, or open a path to the resort for Monica.

When the Portal was open, mist swirling over the snow drift, she turned back to Monica, expecting to grab her hand and lead her through.

Monica was not there. She was wading through the snow toward the approaching alien, and had already reached the edge of the clearing. What in the hell did she think she was doing? Was she being compelled? No,

Alyssa couldn't feel any compulsion at work, whether magic or artificial.

The crazy bitch is doing this on her own, Alyssa thought. But what can I do about it? I don't think I can force her. Not in this snowdrift, and not with her resisting any spell I might try.

Cursing, she closed the Portal. She couldn't keep it open and focus on crazy Monica's cowgirl antics. She decided to risk calling out to her.

"Monica, don't be a fool. Whatever you're doing, don't try it. Come back!" She had to shout, and in the snowy silence her voice rang shockingly loud.

"I know what I'm doing," Monica called back. "You don't know how powerful I've become. I can take this one. I can feel it."

Why, the egotistical bitch thinks she can compel that thing, Alyssa fumed, grinding her teeth in rage and fear. She knew exactly how powerful Monica Gilbert was. The woman's aura was an open book. She was thinking improved skills from better training made her stronger. In a way, it did, but Monica wasn't nearly as Talented as Alyssa herself, and nowhere close to Mitch.

But she doesn't know that, Alyssa realized. Or won't admit it. Her ego won't let her.

There really wasn't anything Alyssa could do except watch, and pray she was wrong. She was otherwise completely helpless. She had never mastered Mitch's Talent for manipulating electronics. She trained the field glasses on the other three figures. They hadn't moved. It would be Monica against only this one.

They approached each other, and stopped about ten feet apart. Monica raised her head to look the creature directly in the eyes. It returned her steady stare, and dropped a long-fingered and somehow oddly shaped hand to a box at its waist. Now she could feel Monica's compulsion, directed at the alien with savage fury, and the counterstrike, emanating from it and its device.

Seconds passed, at least a minute, then longer, as the two stood stark still in their contest of wills. Alyssa allowed herself to hope. Maybe Monica was stronger than she'd thought. Maybe the artificially enhanced alien wasn't as powerful as she feared.

Then, without a sound, Monica Gilbert sank to her knees. The snow came to her chest. Slowly she stretched her arms toward the creature. It waded to her through the snow, lifted her to her feet, and began to lead her toward the alien vessel. Monica, shoulders slumped and head bowed, followed, meek as a lamb.

Alyssa had been expecting something like this, but was still horrified.

"*MONICA!*" Her shout was almost involuntary, and left her lips before she realized it.

Concentrating on the tableau played in the snow before her, Alyssa had taken her eyes off the other three. There was a blinding flash and a wave of heat on her face as a plasma bolt sizzled past her right ear.

Gasping, she hurled herself to her left. She didn't sink far into the snow, and scrambled forward as another bolt split the air where she had stood, leaving a sharp ozone smell. Spitting snow, she uttered the word that would reopen the Portal and crawled through into the clearing up the slope.

She pulled herself up against a tree. This was, she realized with grim self-deprecation, her second ignominious exit this today. And she had lost a team member.

Even if that person was Monica Fucking Gilbert, losing a team member was not likely to meet with Hutton's approval.

And even if it was Monica Gilbert, Alyssa feared for her in the aliens' hands.

She had to find Mitch.

Monica

Monica was stunned. This thing, whatever it was, had her under its complete control. It was leading her back to its ship as surely as if a rope had been tied around her neck and it was pulling it. She was under a powerful compulsion of a type she didn't understand, and she had absolutely no choice. None.

The worst of it, if she didn't count being a prisoner, was that it was so unexpected. It seemed that all of the training, all of the practice, all of the skills she had honed at her sessions at the secret school in the Virginia mountains had no meaning. She had been so confident she could bend this creature to her will. That would have shown Alyssa McCormick and that bastard McCaffrey who was boss Spellcaster.

For a few delirious seconds, it had seemed to be working. The thing was alien, but she was winning. Winning! And then she wasn't. Whatever this thing had done, it had seemed to step on the gas, turn up the juice, whatever. She had simply been overwhelmed.

Instead of scoring a great triumph, she had been humiliated.

Monica ground her teeth as she waded through the snowdrift and blinked still-falling flakes from her eyes. Embarrassment, fear, and rage mingled inside her in equal measure. She wondered what was in store for her. Enslavement? Vivisection? She could imagine all kinds of awful things.

She could sense there were humans as well as more aliens ahead. That meant she might not be killed, anyway. Maybe they could help her. Maybe she could compel them. These things didn't seem likely, but she could hope. She'd find out soon enough, she realized.

Navigating the snowdrift was like walking through waist deep water. It took a few minutes to reach the other three black figures standing before the spaceship. She could sense that two were human, but with an alien tinge. All had face coverings so that only their eyes were visible. There were two sets of light human eyes, blue or hazel – she couldn't tell through the thick snowfall – and, in the case of the tallest figure, narrow-slitted yellow, almost cat-like eyes like her captor's. They made her shudder from more than the winter cold.

Her captor compelled her to stop while he moved forward to confer with the others. They spoke briefly in a language, evidently the aliens' tongue, that sounded like constant clearing of a throat, punctuated by hocking snot. Then, without even turning toward her, the one who had overcome her will compelled her to follow them to the spacecraft. There, a door slid open silently and admitted them to a small bare room, which was evidently an airlock. The outer door closed behind them, and the airlock lit up with wan reddish glow like the light just before twilight in autumn. There was a blast of air from the ceiling that removed most of the snow from their clothes and footgear. Another door in the opposite wall slid open, and she was compelled forward into another, much larger room.

The light was a bit more yellow and brighter here, but not much. The first thing she noticed was a spare and lean figure, even taller than the others, standing before them, dressed in some sort of a uniform tunic with lettering and insignia that meant nothing to her. It was surprisingly human-like, although its skull was oddly elongated. Her eyes were immediately drawn to its face.

Its features were narrow, arrowhead-shaped and tapering to a nearly pointed chin, high cheekbones, a long slender nose but flaring nostrils, above thin, mauve-colored lips. The eyes caught hers and held them. These were, as the others,' narrow, the pupils pale yellow with no evident iris, cat-slitted. The skin was a pale grayish blue. The thing had hair, the brows pencil-thin, as though they had been plucked. These and the hair above the broad, high forehead were a dark purple, short, and flat like a seal's coat.

She had seen something, someone, who looked like this creature, but where. When she realized it, she would have laughed if her circumstances were not so desperate. Except for the elongated skull, the thing looked like the Rasputin character in the old animated feature *Anastasia*.

She noticed another alien across the room, dressed in a similar uniform but wearing a cap oddly like her baseball cap, seated in a chair much too high for humans before a panel with dials and monitors that meant nothing to her, except two of them seemed to show the views outside the craft, one showing the ridge climbing in front, the other showing it descending in back.

Her captor and its companions bowed stiffly to the uniformed alien who stood before her, and she was compelled to do the same. She was permitted no freedom of movement except for her neck, which she was allowed to swivel. The alien before her spoke in the same harsh and impossible language she had heard outside. Its teeth, she saw, were lemon-yellow, blunt except for the incisors, which were very sharp.

Her captor unbuckled its face-covering, which fell to one side of its face, and replied in the same language. She realized there must be individual differences in these creatures, but she couldn't yet ascertain any. They all looked alike to her. While they spoke, she looked more closely at the room. There were exits, both closed, in the rear and to her right. The walls, where not covered with boxes and lighted monitors, were austere, battleship gray in color, and marked or painted with black letter-ing and drawings. A drawing over the console showed a black sun surrounded by stylized planets, none of them the Earth. The large characters seemed slogan-like, but could mean anything, including the name of the vessel.

She saw the two human figures remove their face coverings, and their headgear folded back. They were tall men, short only by comparison with the aliens. The taller, slenderer of the two appeared to be in his early middle years, his hair dark brown with a touch of gray at the temples, his nose long and aquiline, his mouth thin, sardonic and a little cruel, she thought. But she thought him quite handsome.

The other was a bit shorter and more powerfully built. He was good-looking, too, but not as much as the oth-er man to Monica's eyes. His features were square, his nose snub, his hair somewhere between a white and sandy blonde. His lips were thin, and his mouth wide. At least this place had attractive men to offer, she thought. There was that.

The first man smiled and spoke, his voice un-naturally high and cracked in the air she now noticed as much too thin and dry to be really comfortable for a human, although it was breathable. But if she was here long, she realized, her sinuses would give her fits.

"My name is Jean-Pierre Giscard," the man was saying, in a tone that would have been friendly if not altered by the atmosphere, "formerly of the French Air and Space Force. My...colleague here is Jacob Van Der Taalen, formerly of the Royal Netherlands Air Force." His English was fluent, but spoken with a pronounced Gallic accent.

"Jacob and I were collaborating, collecting evidence of UFO sightings and trying to draw conclusions," he continued with a smile. "Then we were collected ourselves. We now serve the" – he made a sound that was even more like spitting mucous than what she'd heard before, that ending in a buzzing noise, but which sounded more or less like *Kraxx.*"

"We are commanded to take charge of you, to find out who you are and who sent you, and to determine how you, too, can be of service. You will therefore come with us. The area set aside for humans is more...comfortable."

At the suggestion she was going to be pressed into service, Monica's heart fell toward her stomach. It must have showed on her face, because Giscard held up a hand and spoke again.

"Do not worry. You will find it is not so bad." His smile widened. "You may like it. In fact, I feel sure you will."

His words did not reassure her, but there was nothing she could do at the moment. Even when she felt the alien who had taken her prisoner release her from compulsion, she didn't dare try anything. Not now. There was no choice but to go along.

When Giscard and Van Der Taalen again bowed to the alien who had greeted them, she followed suit without being compelled. Giscard led the way to the door to the right. Van Der Taalen placed a hand on her shoulder and gently pushed her in front of him. They followed Giscard through the door, which slid open automatically when the man placed a hand on a panel next to it.

He led them down a short corridor with doors on either side until they came to another door to the right. Giscard opened it, and she immediately felt a rush of warmer, more moist, air.

They entered a room that was evidently designed for relaxation and entertainment for humans. There was no carpet on the floor, which, like that in what she had seen of the rest of the ship, was made of some solid but flexible substance that had about as much "give" as all-weather carpet. But there were several brightly covered rugs. The walls held prints of outdoors scenes, some in the Alps and some by a seashore somewhere, she assumed in France or Italy. One wall held a large flat-screen television, hooked to what appeared to be a DVD player.

There were two couches and several chairs, all of which looked comfortable, and low tables that held magazines and coasters. At the rear of the room, flanking another door, there was a small kitchenette, which included an institutional-sized coffee pot. It held real coffee, because she could smell it. Next to it was a cabinet that held what appeared to be liquor and wine bottles.

The Kraxx don't keep their humans without luxuries, she thought. That was interesting.

Van Der Taalen offered to take her coat and head gear, and she accepted gratefully. Giscard offered coffee and brandy. She accepted the coffee and he brought her a cup with cream. He helped himself to a coffee and added both cream and brandy. The Dutchman took brandy only.

"Shall we sit?" Giscard said. He sat at one end of a couch, and Van Der Taalen sat on the other. Monica hesitated, but then sat in an armchair opposite them. It was quite comfortable, and she sighed in spite of herself.

"You are used to comfort, no?" Giscard said, maintaining the smile, which did not appear forced.

She admitted it.

"What shall we call you?" he asked. "*Madame*..."

Monica knew a little French. "*C'est mademoiselle*," she said, adding, "Monica Gilbert."

"Even better," he said, and asked a question in French she could not follow.

Monica shook her head. "I'm afraid my French runs out pretty quick."

His shrug, like his accent, was entirely Gallic. He really was an attractive man, she thought. This may be interesting. She was good at manipulating men even without magic.

"Then we will speak English," Giscard said, "Will we not, Jacob?"

"Of course," Van Der Taalen said. His English contained only the slightest trace of accent.

Giscard's smile abruptly vanished. "Tell us, *Miss* Gilbert, who sent you and how you got here. Tell us whom you work for."

There was no reason, Monica decided, not to tell the truth. At this point, it wouldn't hurt and might help. It might mean better treatment. And besides, those... things could compel her if she refused.

"The FBI," she said. "I work for the Federal Bureau of Investigation. I'm a consultant."

Giscard's smile returned. "Excellent. You will be useful to our...employers indeed." The smile vanished again. "But you didn't tell us how you got here."

Monica hesitated for only a moment. Why not, she thought? They had to know they were facing something unusual.

"Through a Portal created by the woman I came with," she said.

"A Portal? What sort of Portal? How was it made?" Giscard demanded.

"By magic," she said, adding, "I can work magic, too. But," she added lest he demand she create one, "I'm not yet good at Portals."

"Don't lie to me," he snapped.

"I'm not lying."

"Prove it." His tone was alarming.

Monica had set her coffee cup on a coaster on the low table beside her chair. At her subvocalized command, it lifted itself from the table, floated to the urn, refilled itself, and floated back into her hand.

Van Der Taalen had jumped to his feet, exclaiming a startled "*Mein Gott!*" Giscard kept his seat, but his jaw dropped.

"I prefer it with cream," she said, unable to keep from sounding smug. "But you get the picture."

Giscard sat back on the couch, evidently trying to process what he had just seen. He closed his mouth, brought back his sardonic smile, and said, "Jacob, while you are on your feet, would you bring the lady the cream pitcher, please?"

Without a word, Van Der Taalen walked to the refrigerator, removed the cream pitcher, and brought it to Monica. She added cream to her coffee, and placed the pitcher on the low table beside her.

"Thank you, Jacob," she said, in the sweetest tone she could manage.

"Not at all...Monica," the Dutch airman said, resuming his seat on the couch.

Giscard leaned forward. "Okay," he said, "I see we are on a first-name basis now," he said. "Who knows, we may reach 'thee' and 'thou' before the evening is over. You may be a great opportunity, Monica, for both our employers and m – us. But before we explore those possibilities, let me explain why you should join us. Please let me finish before you ask questions."

Monica nodded. "I am your prisoner," she said. "I have no choice."

"Before the day has gone, you may be our colleague," Giscard said. He drummed the fingers of his right hand on a knee. "Where to begin? Ah, I have it.

"I think you must be aware that you live in a society, even in a nation, that is chaotic, divided, undisciplined, and largely unprogressive..."

He talked for a long while, and as she listened, Monica was at first fascinated, then interested, and then persuaded. Jean-Pierre had been right. She did like what he had to say. She liked it a great deal.

"You are very persuasive, Jean-Pierre," she said in what she thought her most seductive voice when he had finished. "I'm sure I can find ways to – help."

"I'm sure you can," Giscard said. "I count on it. But first we must vaccinate you. I was remiss in not doing it before."

"From what?" Monica asked, suddenly alarmed.

"Alien germs, *ma petite,*" Giscard purred. "You must be around the Kraxx, they will insist on it. We must protect you. Jacob?"

Van Der Taalen rose and removed a short rod from a pouch at his belt. Monica shuddered.

"Don't be concerned," the Dutchman said. This is not a plasma rod."

Monica stiffened as he walked toward her. But what could she do? She wasn't sure she had a spell that could free her. And – maybe they were telling the truth.

The rod was cold against her neck, and then she felt a sting.

She realized, as she was losing consciousness, that she really did have some ideas. McCormick and McCaffrey wouldn't like finding out about them.

But she didn't care about what they thought.

Chapter Twelve

THE STORY AND THE CRISIS

Darrel

Darrel Thomas was back to minding the slow-roasting turkey. When he had run inside, drawn by the gun shots like everyone else, he had thought the snowfall was tapering off. But now it was in full career again. The weather reports were saying it would end sometime this evening. It sure didn't appear it was going to be soon.

He was warm enough close to the charcoal fire and beneath the space heater. The turkey was doing fine. This wasn't a hard job. But it was hard to go back to the routine after what had happened. He and his dad had found a tarp, rolled Sorrelli's corpse on to it, and then carried the still-warm bundle to the shed behind the garage, just as Big Jim instructed. That hadn't been any fun.

But he didn't know what was next. He didn't know what was going on now, over in the parlor. The Winchester was still leaning against the wall. He didn't know how effective it would be against... He didn't even know what. He wanted some answers.

The door from the walkway opened, and Sally walked out. She had pulled a coat over the uniform Heather wanted her and Megan to wear. She smiled, walked over, and hugged him. He hugged her back. Without thinking, he looked over her shoulder toward the window to see if anyone was watching; but no one was in the breakfast room.

That was something else they were going to have to do – tell people. He didn't think his folks would be concerned, and suspected they already knew. Sally thought her mom would be cool, but was afraid her dad would freak. But that was the least of their worries at the moment.

"Do you know what's going on?" he asked.

"No," she said. "I'm not even sure what happened. All I know is that the Alvarez woman took Mr. McCaffrey's pistol and killed that Sorrelli guy, and nobody cares. I don't know what happened before that."

She paused and made a face. "I know Megan and I had to clean the carpet and the wall. It made Meg sick, and Laura told her to go lie down. It almost made me sick, too."

"Were you able to get it clean?" Darrel asked.

She shook her head. "Not completely. We did as well as we could. We pretty much got the wall washed, so it's okay except for the bullet holes. The carpet was completely soaked with blood. We got what we could, and threw a sheet over it. I don't see how the Ashworths will be able to sleep there tonight. I couldn't."

"Did you see what Samantha Ashworth did?" he asked.

"No, but I heard she spit on the body while it was still kicking," Sally said. "He must have tried to rape her."

"I think he did. But you heard what Christina said. That guy had some kind of mind control device. He had taken over Big Jim, Jimmy, and Christina. He was already controlling the other people who came with him. I don't know how it worked, but somehow McCaffrey stopped it. He said they were foreign agents."

"You know," Sally said, "there have been a bunch of rumors about Mr. McCaffrey running around at school since they tried to get rid of him last fall. I heard some strange things happened at the hearing.

"But he won't talk about that, and he's been just fine in class."

She moved her body close against his, silently asking to be held, and he obliged. He needed the contact himself.

"I'm scared, Darrel," she whispered. "I'm afraid this isn't over."

He held her tighter. He was scared, too.

And he was sure it wasn't over.

Mitch

Big Jim and Jimmy had wrestled chairs and love seats into a rough circle for the parlor meeting. Laura had brought in a coffee service and left. Mitch was grateful for the coffee, and accepted a shot of brandy in it. He could handle one drink, he decided, but no more. Most of the others took coffee, too. Samantha declined, saying it might make her sick.

She was seated next to her husband on a love seat to Mitch's right, a glass of water in hand. Rob sat close to her, one arm about her shoulders, and the other holding a steaming mug. Lassiter, Miller, and Alvarez were lined up in chairs beyond them. The Tompkins men and Dave Thomas sat on chairs to his left, coffee mugs in hand.

"We'd better get started," Mitch said. Somebody had to be the leader, and he supposed it fell to him. He remembered what Alyssa had said earlier today. "But first, I need to disclose something to everyone that's going to come out anyway.

"I told you that Mr. Sorrelli, Mr. Lassiter, Ms. Miller, and Ms. Alvarez are foreign agents. They are. But I didn't tell you how foreign. The aircraft you saw fly over last night is an alien spaceship. They came here from there."

If he had expected a stir, he didn't get one. Everyone just sat, waiting.

Big Jim said, breaking the silence, "Well, it even makes sense. But if they're from another planet, where are you from?

Mitch actually grinned at that. "Oh, over the ridge and down the mountain outside Martintown. Honest."

But he wanted to get down to business.

"The first thing is to hear your story," he said, his eyes turned directly on Lassiter, Miller, and Alvarez. "But don't all of you speak at once. Who wants to start?"

The three exchanged glances, and he saw Lassiter and Alvarez nod at Karen Miller.

"I will," she said. She drew a deep breath and began.

"I'd better start at the beginning. We were students at James Madison up in Harrisonburg, Virginia, all junior year. This was eight years ago. I was dating Tim. Elena was going out with Drew, but they weren't as serious as we were."

"Hardly," Elena said. "I was going to break up with him after the camping trip. But then we were abducted."

Miller accepted the interruption and continued. "Anyway, it was fall break, and we'd decided to go hiking and camping over in West Virginia, not at a commercial campground but really roughing it. Backpacks, camp stoves, freeze-dried rations, drinking water from streams and springs, the whole nature trip.

"We picked what we thought was a remote area not far from Flatbush, and set out hiking. It was remote, all right. But not too remote that the Kraxx couldn't find us. They picked us up the second night. I guess we're still missing persons. They didn't bother with our tents and stuff."

"The – Kraxx?" Big Jim asked, not coming close to Miller's pronunciation.

She nodded. "That's what they call themselves." She paused and searched for words, then resumed. "You see, that doesn't mean their whole race, their whole species. It's a word they have for their ruling faction on many, maybe most, of their worlds.

"It has a couple of meanings, depending on context. One is 'the Enlightened.' Another, one their top dogs use a lot, is 'the Elite.' I don't fully understand the history. And don't worry about how to pronounce it. I don't think any human can really come close. Mostly, we spoke English.

"That is, when they bothered to speak at all. Usually they just compelled us with their" – she used another alien word – "educators, are what they call them." Her laugh was bitter. "Some education. 'Control' is more like it." She tapped the disabled device at her waist. Her eyes sought Lassiter's. "Tim, can you explain?"

"I tried to learn as much as I could about the history, but I wasn't able to learn much. I think the Kraxx started as a political movement that grew stronger and stronger until it took over their home world, then more. I don't really know much about its origins. Right-wing? Left-wing? I'm not sure those human terms mean much when applied to them. It may have even been a religious movement. They do have some kind of religion, but we know nothing about it. It's for Kraxx only. Their actual race is called" – he used another impossible word – "which just means 'people.'

"They've settled a number of planets, in solar systems spread pretty far apart. Some of them had native populations, which are now on reservations or enslaved. Most did not.

"Anyway, the Kraxx don't control all of their race's worlds. I think they hold more than not. But they have enemies among their own kind. Another faction, maybe more than one, controls some of their worlds. I'm not sure how many."

"What are they called?" Mitch asked.

"The Kraxx usually call them, well, the word means, 'the Enemy.' But the word they call themselves, which the Kraxx usually refuse to use, means something like 'the Liberated' or maybe 'the Free Folk'."

"Thank you," Mitch said. "Go on."

Elena Alvarez took up the thread. "What you need to understand," she said, "is that the official position, what the Kraxx preach and some really believe, is that they know what's best. They're enlightened. They know what's good for their people – for all races." She barked a short, humorless laugh. "They'd tell you they are the instruments of peace, fairness, and progress.

"It's just that so many people don't know what's best for them and have to be controlled, for their own good. That's what they believe, or what they say to themselves.

"But the ones who are really in charge, their...officer class, I think is long past that. They just like power. They just enjoy control."

She broke down and sobbed, head in hands, and then lifted her face. "I can't go back to that. I won't."

"How did you react to all of that?" Jim asked.

"At first we were all in, all four of us," Lassiter said. "We had been exposed to a lot of dissatisfaction with society in school. You know, how our system isn't fair, promotes inequality, tolerates racism." His laugh, like Miller's, was humorless and self-derisive, then he continued his story.

"None of us was really radical, except Drew. He always wanted to tear down everything and start over."

"Yeah, with him in charge," said Elena, who continued, "But we all thought the Kraxx had built a truly equitable society. That's what they say. Of course, someone has to lead, to be in charge.

"That was the temptation for us, and we all fell for it. We could be in charge – not of Kraxx, never that. They were above us. But of other humans."

"Anti-racist, huh?" Miller asked, obviously not expecting an answer.

"But what did they actually want with you?" Tompkins persisted. For now, Mitch was content for him to ask the questions.

Lassiter didn't hesitate. "They want to take over. Here. Everywhere. They already had humans working for them. Some were taken fairly recently. Some already live on some of their worlds. Their ancestors were taken long ago. They wanted agents because they can't move directly against the Earth. They have enemies. Not just the 'Free Folk.' Others, too."

"Other races?" Mitch asked.

Lassiter nodded. "Several. I really don't know all of them. But the Kraxx really despise two."

"Who are they?" Mitch asked. "Where are they from?"

"We don't know where," Elena said. "And I only saw pictures, never one in person." She smiled. "One race we, the four of us, called, 'the Tabbies'."

"Tabbies?" Samantha asked, speaking for the first time.

"They look like cats, but they're not," Elena said. "The other we called 'the Dwarfs,' because they resemble the Dwarfs in *The Lord of the Rings*. They look pretty human, and the Kraxx hate them."

"Anyway," Lassiter said, "they can't just move in, because these other races and the other factions among their own keep track of what they're doing and would stop them.

"But if they can take over from inside, take control of a society here, maybe more than one, the other races won't be able, wouldn't even try, to do anything. It would be, a, a, what's the word?" Lassiter groped.

"*Fait accompli*?" Mitch supplied.

"Yes," Lassiter said, "that's the term. That's where we come in.

"And," he said, "looking directly at Tompkins, "that's where you come in, or would have."

Big Jim started. "Me?" he said.

Mitch leaned forward in his chair. "We need you to explain," he said, "but before you do, answer a couple of questions for me." After no one objected to his interruption, he asked, "First, how do their ships work? How do they fly, and how do they go from star to star?"

"We weren't allowed to learn anything important," Lassiter said. "But they have some kind of cold fusion power. They fly by disrupting gravity fields. They cross interstellar space by making and going through wormholes. As I said, they kept the science from us. From me, anyway.

"I think Drew knew a little more, and Giscard and Van Der Taalen quite a bit."

"Who are they?" Mitch asked.

"They are...well, call them our superior officers. The Dutchman reports to Giscard, and Giscard reports directly to the ship captain. They're both ex-military. I'm going to quit using the Kraxx words, but the title means 'Exalted Ship Leader.'

"Drew Sorrelli was our direct commander."

"Commander, hell," Elena said, "he was our owner." She began to cry again, and Samantha rose, went to her and hugged her.

"That's the next question," Mitch asked, deciding to keep to the technical for now. The emotional context could come later. He was sure it was pretty unpleasant. "How do these mind control devices work?"

"We don't know anything technical," Lassiter said. "But basically, they open a channel from the user to another person, or people, and enable the user to impose his will on them. It focuses brain waves, I think.

"It's not a communications device. You can't read minds with it, although you can sense and channel emotions. When you get the nanite injection, you can work it better, and sometimes control someone directly with it, even without the booster." He tapped his inert device. "And someone who has been injected, but who has no control box, is completely helpless. The boxes are not the same. Some have more...juice than others. We were issued ours before we left on this mission. But Drew's was much more potent. He controlled all of us."

Mitch heard Elena mutter something in Spanish that he didn't quite catch, but was sure was uncomplimentary.

"You see," Lassiter said, his tone more than a little guilty, "this thing about controlling others for their own good was fun at first, especially since we were allowed to control others, especially the humans they have, well, bred as servants.

"But it didn't take that long for Karen, Elena, and I to become disenchanted. It only took a time or two when we were being compelled. But Sorrelli – he was a true believer in the Kraxx credo. He was always more extreme than the rest of us, even at college.

"And he enjoyed it. He liked it.

"But here's the thing: Like I said, it's a mistake using human terms like 'left-wing' or 'right-wing' when talking about the Kraxx. Giscard was as bad as Drew" –

"Worse," said Elena.

"Okay, worse," Tim amended. "But here on Earth, he was right-wing. National Front. A LePen guy. Van Der

Taalen was the same. They talk all the time about what they will do if and when they get control of Europe.

"Giscard told me, 'The Kraxx are superb at controlling those who can't be trusted to rule themselves.' He meant pretty much everybody."

Elena muttered again. She looked as though she wanted to find Sorrelli's corpse and spit on it again.

"And that's their whole society," Karen added. "Control or be controlled. The ones who control the most are the ones who rule, who advance. It's awful." This time she was the one who started sniffling.

"Their human servants are just a reflection of the Kraxx. Giscard, Van Der Taalen, and Sorrelli all find what they want to see in the Kraxx. That may be deliberate on the part of the Kraxx. In fact, it probably is."

She turned her eyes on Mitch and said, "What we don't understand is how you were able to turn our control boxes off, and even disable our nanite nodes. Don't think we're not grateful. But how did you do it?"

"I'd like to know the answer to that one, too," Big Jim said.

Mitch had been expecting that subject to come up again, and gave what was becoming a stock answer.

"You just have to accept that I can, for now," he said, adding, "Just think of it as Above Top Secret."

And that, he thought, is really true. He decided to steer the conversation back to the three visitors from the alien ship.

"But why were you here?" he asked, directing his question to Lassiter. You said something about Mr. Tompkins."

Lassiter spoke directly to Big Jim. "We – they – wanted you. They wanted you under their control."

"Why me?" Tompkins asked. "Why not Musk? Or Bezos? Or Gates?"

"We didn't think we could get near them. They're always surrounded by security. But you, sir – think about it. You have a lot of money. You have influence. And people who aren't predisposed to being controlled trust you.

"With you working for the Kraxx, we could steer your investments, gradually move your corporate policies in the correct direction, put it in terms that would set people on your side of the political fence at ease, get near some of them so they could be controlled. You would fly under the radar for a while. Then you could have a public epiphany, when it was safe to do so.

"It would take time, and other avenues would have to be opened, too; but eventually the Kraxx would be controlling the country."

"But why this country?" Tompkins asked. "Why not the Chinese? These Kraxx sound much more congenial to the way they think."

"The Chinese are paranoid," Lassiter said. "And they're not as gullible as Americans. At least, some Americans."

"I've got another question," Mitch said. "Why do they even want to take over here? From what we've seen, they have to a have a filter to breathe the atmosphere. It doesn't look like their race could live here, even if they thinned our population by force."

"There are two reasons," Lassiter said. "First, this world, once subdued, would be a potent ally in their interstellar rivalries. The other reason is still more unpleasant." He paused and swept the room with his eyes.

"They like slaves. They prefer slaves to robots. Earth has six billion for the taking."

"What are they going to do now, when you don't re-report in?" Mitch asked.

The three exchanged eye contact, and then Tim said, "We aren't sure. Maybe nothing, but that's not likely. They may send another team here. That's a possibility.

"I think they'll wait to be sure we don't come back on-line – I mean, our nanite nodes don't start working again. Then I think they'll take off and destroy this house on the way out. I'm not sure how long they'll wait. But they'll do it while the snowstorm persists."

That created a stir, and everyone began talking at once. Mitch held up both hands.

"We can handle this," he said. I hope, he thought, but he couldn't show any doubt. "But give me a minute to think."

Tompkins probably had a vehicle that could negoti-ate the road. But it wouldn't hold more than a few peo-ple. Mitch could open a Portal, but he couldn't hold it open for more than two or three. That was something he and Alyssa were working on, but hadn't mastered. Hell, if they could have done it this morning, they would have just Portaled to somewhere Hutton told them to go, and brought in a whole squad of special forces. He supposed though, he could make multiple trips, as long as he didn't take them too far.

Damn, he wished Alyssa were here. Two heads were better than one.

"Well?" Big Jim said, his tone demanding, "have you thought enough? What have you got?"

Mitch was saved from answering by Megan entering the parlor, looking a little green but functional.

"Mr. McCaffrey?" she said. "There's someone here to see you. She's out in the hall."

"Jesus, who else is going to show up out of the blue?" Big Jim growled.

Mitch ignored him and followed Megan out into the hallway. Sure enough, there was Alyssa, her face flushed red from snow and wind, but sound, thankfully.

"I need your help," he said without preamble.

"Not as much as I need yours," she said.

"What are you talking about?"

"They've got Monica."

"What? How?" He was dumbfounded.

"I'll tell you in a minute," she said. "But we've got to figure out how to get her out. We can't let the aliens have a Spellcaster."

Chapter Thirteen

COMPLICATIONS

Diana

Diana was just about at her wits' end. She was crazy worried about Mitch, and she could tell Ben was the same about Alyssa. Why weren't they back yet? Had something happened? It helped that she could still feel them with her Talent, especially Mitch. She didn't sense any immediate danger, but what she could pick up, at this distance, from their auras told her they were anxious and concerned about something.

She had felt she needed to share that with Ben, who didn't have a jot of Talent. He'd thanked her but grimaced, showing that he, too, had that cup-half-empty reaction to what she could pick up without knowing anything specific.

To make it worse, Paul and Steve had emerged from their room unhappy that they hadn't been allowed to go back outside, hungry, and completely uncomprehending about why Papa Mitch and Aunt Alyssa were nowhere to be seen.

Thankfully, Ben had helped with that. He'd taken the boys into the great room, sat them on the couch, and told them a version of the truth.

"You guys know your Papa Mitch and your Aunt Alyssa are top-secret government contractors, don't you?" he'd said.

They did. They'd been told that story after the deal Ben had helped cut with the DOJ back in June, with strict instructions not to say anything to any of their friends or at school. As far as she knew, they had kept that promise.

"Well," Ben continued, "they got called in on a project this morning. It can't wait, and they've been working on it ever since, downstairs. They can't be disturbed, so you can't go down there. Your mom only goes down to take them something to eat. We didn't tell you before because we thought they'd be done by now.

"So, they're fine. We just can't interrupt them. And we can't tell you what they're working on. And we've all got to zip our lips about this. Okay?"

"What about Mom?" Paul had asked. "She's a government contractor, too, isn't she? And aren't you?"

"Yes, Paul, she is. But this project isn't in her contract like it is in Papa Mitch's and Aunt Alyssa's. And" – here he'd allowed a rueful smile – "I'm just a lawyer."

This explanation, plus the promise of hot dogs and beans for supper and unlimited binge watching of whatever they wanted, within reason, and the assurance that everyone would be around for Santa Claus in the morning, had calmed them down. Now they had been fed and were in their room watching *Back to the Future*. She'd told them they could watch all three of the films, but she knew they'd never stay awake that long.

She and Ben hadn't eaten hot dogs. She had some leftover beef stew she'd thawed and heated, and that had been enough. Neither of them were very hungry.

They were too worried. They decided they would sit in the great room and listen to music and talk while waiting.

Ben was sipping on a glass of Cabernet. Diana decided she could at least treat herself to a snifter of Grand Marnier. Mitch kept that in the wet bar downstairs. She excused herself to get it.

She was pouring the cordial when she had a sudden sensation of approaching danger, and then felt something cold against her neck, followed quickly by a sting. She started losing consciousness almost immediately, and fell back into to somebody's grasp. She couldn't see who it was, but it felt like a man. The loudest noise she could manage was a muffled cry that wouldn't carry upstairs.

"Bring her now," a voice said. Dimly, she recognized it. Monica's.

Whoever it was picked her up and carried her. She managed to remain conscious, barely, until he stopped walking.

At the very last, she remembered she needed to do something. Summoning the last of her will, she started Blocking.

Monica

Monica was feeling pleased with herself. She was standing next to Giscard in the room where they had taken her, watching Diana McCaffrey slumped in the chair where Jacob Van Der Taalen had deposited her, slowly coming around from her vaccination injection, which, for reasons she didn't understand, caused a brief period of unconsciousness. Jacob stood over Diana.

Monica had already thought of something she could do to show Giscard she was ready to help the Kraxx, who truly were an enlightened race, move American society in the right direction, when she had received her own injection. She'd felt groggy for a short time, but revived when a box on the wall behind Giscard had beeped...

Giscard walked calmly to the wall, pushed a button on the box and spoke a word in the impossible Kraxx language. A voice in the same tongue answered. The exchange was brief, but evidently unpleasant based on the cloud that passed over Giscard's features.

When the conversation concluded, Giscard turned to Monica and Van Der Taalen.

"There has been an unfortunate development," he said. "The ship has lost contact with the team that was dispatched to the Tompkins mansion earlier today. One must assume they have been killed or taken prisoner."

"What are we going to do?" Van Der Taalen asked. "Will the Ship Leader send us after them?"

"That has not been decided," Giscard said, "but I think not. There is not sufficient time. It is more likely the house will simply be destroyed. But we may be deployed there first, once the ship takes off. It is still a setback. Our instructions are to wait for the Ship Leader's orders."

Monica listened with interest, and decided to speak.

"I think I know what has happened," she said, "and I may be able to help."

Giscard raised a brow. "Say on," he directed.

She explained that McCaffrey and McCormick were almost certainly at the Tompkins place, and likely had disabled the team from the ship.

"I will bet you that your team is alive," she said, and amended, "Most of them anyway. They're likely prisoners."

"Can you take us there?" Giscard asked.

Monica hesitated, but decided she had to be truthful.

"No," she confessed. "I am not...fully trained in the... technique for traveling quickly to one place from another." She saw his frown reappear, and quickly added, "but I think I can get us our own prisoner, someone with whom we can barter, if you want."

His broad smile said that pleased him. "Who is that, and how?"

"I can open a Portal to somewhere I have been before. I can take you to McCaffrey's wife. He has a connection, a sensitivity, to her. That will lure him here and we can take him."

She watched as Giscard pondered her words.

"All right," he said. "There is time to try it. Do it now. Jacob, go with her and take a – vaccination. Take this woman, and only her. Don't fail."

Monica felt a rush of adrenalin. She thought she could open a Portal back to the McCaffrey home, to the same room she had left. But it was farther than she had Portaled before.

She inhaled a deep breath and grasped Jacob's hand. She pulled him through mist...

It had worked better than she'd hoped. They'd found Diana alone, concentrating on pouring a drink, her back to them.

And now she was here, her eyes starting to blink at her surroundings without comprehension. Monica felt a brief and unfamiliar pang of guilt. This woman had been kind to her, bringing her a coat and a pair of her own gloves.

The guilt quickly vanished. This woman was married to the source of her greatest humiliation. She was sure Diana Corcoran had gloried in the story of how her skirt had ripped, her buttons popped, and she'd stumbled from the hearing room with her butt spreading for all to see. Well, she'd get her comeuppance now.

Diana moaned softly, then spoke, her blinking eyes directly on Monica. "M-Monica. Where...how? Why?" She was still clearly disoriented.

Giscard didn't give Monica time to answer, but cut in, "Madame, you are our guest. We know it is not your choice. But you will not be harmed. Yet you must cooperate."

He touched a button on a box at his waist. Monica saw it was similar to the one the alien had used to subdue Monica herself.

Giscard frowned. "She is not responding. I don't understand."

Monica felt a blocking aura still emanated from Diana.

"She has...some Power of her own. But I think this is probably temporary."

Giscard considered. "I see. Well, it is enough, for now that we have her.

"Jacob," he continued, "take this woman to a holding chamber and prepare to begin her education. Do not hurt her, but keep her secure."

"Yes, Colonel," Jacob said. He eyed Diana's curvy figure. "With pleasure." He pulled the still-groggy Diana to her feet and pushed her, gently at first, then with more force as she tried weakly to shake off his hand, toward a door, behind which they disappeared.

"I need to ask you something, Colonel Giscard," Monica said when they had gone. "What will be my instructions when I'm released back to where I came from?"

Giscard's smile was almost merry.

"Why, who said you were going to be released?" he asked.

Monica felt the blood drain from her face. "But I thought you promised..." she began.

"I promised you a life of service to the Kraxx," he said, adding, before she could respond, "It is time your own education began. Come, we will go to my quarters. We have a little time."

Monica gasped and began to gather a compulsion spell. But before she could do so, he twisted a knob at his belt, and she felt herself in the grip of an alien compulsion almost as strong as the one that had held her before.

"Follow me," he repeated. "It will not be altogether unpleasant. And don't be surprised. Why do you think you were inoculated?"

He walked toward another door, and she mutely followed.

She had to.

Diana

Diana let herself be shoved along the corridor by the man who had been called Jacob. He was much bigger than she, and something about him made her sure he would get rough if necessary. Besides, she was still trying to shake off whatever drug they had given her.

Inside she was numb. She knew she had been kidnapped. And she knew Monica Gilbert had arranged it. A part of her managed to be angry. If there was any hateful, absolute *bitch* in the whole world who would defect to the aliens, it was Monica Murray Gilbert. She promised herself Monica would pay for this.

They finally reached a door that slid open when her captor pressed a palm against an adjacent panel. They entered into a small room, perfectly square, with no windows, but lit well enough by something like track lighting. It held a cot with a pillow and mattress, a cushioned chair, an exposed metallic toilet, and a metallic sink. There was nothing on the dull gray walls but writing. No pictures, nothing. There were no amenities beyond a cup that looked ceramic in a holder beside the sink.

Jacob pushed her onto the chair, not violently, but roughly enough to make the point that he was in charge.

"Rest," he commanded. "I will return presently." He bared his teeth in an unpleasant smile. "Perhaps I will bring you food. We will talk. We will get to know each other well, *nein*?" His English was very good, with only the slightest of accents. German? Dutch? She couldn't tell.

Without waiting for an answer, he turned and left the room. When he was gone, she looked around. She assumed there was a microphone and a camera somewhere, but she couldn't spot anything.

She studied the writing on the walls. There was print in English, in languages she recognized as French and Spanish, in what she thought was German, and something she believed was Arabic. There were other languages, too, but she couldn't place them, except for some symbols she thought must be Chinese or maybe Japanese. They must all say the same thing, she thought. The English was in large block print, all in capital letters, and said –

SERVICE IS FREEDOM

SERVICE IS FULFILLMENT

SERVICE IS JOY

Her head was now clear, and she felt herself, except still being dazed by what had happened. She remembered calling up her Blocking Talent. It was still engaged. She had used only to surround herself. She was capable of projecting it over a wider area, and the area had grown with practice.

She decided to let it dissipate, so she wouldn't tire herself any more than she already was. She would engage it again when Jacob returned. She wasn't sure her Blocking Talent would help, but it might. Alyssa had said she and Mitch had been able to block the aliens, and she was supposed to block spells better than either. The aliens used something like spells with their gadgets.

Mitch could find her more easily with her Talent off. He would come for her. She knew he would. He had to. She clung to the thought.

She was suddenly very thirsty. She rose from the chair and unsteadily made her way to the sink. It took her a moment to figure out the button that brought water. When she did, she filled the cup and drank. The water was cool and tasted slightly metallic, but not bad. When the cup was empty, she refilled it and drank another cup-ful.

She felt an urgent need to pee. The toilet was hardly private, but there was no one in the room. She walked to it, pulled down her sweatpants and panties, and re-lieved herself. When she was done, she rose and looked for something that would flush. But she saw the toilet bowl was frictionless or something, because her urine was fast disappearing.

Her urine sparkled, as though there were tiny bits of metal in it. That was odd.

What could that be? Something that had been in the shot they'd given her? She guessed it was.

She sat again and felt the tears come. Fear, sorrow, and anger mingled to produce them. She sobbed for a minute, and then found her self-control.

She could do nothing but wait.

Mitch, she pleaded silently, come to me soon. Please. Oh, God, please let him come soon.

Chapter Fourteen

THE PLAN

Jim Tompkins

There were two conversations, both conducted in low tones, going on the parlor in Mitch's absence. On one side of the empty chair McCaffrey had occupied, Christina, Samantha, and Rob were talking with Lassiter, Miller, and Alvarez. On the other, Big Jim, Jimmy, and Dave Thomas were mostly silent, but every now and then, one of them would wonder out loud what was keeping Mitch.

Tompkins could only catch a word or two of the other conversation, but evidently the latter three were talking about their life among the Kraxx. The two women were crying, and Christina and Samantha were crying with them. Rob wasn't saying anything, but his eyes were wide, and he was grinding his teeth. As he watched, he caught a bit of what was being said, when their voices raised just a little.

"But Elena, Karen," Samantha was saying, "how did you keep from getting pregnant? Did they give you birth control?"

Miller's sobs began again, leaving it to Elena Alvarez to answer.

"At times," she said. "But the truth of the matter is that Karen and I have both been pregnant several times."

"Your babies have been aborted?" Samantha asked.

Elena shook her head. "No. Harvested. We don't know what was done with them. We...think some were destroyed. Others were implanted in host mothers and brought to term. We never saw them. We only heard rumors."

Then her tears began again.

Jim shuddered when he heard that exchange. Jesus, was this what they were dealing with? Was this what McCaffrey had saved them from?

He decided to interrupt.

"Christina," he called. "Do you know exactly who is with McCaffrey?"

Christina rubbed her wet eyes and answered.

"It has to be Alyssa McCormick," she said. "I've known her for a long time. She is a very accomplished Witch. So is Mitch, evidently. I suspected they were working together when I saw the news reports last spring."

Big Jim shook his head. Aliens. Witches. This stuff was a lot to process. But the evidence was pretty stark. Lassiter and Miller really had taken control of him, Jimmy, and Christina. Then McCaffrey had come out of nowhere and freed them in some way he didn't understand. And now another visitor had simply appeared out of nowhere. He needed to talk with Dave and Jimmy in private, he decided. He stood.

"I need a smoke," he announced. "And I need to use the bathroom." His eyes swept his son and his groundskeeper. "You two want to come?"

"Dad, you know I don't smoke," Jimmy said, "but I do need to pee. So, sure, I'll come."

"A cigarette would be good," Dave said, getting to his feet.

When they were in the hallway, they saw McCaffrey sitting on a cushioned bench with a woman who was bundled up. He noticed there was a revolver at her hip. McCaffrey looked up at them and called.

"Don't leave," he said. "We'll be through in a minute, and then we'll need to speak with everyone."

Big Jim promised they would return very shortly, and led Jimmy and Dave to the back stairs. When they arrived in his study, he immediately bolted for the bathroom, and found Jimmy waiting at the door when he emerged. He was loading his pipe, and Dave already had a cigarette going, when Jimmy returned and took one of the chairs across from the desk. Dave had the other one. Jim lit his pipe.

"Dad," Jimmy asked, "when you peed, did your urine look, you know, *sparkly*?"

"It did," Jim answered. "Did you flush?"

"Yes."

"So did I. Maybe we shouldn't have. Somebody might want to analyze it, after this is over."

These words were met with silence. No one would voice what they were all thinking. Was it going to be over? Would any of them be alive, or free, when it was?

"Well, we don't have time to think about that now," he said. "What I want to know from both of you is this: Is this real? And can we trust McCaffrey and that woman Christina says is a Witch?"

"Dad," Jimmy said, "we know it's real. We know what happened. We can't explain it, but we know.

"Yes, I think we can trust them. McCaffrey did save us from...those people. Rob vouches for him. Christina vouches for both of them. I think we have to trust them."

Jim blew a cloud of aromatic smoke and turned to Thomas.

"Dave, what about you?"

Thomas stubbed out his cigarette and reached for another.

"I don't really know what's going on," he said. "But I think I agree with Jimmy." He lit the second smoke and smiled. "I like the guy. He may be an Army puke, but he listens to sergeants."

Big Jim and Jimmy laughed, and the latter said, "Don't ask me. I was Air Force, and didn't get past airman first class."

"Hell," Dave said, "you didn't even have basic training to amount to anything.

"But Jimmy's right that we don't have any choice. Did you hear what they said about the aliens bombing the house on the way out? We can't get anywhere on foot. We'll freeze in the woods. We have only the Land Rover. It can't hold everyone, and I don't know if it can make it down the mountain in this weather. Not in the dark. And it will have to have the headlights. Easy to spot.

"And it will be slow. Hell, if those things, whatever they are, can see the house from the air, they can see a vehicle on the road. Look, I don't know how McCaffrey and the woman can zip from place to place like that.

"But if there is a chance of getting everybody out, they're it."

Big Jim knocked out his pipe.

"We're wasting time," he announced. "Let's get back downstairs."

Mitch

"Tell me what happened to Monica," Mitch said. "How did they get her?"

Alyssa told him what had happened.

"Damned, arrogant, stupid woman," he muttered. "But I'm not surprised she pulled a trick like this.

"Hell, she's probably on their side by now. We ought to let 'em have her."

Alyssa removed her caps and shook out her hair, turning the gesture into a shake of her head in the negative.

"Mitch, you know we can't do that. Having her means the aliens will find out about the Talent. If she's under their control, they'll use her whether it's voluntary or not. We have to go in and get her."

"I know," Mitch sighed. "I was just venting. Sorry."
"Now you tell me what happened here," Alyssa said.

Mitch tried to summarize what had happened as quickly as possible. Valuable seconds were ticking away. But she had to know about the Kraxx. She had to know what they were facing.

He was about two-thirds through the story when he felt it. He stopped talking in the middle of a sentence and gasped. Alyssa's expression told him she'd felt it, too, but not as strongly. She was bonded with Diana, but not like he was.

"They've – got Diana," he whispered. "She's alive, but she's a prisoner. How? How did this happen?"

He saw Alyssa's eyes fill with tears. "Oh, Mitch," she said, "I'm afraid this is my fault. I was the one who took her to your home, and put her around Diana. I-I'm sorry."

Mitch found his own tears, hot and sudden. He was paralyzed. All he could think of was his Diana – his beautiful, loving Diana – in the hands of someone like Sorrelli. Maybe someone worse. Someone's puppet. Controlled, ravished, raped.

Then, pushing through the fear and sorrow, came the rage. Monica Gilbert. Every time he turned around, there she was, up to no good. His anger toward the aliens paled next to how he felt about her. That's all he could think of. He didn't even consider believing she was being controlled. She'd done this willingly. She had enjoyed it. He was sure of that.

He unleashed invectives against Monica that surprised even him. Irrationally, he included Alyssa, cursing her judgment. He wasn't given to that type of talk. Alyssa sat regarding him with pity.

When he'd run out of steam, she said, "Mitch, I understand. But I need you, and Diana needs you, completely rational right now. We are going to get her out. We will. But we have to plan our next move. I can't do this by myself."

That brought Mitch up short. He blinked, breathed deeply, and said, "You're right. And – and I'm sorry. Monica has been in our home before today. She was there with the FBI last spring. And, hell, I was the one who said we needed her. I shouldn't blame it on you.

"But what I don't understand is how she did it. I didn't think she could use Portals."

"Mitch, let's not spend a lot of time worrying about that," Alyssa said. "But I'm sure she's had some training, since we had to introduce it under our contracts. I didn't think she was any good, either. And I'll bet she's not.

"But the first thing you learn is how to open a Portal between you and somewhere you know, or someone you know. I'm betting she took a chance she could get to your house, and it worked.

"But now let's concentrate on how to get her out."

"I can Portal right to her."

"They'll be expecting that. Then they'll jump us and have two Spellcasters rather one. Or three, because you're not going in there without me."

"Okay, then. What should we do?"

"We have to create some type of diversion, and then go get her. And we're going to need help to do that."

They discussed and discarded a couple of plans. As they talked, Mitch found himself able to think better. He reached, reluctantly, a couple of conclusions. He'd better share them now, he thought.

"Alyssa," he said, "there's more." He told her about what Lassiter had said about what the aliens might do once they realized they had no contact with him, and Miller and Alvarez. "We have to do something to get these people out of harm's way."

Alyssa bit her lip. "I hear you. I suppose we could ferry them over to your house, temporarily. It would take a little while, and we'd have to do it in stages."

"If they'll go. I'm not sure Big Jim will. We have to offer, I agree. But there's something else, 'Lyssa."

She said nothing, waiting for him to continue.

"I don't think we can do just a 'snatch and run.' It may come down to that, if we have to bug out. But there are too many people at risk, too much chance of a slip." He fixed her eyes with his own and said, "We have to neutralize the aliens. We have to take the ship."

She closed her eyes, evidently thinking. Then she said, "All right. I agree. But how are we going to manage that?"

"You were more right than you knew a minute ago," he said. "We need help. I think we can get it. Those three abductees we freed are just aching for a shot at the aliens and their human thugs. I think the others will help. But...but I don't know how we can get them there."

Neither he nor Alyssa had been able, no matter how much experimenting they did, to keep a Portal open long enough for more than three people at a time. If they had been able to do that, they would have brought a team from Quantico in this morning. He didn't see how they could do a staged surprise raid on the alien spacecraft.

But Alyssa surprised him by saying, "I think I know of a way."

Her plan was simple, but Mitch's heart rose to his mouth considering the uncertainty. He and Alyssa had been working on a joint spell so that, working together, they could hold a Portal open for a larger group of people. They almost had it. They would soon perfect it.

But almost didn't count.

Alyssa finished with "Let's go see how many volunteers we can get, then you and I can put it together."

They had seen Big Jim, Jimmy, and Dave Thomas walk back into the parlor a couple of minutes earlier. Both he and Alyssa rose without another word.

They had no time to waste.

Ben

Ben Callahan didn't miss Diana for a few minutes. When she didn't return upstairs, he went to the stairwell and called for her. When she didn't answer, he retrieved his handgun from the great room and went down the stairs as quietly as possible.

He found an open bottle of Grand Marnier and a partially filled snifter on the wet bar, a few spilled drops glistening on the granite counter. But no Diana. He called again. No answer.

He quickly checked the bedroom, even the closets and bathroom. She wasn't there. The sliding door to the outdoor patio was locked and secure. No one had entered there. She hadn't stepped outside, although he turned on the outdoor light and looked anyway, because the door would have been unlocked.

He was sure she hadn't sneaked past him upstairs. He would have heard her. And she wouldn't have left her snifter and an unclosed bottle where they sat now.

A cold chill ran down his spine. Someone, or something, had entered the house without using a door and taken Diana. That someone couldn't have been Alyssa, or Mitch. Diana had been abducted.

He went to the guest bedroom where he and Alyssa were staying and changed into heavy clothes. He pulled on boots, and belted on the holster Mitch had given him for the pistol. He removed his winter coat and his cap with furred earflaps.

Then he returned upstairs, carrying the coat and hat in his arms. These he threw over the dining table for quick retrieval. He checked the loads in the shotgun and the pistol. He had to be ready for — well, he wasn't sure what.

He looked outside. The snow was still coming down, but not quite as heavily now. He considered risking a cell phone call to Alyssa, but he'd been told not to do that. He decided he would call Hutton if no one appeared within the next half hour. He, too, had a secure phone.

There was one more thing. Before long, Paul and Steve would wander in, wanting their mother. He had no idea what he'd tell them.

Mitch

When Mitch and Alyssa entered the parlor, they found seven pairs of expectant eyes on them. Everyone was looking to them, to him especially, he realized, to tell them what needed to be done. He remembered what it was like to lead a platoon in Iraq. He thought he'd long finished with that type of leadership.

Suck it up, buttercup, he told himself. You need to do this if you're going to get Diana out of that spaceship. He glanced at his watch. Six-twenty. Not as bad as he'd feared, but no time to waste. He cleared his throat.

"This is Alyssa McCormick," he began. "Like me, she is a government contractor. We're here because there was no one else to send. We're not heroes, but we're what you've got, I'm afraid.

"We just found out that the aliens are holding two Americans they've kidnapped. One of them is another contractor. She was with Alyssa when they got her." He paused and swallowed hard. "The other is my wife."

There were gasps and stares from around the room. Samantha Ashworth uttered a startled cry, a hand flying to her mouth.

"Alyssa and I are going to get them out," Mitch went on. "We need your help to do that, but we can't make anyone put themselves at risk. And we need to keep everyone else safe."

His eyes swept the room. No one said anything, and he didn't sense any hostility, only concern. Adrenalin was already flowing. That was good. Some of them would need it.

"Alyssa and I have a plan. We need to share it. You need to help us fine-tune it. But before we get into that, we need to get everyone in the house in here. We don't have time to waste, so we need to get them here right now."

"I'll get them," Dave said, and headed for the door, walking fast, but not running.

"While we're waiting, can you tell us how the aliens were able to kidnap your wife and the other woman?" Big Jim asked, his tone expectant but not belligerent.

"I'll tell you what I can," Mitch said. Inside, he was fuming that he was not already on his way to find Diana, that this was taking so long, but if he was going to get these people to help him, he had to be as transparent as possible. "As you are already aware," he said, "some of us have a top-secret way of moving rapidly from place to place."

"By — magic?" Big Jim asked, almost choking on the second word.

"That's as good a name as any," Mitch said. "You need to accept that. You've seen it."

"Do the partners in my firm know about this?" Rob asked.

Mitch allowed a grim smile, realizing the light bulb had turned on in the young lawyer's head.

"Some of them," Mitch said, and then plunged on to answer the rest of Big Jim's first question. "The other contractor, a woman named Monica Gilbert, tried to take control of one of the aliens. Instead, he took control of her.

"Not long after that, Gilbert traveled to my home. We don't know if she was being controlled, or whether she'd been turned. We think she must have taken an alien, or one of their human lackeys, with her. They returned to the ship with my wife, Diana."

"Mitch, I think we have to assume Monica did it voluntarily," Alyssa said. "I don't think she could have concentrated enough to open a Portal while under a compulsion. I could be wrong. But we should assume she's helping the, uh, Kraxx because she wants to, until proven otherwise."

At this point, the door opened and Dave entered, followed by Laura, Sally, and Megan, all wearing aprons, with Heather and Linda trailing close behind. Seconds later, Darrel entered, still dressed in his outdoor clothing.

"Sorry," the young man said. "I had to bank the fire."

Dave and Laura walked to the chair where Dave had been sitting. Laura sat, while Dave stood behind the chair. Big Jim and Jimmy did the same for Heather and Linda. Mitch's chair was empty, and Megan took it. Darrel and Sally stood together next to Mitch and Alyssa, holding hands. Dave's brows raised at that, but he said nothing. All of the women except Sally looked bewildered.

Mitch realized he would have to repeat himself. He stole another look at his watch. Only six minutes had passed, but these preliminaries seemed to be taking forever. He raced through the status summary as fast as possible.

"Do you want to take over for a minute, Alyssa?" He asked. This was her plan, after all.

Alyssa's explanation was brief and well-organized. She explained why it would be necessary to take the ship, and why they needed help to do it. They needed Lassiter, Miller, and Alvarez as guides. They needed armed back-ups. In the meantime, just before they assaulted the spaceship, they could move everyone else to safety at Mitch's home.

"That's just temporary," she said. "We hope everyone will be back by midnight." Her eyes swept the room. "We think we have a very good shot at pulling this off," she finished. "Mitch has mastered the, uh, technique, of turning off or disabling electronic devices. He can disable the aliens' weapons, and their compulsion hardware. We just need backup."

God, she's lying through her teeth, Mitch thought. They did have a chance, but he wouldn't call it "excellent." But he hoped the confidence she was projecting was contagious.

"Why not just disable their whole ship?" Big Jim asked. "Right now, I mean. Then we can just wait for the weather to clear and let the Army handle it."

Mitch had been expecting the question. "I will if I can, if I think it's safe. But some systems may have too much shielding. And I don't want to risk throwing some switch that will blow up the ship with my wife in it.

"And regardless, I can't do it from here." He managed a weak smile. "I'm good, but I'm not that good."

"Can't you just speed in and get the prisoners?" Jimmy asked.

He'd been expecting that one, too.

"That's the back-up plan if we're losing," he said, "but we don't dare leave active shooters to lift off and follow us, or to follow us by Portal, especially if Monica Gilbert is working with them. It's much better to subdue the whole ship."

"Well, we're in," Lassiter said, referring to himself and the other two erstwhile abductees. "We all want payback.

"And," he said, "we can shoot, too. We've all had firearms training." His smile was wicked. "Of course, they thought we'd be under control. Now we're not."

"Do you know the layout of the vessel?" Alyssa asked.

"Yes, we do," Miller said. "Well enough, anyway. We weren't allowed in the control room long enough to learn anything. But we know where it is. I can draw a diagram if someone can get me some paper."

Jimmy turned and walked to a small table that held a landline telephone. He picked up a pen and a small notepad, passed it to Linda; and she took it to Karen Miller, who immediately began drawing.

"Well, I'm not going anywhere," Big Jim said. "This is my home. I'm not going to be run out of it. If what you're going to try doesn't work, we're probably dead anyway.

"And think about it. You said they might send someone here. If that woman you say is working with them can whizz around like they say, what's to stop them from coming here and ambushing us when we come back? Someone needs to stay here and guard the house. That's me."

There was some truth to what he said, but plenty of holes in it. But, Mitch realized, Tompkins had made up his mind. He just nodded. Alyssa had opened her mouth to argue, but when she saw Mitch's nod, closed it.

Heather turned in her chair and grasped her husband's hand. "If you stay, I stay," she said.

"That goes for me, too," Jimmy said. "Unless," he added, "I'm needed to go with you to the ship. But I want Linda safe."

"I'm not leaving without you," Linda said.

Mitch decided to take control of the conversation.

"I've been giving this some thought," he said. "Alyssa and I have to go. I'd rather leave her here, if anyone is staying, so she could get them out in a hurry. But we have to have two Spellcasters. Two to Gilbert's one, assuming she's working with them.

"And we're going to have to split into two groups. One to find Diana...and Monica, if she's a prisoner. The other to take control of the ship. We have to decide the rest of the team."

His eyes traveled to Dave Brown. "If you're willing, Dave, I want you. You've seen combat."

Brown hesitated only a moment. "Sure," he said, and then, smiling, added, "Ooh-rah."

"Dave!" Linda yelped, her right hand flying to her mouth. But then her husband's eyes caught hers and she said, "Well, that settles it for me. I'm staying here. Someone has to mind the turkey."

"And it goes against my grain as a father, but Darrel needs to come. He's a better shot than any of us," Dave said, sparking another protest from Linda.

"I'll do it," Darrel said. "You lead the way."

"I want in," Rob Ashworth said. "I want a piece of those bastards who tried to make a slave of my wife." That provoked a startled cry from Samantha, and more tears, but he continued, "Honey, you have to go somewhere safe." Turning his eyes to Mitch he said, "You and I have hunted together. You know I can shoot."

"And I," said Christina. "I can take a bow."

Mitch paused, intrigued. That might come in handy. He might not be able to turn off the Kraxx suppression field right away. A well-placed arrow could buy time.

"All right," he said. "But I would like one more gun. And I think I know where to get it." He turned to Sally, and then looked down at Megan. "Can either of you use a gun?"

"No!" Laura put in. "Not them. I'm thinking about guards for Diana's kids."

This time it was Alyssa who protested. *She realizes what I am thinking,* Mitch thought.

"No," she said. "Not him."

"Yes," he answered. "Him. I want Ben."

She lowered her eyes and nodded.

"Sally, Megan, can you use guns?"

Both of the young women laughed.

"My dad and mom are preppers," Megan said. "I had to have firearms training and keep it up. You bet I can shoot.

"AR-15s?" Mitch asked. "And what about you, Sally?"

"Oh, yes," said Megan. "And shotguns. And pistols. And deer rifles."

"Me, too," Sally said. "My dad was a Ranger. After he left the Army, guns have been his hobby. I was a tomboy and followed him around. I aggravated him until he taught me."

"Great." Mitch said, and directed the next question to the Tompkins men. "Do you have firearms?"

Big Jim stood.

"In the gun room," he said. "Let's go."

Chapter Fifteen

THE PLAN UNFOLDS

Alyssa

While all of the men, plus Christina, headed for the gun room, Alyssa huddled with Karen and Elena over Karen's drawing while Samantha watched. Heather, Linda, and Laura excused themselves to go back to the breakfast room for more coffee.

Karen had drawn an ovoid sphere with boxes connected by channels inside. The channels represented hallways, she said, cautioning she was drawing only the more important areas and that her drawing omitted a number of details.

"The main airlock is here on this side, which is the one facing the ridge," she said. "Just beyond it is a large room, big enough to hold a number of people who have just entered, or are getting ready to leave, the ship.

"There is a monitoring station, with screens showing the outside, on the left side of the room. It has control of the outside door and the airlock, and there is always a subordinate Kraxx on duty. Most the time, there are two. They are armed."

"How?" Alyssa asked.

"They have a control box with enough power to control a human, or another Kraxx who is subordinate to them. Each of them also has a plasma rod. It can be set to discharge a single bolt, if on full power, or up to four at lower settings. The more charges, however, the lower the power and range.

"There are more powerful plasma blasters that can hold more charges. These are kept in a locked arms locker in the control room, and released only on the orders of the Exalted Ship Leader.

"The plasma bolts are deadly. Even the Kraxx armor won't deflect them."

Karen saw Alyssa's grim nod, and continued.

"They also have little guns that fire pins with a sleep-inducing drug. These are also in the arms locker. They don't have much range or power. A heavy coat might stop them.

"Do you want me to show you what the rest of the ship holds?

"Please," Alyssa said.

Karen tapped slash marks on the right side of the entry chamber. "This door leads into a hallway that takes you to the part of the ship that is climate-controlled for humans. That's where we were housed. That's where you'll find Mitch's wife and the other prisoner – well, the other woman, whether she is a prisoner or not.

"The Kraxx can enter this area at any time, but humans are allowed in the Kraxx part of the ship only if escorted by one or more Kraxx. They let their head flunkies go armed in the human section, but not in the Kraxx section."

"Who are they, and how many?" Alyssa said.

"There will be a total of six, but the only two who will give you trouble are Giscard and Van Der Taalen. Sorrelli was a level beneath them, and we were a level below that."

"Bastards!" Elena put in. "Worse than Sorrelli...if possible," she added.

"Who are the other four?"

"No one who will give you trouble. I hope we can free them, too," said Miller. "They were born on a Kraxx world, or were stolen as infants. They are there to be servants for the rest of us. Two men and two women. Karl, Jose, Darlene, and Carmen. They prepare food, and" –

"Are sex toys," Elena finished for her, her tone contemptuous. "For us, too, if we wanted it. Karen and I tired of that long before we were assigned to this mission. Tim, too, not long after." She looked as though she wanted to spit again. "Drew never did. Giscard and Jacob Van Der Taalen never will."

From the corner of her eye, Alyssa saw Samantha shudder.

Karen moved her pen back to the entrance chamber and tapped another pair of slash marks leading to a hallway, which in turn led to a large box in more or less the center of the drawing. She had placed other slash marks along the way, but didn't show what was beyond.

"This is the door to the Kraxx part of the ship. The large box is the control room or command center. The Ship Leader is usually there if he is not in his quarters or office. There will be others on duty. Some will be armed.

"The rest of these rooms lead to crew quarters, kitchen and dining areas, and so forth."

"How many are there?" Alyssa asked.

"Fourteen, but only ten will be dangerous. The other four are Kraxx servants. Three are female. They serve the same purpose as the human servants, but for the Kraxx officers. They are not of the ruling class. They are shorter, stockier, and their skin color is a little paler blue. Their heads are rounder." She sighed. "I think they are the most pitiful of all. The officer class treats them like dirt. For their own good, of course."

"Are there other Kraxx females?" Alyssa asked.

"One," Miller said. "The Exalted Ship Leader's mistress, for lack of a better word, and second in command. She'll mostly likely be with him, and she'll be armed, too.

"The upper-class Kraxx believed they have evolved beyond mating rituals, but women – females – don't have very high status, except in the officer class."

Alyssa was already planning. If she and Mitch could get everyone Portaled into the entrance chamber, and take care of the Kraxx on duty, she could take a team to find Diana; and Mitch could take another to go for the control room.

Mitch wouldn't like that division of labor, but it had to be that way. He was the one who could neutralize the Kraxx weapons. She'd take Elena and Karen with her, and...Ben, probably, but maybe Christina. Mitch could have Dave, Darrel, and Rob. Maybe Ben. They'd work it out.

Just then, the men returned from the gun room, arms loaded and Dave pushing a hand cart. They have really loaded up, Alyssa thought.

"Mitch," she called, "let's talk."

She took the sheet of paper with the drawing from Karen and led him to a corner of the room. She showed him the drawing and whispered rapidly, repeating what Karen had told her and adding her plan for the two teams.

"I know you want to find Diana," she finished. "But it has to be this way. You know it."

Mitch made a sour face, but sighed and said, "Okay. You're right. But you take Christina."

"Don't you want her? You're one who liked the idea of an archer."

"Yes, I do. But think about it. You can block spells and compulsions. But they'll have that suppression field, like you said. And you can't turn it off. That compound bow can't be turned off."

It was Alyssa's turn to give in.

"All right," she said. "Let's go get this organized."

In the Gun Room

When they reached the gun room, Jimmy Tompkins took charge. He led them to the cabinet on the wall to the right. He opened it, revealing the AR-15s.

"We've several of these," he said. "And" – he reached in and pulled out a rifle that looked much like the AR-15s, but wasn't one – "this is something we're not supposed to have, but we do. This is a military-grade M-16. It really is an assault rifle. It can fire three-round bursts."

"That's mine," Dave said. No one argued.

"Do you want the armor-piercing rounds?" Jimmy asked. "We have them."

"Yes," Mitch said. He told them about the Kraxx armor. "It stopped my bullets, but not their force. The armor-piercing might not get through, but they would have a better chance.

"Of course," he added, "a head shot will work, too."

Lassiter wanted one of the AR's, and Jimmy handed him one.

"Rob?" Jimmy asked.

"I think I'd better have one of the Ranch Rifles. I've used one before," Rob said.

"Why don't you take the .223? It will take the armor-piercing rounds," Jimmy said. "We'll remove the 'scope."

Rob nodded.

"I think I should take the .338 I've had outside," Darrel said. "I know we only have soft-nosed hunting cartridges for it, but from what Mr. McCaffrey says, it won't have any trouble knocking them down.

"And," he added, "I think I can make a head shot or two."

"He can," Dave said.

"What about you, Mitch?" asked Jimmy. "Do you want a long gun?"

Before answering, Mitch turned to one side and muttered a word. When a cloud of mist formed, he reached inside and pulled out his rifle, ignoring the dropped jaws around him.

"I'm going to be busy with trying to turn off the Kraxx devices," he said. "I won't primarily be a shooter. But if I need my rifle, I'll reach for it. I would like to top off my magazines, though."

Jimmy opened one the cabinets and took out Rob's rifle. He handed it to Darrel to remove the telescopic sights. At his father's request, he took one of the Winchesters from a cabinet and handed it to him. He gave Lassiter an AR, and placed three more on a trolley, one for himself, and the others for Megan and Sally, and then started pulling out boxes of ammunition and spare clips from the cabinets. Big Jim helped him. These went on the trolley, too, along with Berretta pistols and magazines for Elena and Karen.

"And there's two more things," he said, pulling a large box out of the same cabinet and setting it on a table, then removing a narrow rectangular box and doing the same. He opened the latter first and removed four arrows with narrow, needle-nosed steel tips.

Christina had already grabbed the compound bow and a quiver filled with broad-bladed hunting arrows. Jimmy handed the arrows he'd just pulled out to her.

"I had a blacksmith run these up just for grins," he said. "These are classic bodkin points. They could pierce mail armor, back in the day. The compound bow you have doesn't have the pull of a longbow, thanks to the pulleys. But it's just as powerful."

Then he opened the larger box and removed a short tubular object with a ring and lever attached. Dave and Mitch knew exactly what it was, but Jimmy explained anyway.

"Flashbang stun grenades," he said. "We're not supposed to have these either."

"I've used them," said Mitch. "They may make a difference."

Mitch took two and gave two to Dave.

"Let's get going," he said. "We've no time to waste."

Ben

Ben was stressed. First, he was sick with worry about Alyssa, and now about Diana, too. Secondly, he was sure someone bad had been able to spirit Diana away; and he was afraid for the boys and even for himself that whoever it had been would be back.

And to make everything worse, Paul and Steve had shown up, wanting to know why he was wearing a coat and carrying a gun, and demanding to speak with their mother. Ben really didn't know how to answer, but he had to tell them something. And it had to include at least some of the truth. They were smart enough to know that no one was going anywhere on foot tonight.

He asked them to sit on the couch in the room Mitch insisted on calling the library and he thought of as Mitch's man-cave, cleared his throat, and began.

"We talked to you earlier about your mom and Papa Mitch and Aunt Alyssa being government agents. You remember that, don't you?"

"You said 'government contractors,'" said Paul.

"Same thing. Well, we couldn't tell you earlier; but Aunt Alyssa and Papa Mitch have been away on a secret mission. They used a top-secret way of going from place to place.

"Aunt Alyssa came back a while ago to get your mom to come help. She asked me to stay here and protect you guys, and told me to be ready to take you outside if necessary. That's why I have my coat on, but I'm going to take it off in a minute.

"You two with me so far?"

They nodded, wide-eyed, but Paul, the older said, "I don't understand how they could go anywhere."

Ben decided to level with them. "I don't either, but for now, you just have to know they can and did. What we're going to do now is to go upstairs and get your coats, and hats, and boots and bring them down here. You'll have to put your boots on in case we have to leave in a hurry, but you won't have to put on your coats.

"We're going to stay downstairs. You two can go back in the bedroom, the one Alyssa and I are staying in, and you can watch TV if you don't turn the sound up too loud. I'm going to stay on guard out here.

"Everyone will be back in time for Santa Claus." I hope, he thought as he said it.

The minutes later, despite some protest, the boys were back in the bedroom, wearing their boots, their coats draped over a chair, the television a low noise but not obtrusive. He was sitting on the couch, his own coat hanging on a corner rack, the shotgun beside him, safety on, and holiday music playing on the CD player. He didn't dare read or watch TV because he had to stay alert.

He shifted uneasily where he sat. He was going to have to get up and walk around in a minute. He didn't dare risk dozing off.

He had just risen to his feet when he saw a cloud of mist swirling to the right of the television. There were figures emerging. He grabbed the shotgun and pointed it at where they would come out.

Then he heaved a sigh of relief, snapped on the safety, and lowered the gun. It was Alyssa. She ran to him, and he tossed the shotgun on the couch and gathered her to him.

Looking over her shoulder. He saw Alyssa was not alone. She'd been followed by three young women. One was Samantha Ashworth, Jack Melton's daughter and Rob Ashworth's wife. He had met her at firm social events. The other two appeared to be in their early twenties. One was white; the other, black. The white girl was quite pretty, and the black girl was stunning. But that wasn't the first thing he noticed about them.

They were carrying AR-15s.

The young black woman spoke first. "Mr. Callahan," she said, with a dazzling display of even white teeth, "I know who you are. Tiff has told me all about you."

That's who she looks like, Ben realized. This girl had to be related to Tiffany DeRatt, a paralegal at the law firm.

He was sure he was gasping like a fish out of water. Stepping back from Alyssa, he stammered, "What? How?" He forgot to greet Samantha. It didn't seem to trouble her.

At that point, Paul and Steve showed up, babbling questions like mad. Thankfully, Alyssa took charge. He was too confused.

"Boys," she said. "Papa Mitch sent me to get Mr. Callahan to come and help him and your mom. But we can't leave you by yourselves. So I brought baby-sitters."

"We're not babies!" Paul protested.

"Bodyguards, then," Alyssa amended.

That seemed to pacify Paul. His eyes went to Megan and then to Sally. He was starting to be curious about girls, but didn't know why.

"You're pretty!" he told them.

"Yeah!" his brother said. "And they got guns!"

"Mr. Callahan and I have to go. Right now," Alyssa said, noting with approval that Ben was already zipping up his down jacket. "You boys mind Megan and Sally, y'hear?"

As Ben was pulling on his winter hat, she stood on tiptoe and whispered in his ear.

"The aliens have Diana. We think Monica is helping them. Mitch told me to come get you. He wants another shooter, he said. He remembered you were in the Army."

"I was in JAG," Ben muttered, but his voice was drowned by shouts of "we want popcorn" behind him.

It was just as well. He had to go.

He set his jaw and followed Alyssa into the mist.

Chapter Sixteen

THE ASSAULT ON THE SHIP

Mitch

Mitch inspected the small force they had gathered in the mansion's entrance hall. All were dressed for winter weather. All were armed. They were as ready as they were going to get.

And all of us are scared, he thought. No wonder. The first assault on an alien spacecraft in history is being undertaken by, well, amateurs.

He didn't minimize his own Talent, or Alyssa's, as an advantage. He realized that both he and Dave Thomas had experienced unfriendly fire before. He thought the plan good – if it survived contact with the aliens. But he also knew that this group was like an old "forlorn hope" from the 18th century, dispatched to be the first over enemy fortifications.

But there was no choice. Not if he was going to see Diana alive.

And he was in charge, the "officer commanding." It wouldn't do for him to appear doubtful.

They'd just said their good-byes to those who would remain in the house, and closed the doors to the hallway. The Portal spell would work better if there was only a static view in front of him. He would go in front, along with Dave, Darrel, and Tim Lassiter, with Tim standing next to him. He wanted the anchor of someone familiar with the destination close-by. Ben and Christina would be next, with Karen, Elena, and Alyssa at the rear. That was too much clustering, and Dave hadn't approved at all; but they had to be close when going through the Portal he would open. Alyssa's job was to keep it open until everyone was through.

If the spell worked. It should. There was no reason it wouldn't. But...Unbidden, the vision arose of his arriving in the alien craft alone, or with only one other person. He gritted his teeth and concentrated. He didn't need any doubts now.

Someone tapped him on the shoulder. He almost jumped, but didn't. He turned to see Alyssa.

"Mitch," she said, "I've been thinking."

"Yes," he said, irritated. They needed to get going.

"When we take the ship – and we're going to – we can't take prisoners. Not among Kraxx upper class."

Now he really was irritated. She was thinking about this, now? All he wanted was Diana.

But he asked, "Why not? Hutton would prefer it."

"Because there are too many Monica Gilberts in the intelligence services. We don't want the mind control technology in their hands. Think about what Karen and Elena have told us about Sorrelli. Some of them would be as bad as the aliens."

He realized she was right, but he still didn't want to think about that right now. And murdering what amounted to prisoners of war went against his grain.

He just nodded and said, "Well, let's take the ship first."

"Think about what I said."

She turned and walked back to where Elena and Karen stood.

"I'm ready," she called.

He waved to her, turned to face forward, and said, "Now!"

And he walked through mist into the alien vessel.

The entrance chamber was exactly as Lassiter and Miller had described. It was empty except for an impossibly high console desk in front of him and a series of monitors against the wall to his left. Aliens sat at both. The one in front wore a black armored jumpsuit like the ones he had seen earlier. The other did not.

For an insane moment, the two sat staring at their surprise intruders. The second had to turn his body to do so. Mitch could see their open mouths and yellow teeth. Then they moved fast. The one in front jumped to his feet, yelling in harsh Kraxx, and reaching for his belt.

Whatever he was going to do didn't happen. Mitch heard the boom of Darrel's .338 magnum, and another gunshot to his left at almost the same moment. The heavy slug lifted the Kraxx off his feet and hurled him backward, toppling the tall chair and ending against the wall. The Kraxx was sliding down the wall when the big rifle spoke again. This time the slug hit the alien in the neck, almost severing the head.

Mitch turned to his left and saw a headless Kraxx corpse sprawled on the deck, thrashing and spewing reddish-purple blood. Ben stood gawking at him, the barrel of the twelve-gauge smoking.

"Good shooting," Dave told him. "But next time aim at the torso, if it's unarmored. Chances of hitting it are better."

"I-I was aiming at the torso," Ben muttered, provoking a grim chuckle from Dave.

"Well, when you tell the story, leave that part out."

Alyssa walked up to Mitch and said, "So far, so good. Two out of ten down. My team had better get going."

She gathered Christina, Karen, and Elena and walked to the door on the right side of the chamber. It opened to Elena's palm print, and they disappeared into a corridor, the door sliding shut behind them.

Mitch breathed a prayer of thanks. They had made it in.

But, he admitted to himself, we haven't made it out. We surprised them that time, and they hadn't engaged a suppressor field. We won't take them off-guard again. I'm going to have to start using spells to turn off their gear.

Darrel spoke up, the old gunnery sergeant coming to life.

"All right, people," he said. "Get ready. We've still got a mission.

"If we don't have company first," he added. "They may have heard the shots, probably did."

Mitch extended his aura into the corridor beyond the door at the rear of the chamber and felt three — no, four, alien presences coming toward them.

"We will have company," he called out. Everyone out from in front of the door. Tim, with me on the right. Dave, Ben, and Darrel on the left.

"Dave, you remember what we discussed."

Dave replied with a jerky nod.

Chapter Seventeen

THE END GAME

Alyssa

"The doors to the left lead to storage, except one that is a kitchen," Elena whispered as they walked, as rapidly as possible but staying alert, down the corridor. "There is a lounge up ahead to right. Beyond that there are a couple of rooms to hold new...guests. The more favored living quarters are beyond that. The servants' rooms, just cubbyholes, really, are against the bulkhead at the rear to this section."

Alyssa extended her aura.

"I don't feel anyone in the lounge," she said, "but I guess we can look."

Sure enough, the room was empty.

Alyssa stiffened. Something was coming. Something alien. Something Kraxx. But the corridor ahead was empty.

And then it wasn't. A door down the corridor slid open, and a Kraxx in an armored jumpsuit emerged. It was wearing a breathing filter over its lower face.

It saw them immediately, hissed, and grabbed something at its belt.

Elena and Karen had both raised their pistols, but nothing happened. The creature had engaged a suppressor field. It was still pushing buttons on its belt.

Summoning help, she thought. But Mitch's team has its friends occupied. I hope.

She felt a compulsion wave but blocked it with a spell. She didn't understand the Kraxx language, but suspected she was hearing curses.

Then Christina's bow thrummed, and an arrow shaft appeared in the Kraxx's chest. The bodkin point didn't penetrate, but the force rocked the Kraxx back a step.

The second arrow went in its right eye. The bodkin point went all the way through the skull. The Kraxx fell and did not move.

"What is it doing here?" Alyssa asked, keeping her voice low, even though the falling body had made a noise when it hit the deck, a low thud on the carpet-like floor covering.

"Probably checking on your friend," Karen whispered back. "Shouldn't we try to hide the corpse?"

"No. Leave it," Alyssa said, a bit louder this time. "We don't have time. We have to find Diana."

Diana

Diana didn't know how long she waited. There was nothing in the cell to occupy her, except her fear and anger. That was enough. She diverted herself by imagining what bad things she could do to Monica Gilbert and Jacob Van Der Taalen to keep the fear from overwhelming her. It worked for a while, but at last she sat and let the tears flow.

The door opened and she looked up, blinking her tears away. Van Der Taalen entered and, seeing her wet face, smiled. Behind him came the first Kraxx she had seen. Her eyes widened at the tall, thin creature in the black jump suit, with some sort of breathing mask hiding its face except for the yellow cat-eyes.

"The nanite injection did not work," it said in English. The voice was guttural, harsh. "It happens sometimes. You'll have to inject her again. Be sure you do a proper job of it this time, and inform me when she has been subdued."

"Yes, Exalted Group Leader," Van Der Taalen said. "Should I inform Colonel Giscard also."

"When he asks you," the thing said. "He is occupied with our other guest at the moment."

Van Der Taalen's answering smile was smug and knowing. "As you say, Exalted One."

The alien turned and left without another word. When he had gone, Van Der Taalen pulled a small tube from a pocket.

"Please do not resist," he said. "This will not be painful. Resistance will be both painful and futile. I am much stronger than you. But I do not wish to cause you pain. I would rather we be good friends." The smug smile again. "We will be in any case. Very good friends."

Diana stood, extending her arms. "No. No, please."

She let her shoulders slump. This was something she'd planned.

There was a dull thump from outside, and Van Der Taalen's head swiveled to the door. Diana made her move.

Diana had always been a fitness fanatic. It was something she had in common with Mitch. In recent months, Alyssa, who herself had been trained in unarmed combat by the SAS in Wales, had been teaching her self-defense. She wasn't nearly as good as Alyssa, but she knew some moves.

Her roundhouse kick took Van Der Taalen in the scrotum. He did what any functioning male would do when that blow has been delivered: He collapsed groaning on the deck. She saw he had an automatic pistol strapped to his waist. She snatched the gun from its holster, jacked a shell into the chamber and held it on him, using the two-handed grip Mitch had taught her.

"You – you are making it worse on yourself, you fool," Van Der Taalen muttered between groans. He finally was able to sit up.

The door opened again, and Alyssa McCormick walked in, followed by two women who carried pistols. Diana didn't know them.

One of the two women, the one with blonde-brown short hair walked over to Van Der Taalen and without saying a word shot him in the face.

"Goodbye, asshole," she said to the twitching corpse, her tone matter of fact. "You won't have any more slaves."

"Diana, are you all right?" asked Alyssa. "Did they inject you?"

"Yes, but it didn't take," Diana said. "I think...I think I blocked it. I peed it out."

"Good...Look, I don't have time for introductions right now, but these are friends. We're here to rescue you. Right now, we have to find Monica. Then we need to rejoin Mitch and get out of here."

"Mitch? Where is he?"

"I hope he's taking over the ship about now. But hang on to that gun and let's go."

"Why don't we leave Monica Gilbert? She deserves it," Diana asked as the left her cell.

Alyssa turned down the corridor and said, "We can't. We can't let the aliens have her."

"Then why not kill her?" Diana snarled.

"We may have to," Alyssa said, walking. "Do something else for me, Diana."

"What?"

"Turn on your blocking. If you can, extend it over this side of the ship. But no further."

Diana didn't understand, but did as she was asked. It was second nature by now.

Monica

Monica Gilbert was naked, on her knees, in Jean-Pierre Giscard's quarter, cupping her bare breasts in her hands and being made to offer them to him, while he was watching her with a lascivious smirk and touching himself suggestively, when it happened. She was suddenly free of compulsion. Someone was blocking it.

She didn't move right away. She wanted to plan what to do now. The last while had been the most humiliation she had ever endured. The embarrassment caused her by McCaffrey at the hearing last year was nothing beside it. Giscard was toying with her, preparing to use her. Still worse, he was manipulating the pleasure centers of her brain, turning her on, making her like, at a surface level, what she was doing, while deeper she was being reduced to insignificance, a plaything, and being made to like it.

Just before the compulsion was lifted, she had just heard herself whimper, "Oh...please. Now."

She had always prided herself in being able to manipulate people, especially men. Now she was being manipulated. She felt violated even though Giscard hadn't touched her. This was not the exalted future she had imagined.

If this was the scientific, progressive future under the Kraxx Giscard had promised her, she didn't want it. Her surface thoughts were being compelled to long for Giscard's touch, to beg for it, plead for it. Underneath, layers of consciousness down, she was beginning to question many things.

Close upon the lifting of the compulsion field, the communicator on the wall behind the couch where Giscard sat beeped. He instantly muttered, "*Merde*," and jumped to respond. She heard Kraxx words that sounded urgent, and he immediately swore again and bolted for the door, which closed behind him.

The son of a bitch was going to leave me on my knees, she thought.

The compelled lust was gone, but her heart rate remained fast. She rose to her feet, her legs trembling, and reached for her clothes. The first thing she thought to do was dress.

While she was lifting her panties, she heard a hail of gunshots from the corridor outside. She thought she heard voices, but could not be sure of that. She dressed as quickly as possible without the aid of spell craft. This, she had sought to use; but something was blocking her, too. She decided to throw on her coat. She might need it.

She went to the door, but didn't know how to open it.

Then the door opened. She found herself looking at Alyssa McCormick. Behind Alyssa were Diana McCaffrey and three women she did not know. One, with bright auburn hair, held a compound bow. The others, including Diana, all held pistols.

"Come with us," Alyssa said. "Now."

She followed them into the corridor. There, in the middle almost directly before the door to his quarters, lay Jean-Pierre Giscard, an arrow in his neck and his body riddled with bleeding bullet holes. There was no question he was dead. As she watched, two of the women leaned over and spat on his corpse. She didn't know them, but she approved of what they did. She wanted to spit on him, too.

Monica's eyes darted from Alyssa to Diana. "I-I'm sorry," she said, her voice barely above a whisper. "You don't know how sorry. I...understand, now."

Diana wasn't having her apology. "You ought to be sorry, you bitch," she said, her voice a snarl. "You sold me out to those...things. To them!" She pointed to Giscard's body.

Monica started to answer, but Alyssa cut her off.

"We don't have time for this right now. We need to go find the others. Let's move."

Diana subsided with a hate-filled glance at Monica. Monica decided to say nothing, but simply nodded.

They heard voices, human voices from the corridor ahead of them. Monica turned to see four people coming toward them, people she did not know.

One of the women, a brunette who looked Latina, said to Alyssa, "These are the servant humans."

She heard Alyssa address the newcomers, two men and two women.

"We're here to get you out," she said. "Do you understand me?"

When they nodded, Alyssa continued. "Go get warm overclothes. Get a coat for this woman." She pointed to Diana. "Come back as soon as possible."

They turned and ran back up the corridor. Monica remained silent. Diana said nothing, but continued to look daggers at her. Just as the four "servants" returned, wearing coats, and carrying one for Diana, lights in the corridor started flashing and there was a loud beeping.

One of the women with pistols said, her voice panicked. "The ship is preparing to take off. It won't be but a few minutes."

"Let's go," Alyssa commanded.

No one argued. They all ran back down the corridor toward the entrance chamber.

Mitch

"All right," Mitch called to his team, "I'm going to open the door. Get ready." His voice sounded oddly squeaky in the thin alien air, but they heard him, raising thumbs he saw from the corner of his left eye.

Thanks to his experience that morning, he was able to wrap his spell around the alien door controls, and the door slid open. Immediately, four plasma bolts, spaced close together, blasted through the doorway and hit sizzling on the opposite bulkhead. Their passing added a slight ozone smell to the already uncomfortably thin air.

Poor tactics, he thought. They're bunched together and easier targets.

Their auras were easier to locate, too; and his next spell, designed to disable the plasma guns, found them easily.

"Now, Dave!" he shouted, removing a flashbang grenade from a pouch hanging on his left side, pulling the pin, and tossing the grenade up in the air before the doorway like lobbing up a tennis ball to be served. Dave did the same, and then another spell sent the grenades flying through toward the aliens, whose strangling cat language he could hear in the corridor. Evidently, they were trying to comprehend their plasma guns not working.

The grenades exploded almost simultaneously. Their detonation was Dave's signal to move out the "troops."

"Go! Go! Go!" he yelled, the words oddly squeaky but loud.

Dave, Darrel, and Ben darted into the corridor and edged up its left side, while Lassiter and Rob did the same on the right, Mitch following because he was holding no firearm, and would depend on spellcraft, at least for now.

The four aliens he had sensed were bunched up in the center of the corridor about a third of the way between the door to the entrance chamber and another door at its far end. They were clearly dazed, stumbling and coughing. Easy targets, Mitch thought.

And so they proved to be. The aliens were wearing the jumpsuit armor, and all had head pieces of the same material, but their faces were uncovered. Dave picked a target and walked a three-round burst up his torso. Even the armor-piercing bullets didn't penetrate, but they rocked the creature back. The next burst caught the alien in the face, and he collapsed.

At the same time, Darrel had picked out a second alien, who had turned to stagger off toward the opposite door. The magnum slug caught him in the back and sent him sprawling. Darrel, with Ben close behind, caught up to him before he could regain his feet. They flipped him over and Darrel's hunting knife flashed.

Mitch saw that Tim Lassiter and Rob were having a little tougher time. Tim's AR could not fire bursts. Most of his rapidly aimed shots hit and rocked one of the aliens. Two went high and ricocheted off the bulkhead at the end of the corridor. The ricochet did not hit anyone, but made Mitch wince.

Rob hesitated before shooting, and Dave had to call, "Rob, we need help!" to him. Mitch knew that even some trained soldiers couldn't bring themselves to shoot in combat, and loosened his revolver in its holster. But then Rob shot, and shot again. Both his shots hit, and his target fell over, scrambling to regain its feet.

"Come on," Mitch yelled, and the three charged toward the two creatures. The one still on his feet, but still stumbling, fell to a short range shot from Rob's Ranch Rifle. Seconds later, Lassiter's knife, loaned to him by Jimmy Tompkins, found two Kraxx throats, and their purple blood spurted over the springy deck of the corridor.

Mitch looked up the corridor. Nothing appeared, from either the door at the end or any of the doorways to the side. Miller had told Alyssa there were only ten aliens that were dangerous. Four were down. So far, Alyssa's admonition to take no prisoners had been followed to the letter, even though he hadn't ordered it.

For these four, Mitch didn't care. These Kraxx had been shooting at them, or preparing to do so. This was war.

And so far, so good. Mitch realized they had been aided by surprise and by the Kraxx being unprepared for spell craft that could neutralize or disengage their devices. He felt sure they had been so confident of their technological superiority over anything short of self-propelled artillery, and maybe that, too, that they had never trained to repel boarders.

His throat ached and his sinuses hurt. Lassiter had told them the air was thin, but breathable. It was, but all of them appeared to be panting from their exertions, trying to gulp in air that seemed inadequate. They needed to complete the mission and get to better air, Mitch realized.

"All right people," Dave called out, not waiting for Mitch. "We're too bunched up. Same drill as before. Spread out against the walls."

Mitch followed Dave's directive and was grateful to get it. Any officer who didn't let his sergeants do their jobs was nuts. He saw Lassiter pick up something that looked like the nozzle of a garden hose with a pistol grip. It must be a plasma blaster.

"Can you turn this back on?" Lassiter asked.

"Yes, but not now," Mitch said. "I've got to concentrate on other spells."

They made their way down the corridor rapidly but cautiously. There were two doors along the walls on each side, and Mitch opened all four with spells. The two on the left held only storage or instruments; and those on the right opened to empty corridors, neither as wide as the one they were in.

They reached the end of the corridor, and huddled in two groups on either side of the door, just as they had before.

"All right," Mitch said, not trying to whisper. "The command center should be just beyond this door. We expect another four Kraxx, all armed and dangerous. We'll do the same drill as before. I open the door and then we use flashbangs. Then we go in. I'll try to disable their guns first, so wait for my command."

Right after he spoke, they felt a lumbering vibration under their feet, and then heard a beeping noise.

"What's that?" he asked Lassiter.

"They are warming up the gravity generator for take-off," Tim said. "They brought it down when they landed. The beeping is to tell the crew to strap in."

"How long will it take?"

"Not long. Less than five minutes."

We have to move now, Mitch thought. Once we're in the air, this thing can get to orbit in seconds. Then we're dead.

He breathed deeply of the unpleasant air to steady his nerves, and reached out with a spell to the control mechanism. The thing had some kind of security lock, and it took longer than expected to get it open. He lost seconds only, but every second was precious.

The stun grenades flew and detonated, and then the team was inside the control room. Mitch saw only three Kraxx. Where was the other one? One sat behind some kind of screen in front of the other two, who sat side by side in the tall chairs behind him, their hands, now shaking after the flashbang, poised over knobs and levers. All had armor, but the rear two had no head armor.

He first moved to disconnect their blasters, beginning with the two closest. He was just a second or two late with the third, but that instant gave it time to turn in his chair and fire a snap bolt. Fortunately, it was dazed from the stun grenade; and its aim was poor. Still, it managed to set fire to Ben's cap and singe his hair before crashing into the bulkhead. Ben shouted and danced on his burning cap.

Mitch heard the boom of Darrel's Winchester, and the alien's head exploded. He dropped the blaster. But the floor continued to vibrate and the beeps continued.

"Can you turn it off?" Mitch asked Lassiter. He had no confidence his spell craft could take control of the whole vessel in time.

"I think so, but we have to neutralize the ship leader and his female first," Lassiter said, referring to the other two, whose hands were now shakily flying over the control knobs and levers.

"I can handle that," Mitch growled, or rather squeaked. He wasn't sure what he could do with the entire control panel in the time remaining, but he could stop those two. He had no qualms about using a compulsion spell with the Kraxx. Compelling two at the same time was challenging, but he could do it.

Again, it seemed as though it took forever, even though he knew it had been seconds. But he saw the two lower their hands from the controls and sit glaring at him. He was compelling them to keep their hands in their laps and sit still.

Lassiter slung his AR and walked to the control panel before the two aliens, who moved their glares to him and spoke to him in Kraxx. He ignored whatever they'd said. He studied the panel for what Mitch thought an eternity, but wasn't, and flipped switches and pushed buttons. The beeping stopped.

Then he walked away from them and down a step to where the third alien's corpse was draped over its chair. Lassiter studied that panel, too; and finally pushed two buttons. The deck ceased to vibrate, and they heard only a low humming. Mitch realized the humming had been with them since they'd arrived on the ship. It must be the engine idling. Or something.

He looked over at Ben. "Are you all right?"

"Well, the top of my head is blistered, and it hurts; but I'm okay," Callahan answered.

"Mitch! Mitch!" To his joy, he heard Diana's voice from the doorway. He turned and gathered her into his arms as she ran to him, almost losing control over the two aliens.

Over Diana's shoulder, he saw Alyssa.

"'Lyssa," he said, "Can you take over for me?"

She nodded, and then Monica Gilbert stepped up beside her.

"If you take the one on the left, I'll take the one on the right," Monica said.

Mitch started to protest, but Alyssa spoke.

"It's okay, Mitch. She'll do it."

Mitch's instinct was to not trust Monica Gilbert with anything. But he did trust Alyssa. He relaxed his spell, feeling theirs rush in behind him, and feeling the venom in Monica's compulsion. It actually made him shudder. Whatever had happened earlier today, Monica definitely didn't like the aliens now.

He looked around for Lassiter.

"Tim," he said, "can you find something to bind these two. Keeping them under control is going to tire us out."

Tim nodded and walked to a door on the other side to Mitch's right. Mitch opened it for him, and he walked into another corridor. Within minutes, he returned with something like a bag. It held two other blasters and something like zip ties.

Dave and Tim went to work and soon the aliens, who had kept a gargling fusillade of hateful sounding words directed at Lassiter (and, Mitch assumed, Elena and Karen), were bound at wrists and feet.

There was another Kraxx voice from the doorway Mitch had opened for Tim. He whirled, expecting a plasma bolt. There was still one Kraxx that hadn't been accounted. But instead, four short, stocky Kraxx, all dressed in shapeless tunics, walked in, their bearings diffident.

These must be the Kraxx servants Alyssa had told him about, Mitch realized. He couldn't tell which one was the male, and which were female. The sexual differences, whatever they were, were not pronounced to his untutored eye.

"Can you tell them they will be well-treated?" he asked Lassiter, who nodded and spoke to the four in Kraxx. He was sure Tim was taxing his command of the language, but the four appeared to understand. They just stood with darting and, he thought, uncomprehending eyes.

Alyssa walked to where Ben stood. "Darling, you've been hurt." She placed a palm to his cheek and hummed a spell. Mitch saw Ben's eyes widen and a wide grin appear as his blisters were healed. Alyssa was pretty good at healing spells.

Then Alyssa turned abruptly and walked back to Mitch. She pointed at the two bound aliens, who were now silent, but who still looked daggers at the humans.

"You know what we have to do, Mitch," she said.

Mitch drew a deep, ragged, and painful breath. All of his training on the Geneva Convention, all of the hours Jim McCormick had spent pounding the ethics of magic, all of his upbringing were screaming at him not to do this. And not to permit it.

"No," he said. "No, we don't have to do it. No, we won't do it. I won't, and I won't let you. We do not kill helpless prisoners. That's what the Taliban does. If we do it ourselves, we're no better than they are. We're no better than Kraxx."

He saw Alyssa open her mouth to answer, but then two shots, almost simultaneous, shattered the thin air. Mitch whirled. He had not accounted for Elena and Karen. While he was confronting Alyssa, they had walked around him and now stood, Berettas smoking. They lowered them as he watched.

"Alyssa was right," Miller said. "These two are too dangerous — and too evil — to be allowed to live. Maybe especially among humans."

Mitch was nonplussed. He started to say something, but Dave Thomas spoke first.

"Captain," he said to Mitch, "sometimes things have to be done that officers can't order, and shouldn't see. Just be thankful you were looking the other way."

The command center was deathly silent. Then Christina spoke.

"I've got a very bad feeling," she said. "We shouldn't stay here. We have to get off the ship now."

Mitch locked eyes with Alyssa. Now he felt the premonition. Her nod told him she felt it, too.

Then the beeping began again, somehow more urgent this time.

Chapter Eighteen

OUTSIDE THE SHIP

Alyssa

The beeping grew more rapid, and Alyssa's eyes swept Lassiter, Miller, and Alvarez. Their alarm was evident in their wide eyes, open mouths, and suddenly rigid posture.

"What's going on?" Mitch demanded, directing his question to Lassiter. "Is the ship still going to take off?"

Lassiter's head shook vigorously. "No," he said. "It's a countdown to destruction. The ship is going to implode. The Ship Leader must have set the dead man's switch to start the process if the ship didn't lift off."

"It's going to blow up?" Mitch asked.

"No," Lassiter replied. "Like I said, it's going to implode, collapse in on itself."

"Can you stop it?" Mitch asked.

"No. Only the Ship Leader or his second-in-command could do that."

Mitch cast reproachful eyes on Alyssa before he looked down on the alien corpses. She felt herself stiffen. Damn it, she hadn't pulled the triggers.

"Well, they can't do anything now," Mitch said. Then his head swiveled toward Lassiter. "How long do we have?"

"Not long. Minutes."

Alyssa saw Mitch straighten. He had made a decision.

"All right, Tim, tell those Kraxx to go get warm coats and as much food and water, and as many breathing filters as they can carry, and come to the entrance chamber. Tell them to be quick about it.

"Everyone else, grab what you can, but don't load yourselves up and get to the entrance chamber. Now! Alyssa, you're with me."

"You heard the man," snapped Dave Thomas. "Get going."

Alyssa had to admire how quickly Mitch had gone from reproach to command. She walked next to him, Diana on his other side. As they walked, she asked, "What have you got in mind?"

"We're going to take a Portal out of here, the same way we came. We'll never get anywhere on foot," he said, stooping to pick up a plasma blaster from next to a dead Kraxx and shove it into a pocket.

Alyssa considered. "I agree," she said, "but Mitch, I don't think we can risk going back to the Tompkins house. We have too many people. I'm afraid we would lose some."

"We can't risk doing it in shifts," he said. "It would take too long. Could we take everyone a shorter distance?"

She thought about that as she stepped around another Kraxx body.

"I think so," she said. "What have you got in mind?"

"What about the spot at the tree line where we ran into them this morning?" he asked. "We've both been there."

Yes, she decided, that will work. Probably. She told him so.

By now they had reached the entrance chamber. Mitch and Dave Thomas immediately huddled, and then Thomas started organizing everyone in preparation to Portal out. Again, Mitch would open it, and Alyssa would keep it open. There were more people but not as far to go.

Mitch was looking back down the corridor, and back into the corridor that led to the human section of the ship.

"There's still a Kraxx we haven't accounted for," he said.

"Actually, there's not," Alyssa told him. "Christina took care of him." She explained quickly, and they resumed preparing to exit the ship.

It ought to work, she thought. I pray that it does.

They had to wait some minutes on the four Kraxx servants. While they were waiting, Alyssa walked over to Lassiter, Miller, and Alvarez. She whispered to them, and without a word they unclipped their control devices, the ones Mitch had disabled, from their belts and tossed them to the side. The devices bounced on the springy deck. Then Alyssa walked to Mitch and whispered to him.

Thankfully, she got no argument. Instead, he called out to the others, "Listen, if any of you picked up one of those mind control gadgets, toss them away. Those things are too dangerous to turn loose on Earth."

"More dangerous than these blasters?" Rob asked.

"The blasters are only firearms," Mitch said.

Without further argument, the others tossed their scavenged devices aside.

Just then, the four Kraxx appeared wearing bulky coats with bundles strapped to their backs. They lost another minute or two while the four fitted breathing filters on their faces. Alyssa placed them next to Lassiter, who stood directly in front of her, so someone could talk to them, at least a little.

The beeping continued. Alyssa imagined it was more urgent than ever. She shoved down her fear and joined her aura to Mitch's. He spoke firmly and rapidly. Mist appeared before him, and they all walked into it.

Alyssa exhaled with relief when she found herself wading through a snowdrift. Looking ahead, she saw everyone had made it. The trees were close in front of them.

"Everyone into the trees, right now," Mitch ordered, his command echoed by Dave Thomas. Within seconds, they were inside the tree line. Everyone automatically looked toward the ship, Alyssa included. They saw only a dome covered with snow.

Looking up through the branches, she saw the snow had stopped falling. There were patches of clear sky visible. She could see stars, and shuddered at the knowledge that some of them were hostile. Then she remembered what night it was, and thought of a long-ago star that brought hope. She crossed herself and prayed.

She heard Mitch's voice break the silence. "Tim," he called out, "is this far enough, or do we need to keep moving?"

"It is," Tim answered. "Remember, this will be an implosion, not an explosion. We'll be able to hear a whine when it starts. We'll need to hunker down and avert our eyes. There will be a painfully bright flash."

They all stood, staring at the alien ship and waiting. Alyssa noticed that it was getting much colder and that the breeze had picked up, causing snow to drop from the branches overhead. The air was still moist from the snowfall, and she gratefully inhaled the mountain air, after her time on the Kraxx side of the ship. She hoped the Kraxx weren't suffering too much. At least they had breathing filters, which was more than the humans had had in the ship.

She heard Diana complain about her cold feet. No wonder. The poor woman was wearing Nike running shoes. Mitch had her sit on the boulder that had sheltered them this morning, while he held her feet and muttered a warming spell. Good for him.

Minutes passed. Nothing happened. They couldn't hear the beeping from here, well outside the ship. Then they heard a low whine from the ship, rising in intensity until it became shrill and unpleasant. She thought the alien craft was vibrating. Yes, it was. Snow shook loose and fell from the craft.

Then the snow-covered dome lit yellow, which quickly became orange and then an angry red.

"Everybody down!" Mitch ordered. "Close and cover your eyes."

She assumed everyone obeyed. She certainly did.

The intense white light that followed penetrated her eyes even with her head down and her eyes closed and covered. It lasted only seconds, and then there was a loud crack like sonic boom from a fighter jet, except much louder. Then she heard a hissing sound.

"You can get up now," Mitch shouted.

Alyssa rose to her feet, her knees wet and cold. Her ears rang, and spots danced before her eyes as she blinked them into focus. Looking ahead, she saw, where the ship had been there was only a round hole that glowed red and hissed as snow cascaded in and melted.

She realized the flash of the implosion would have been seen for miles. She hoped no one had been looking directly toward it when the ship collapsed on itself. She wondered how the government would explain it. Well, she thought, that will be Hutton's problem. Or somebody's.

Overhead, the sky was now completely clear, the stars bright where the glow from the crater did not obscure them. The wind was picking up still more, and she was cold even through her heavy coat. Alyssa was suddenly so tired she wanted to go to sleep. Right now, in the snow.

Ben walked to her and hugged her. She hugged him back fiercely. He had been through the fire, too, she realized. Everyone stood, staring at the glowing pit, which now was glowing less brightly.

Then she heard the helicopter rotors behind her, passing over the ridge behind them.

Mitch

When the shrill whine from the spaceship amped up, Mitch pulled Diana behind the boulder, pushed her down into the snow, and knelt beside her, this body partially covering hers and his face, eyes tightly closed, buried in her hair. He realized, as the ship imploded, he was going to have to find something to cover her ears.

Thus, when they rose, he found that the boulder had given some protection from the flash, and their vision returned before most of the others found theirs. He stared at the glowing, hissing crater for several seconds; and then, his mind working again, he removed his hat and the stocking cap beneath it, pulling the latter over her head and ears.

"I should have done this before," he said. "I'm sorry."

She smiled up at him and squeezed his arm. "You had a lot on your mind," she whispered.

He was about to answer when he heard the helicopter rotors overhead.

Mitch walked through the trees to the edge of the clearing. He sensed someone to either side, and saw Diana, Alyssa, and Ben. Looking up, he saw two Chinook helicopters, cargo and troop carriers, pass overhead. They were flanked by a Blackhawk, a reconnaissance and gun ship.

"Dave," he called out. "Keep everyone else in the trees for now. We'll find a way to make contact."

"Aye-aye, sir," David called back. Mitch allowed a rueful smile. He wished Thomas would quit calling him an officer. That part of his life was well behind him. All he wanted to do was teach English.

But then he realized he actually had been an officer, at least of sorts, tonight, and maybe he ought to continue acting like one, for now.

They watched the choppers fly over to the glowing crater. They did not go directly over it, but hovered outside the rim. Afraid of radiation, he realized. Then he shook himself. He'd better find a way to make contact.

Reaching into his coat pocket, he pulled out the plasma blaster. He mouthed a spell that he hoped would reactivate it. Evidently the spell worked, because he felt a slight vibration in the long grip, which, designed for a bigger Kraxx hand, jutted out from his fist. Pointing the device straight up, and taking care it was not pointed at one of the helicopters, he touched a button under his thumb, hoping it was the trigger.

It must have been, because a searing bolt leapt into the air, lighting up the snow around them and cracking like thunder in the thicker atmosphere of Earth. That got the choppers' attention. They turned back toward the trees. As they did, he stole a glance at his watch. Ten-oh-five.

That brought an odd thought.

"'The spirits have done it in a single night,'" he said aloud, quoting Dickens as best as he could remember. "'Well, of course they did. They can do anything.'"

"What?" Diana said.

"Just a Christmas story, honey," he said.

Then he thought there might have been a less melo-dramatic way to make contact. He shoved the plasma blaster back into his pocket, spelling it back into sleep, and found his cell phone. He placed a call to Hutton.

Hutton answered immediately.

"Mitch?" he asked, his voice anxious.

"Yes, it's me," Mitch said. "We have a bunch of people here. Some of them are refugees. No one is hurt, but we've really been through it. We've been inside the Kraxx ship."

"Kraxx?"

"The aliens. We need some help, and we'll give you a full report. But we're all pretty tired, and we all want to get home for Christmas."

"Okay, stay where you are," Hutton said. "We'll get you."

They watched the Chinooks land in front of them, blowing show onto their faces. The Blackhawk continued to hover. A door slid open in the side of one of the choppers, and four men, each in arctic gear and carrying M-4 carbines, jumped out, followed by another man in a heavy coat and boots, who walked toward them.

As he neared, they could see his features under the parka. It was Fred Hutton.

Mitch could sense his Talent. Hutton's wasn't nearly as strong as his own or Alyssa's, but it was definitely there.

"You people don't know how worried I've been," Hutton said. "I can't wait to hear the story."

"It's good," Mitch said.

"It had better be. I moved heaven and earth to get troops here on Christmas Eve."

Mitch and Alyssa

Within minutes, everyone was inside the second Chinook, and Mitch and Alyssa were sitting on camp stools being debriefed by Hutton. The Chinook Hutton had ridden held two squads of Delta Force out of Fort Bragg.

The other contained a team of medics and a small field kitchen. The small task force had worked its way south and west around the edge of the front, refueled outside Rutherfordton, and followed the moving front north to Johnson's Mountain.

Now, Hutton had released the Blackhawk to return to base, seeing no more need for an escort gun ship. Everyone who had escaped the spaceship was inside the second Chinook. Most were sipping coffee and eating prepackaged snacks. Alyssa felt sorry for the four lower-caste Kraxx, who couldn't eat or drink, and were doubtless bewildered. But at least, she consoled herself, they were alive and together.

It didn't take long to make their initial report and come up with a plan. Hutton at first wanted Alyssa and Mitch to come to Washington immediately for a thorough debriefing, but Mitch persuaded him that it would be just as well to wait. Not everyone who wanted in on it would be available until after the holidays. In the meantime, Mitch and Alyssa would write a full report and send it by secure upload.

When they described their use of Portal spells to move a number of people, Hutton interrupted, "I thought you couldn't do that."

"We didn't know we could," Alyssa said. "It was just something we had been discussing. And we were afraid it wouldn't work."

"What if it hadn't?"

Mitch answered this time. "Well, Alyssa and I would have gone in, by ourselves or with another one or two people, and tried to snatch Diana." After a quick pause, "and Monica, if we could."

"Maybe that's what you should have done anyway," Hutton suggested. "What you did was way beyond your mission."

Alyssa was ready for that one. "Fred," she said, "if we had done that, we very well might have failed. At the very least, we probably would have lost all or most of everyone at the Tompkins house. There just wouldn't have been time to get them all out, one or two at a time."

"And then," Mitch said, "we'd have that our conscience and you wouldn't have all the new friends we brought you."

"All right," Hutton said. "I get it."

Alyssa tried to persuade Hutton to allow Lassiter, Miller, and Alvarez to spend Christmas at the Tompkins house. "After all," she said, "they haven't had a real human Christmas in years." But Hutton flatly refused. He couldn't leave the human servants and the lower-caste Kraxx here, and the three humans who had enjoyed at least slightly more privileges with the aliens were a necessary liaison.

"All right, Fred," Alyssa said, "I give. But remember these three are Americans. They have rights. You just can't keep them locked away for life."

"They were helping the aliens try to infiltrate the United States," Hutton said. "They could be tried for treason."

"Major Hutton," Mitch said, "you know that's not going to happen. There would have to be a public trial. But more to the point, they were being mind-controlled." He looked over where the three sat in earnest conversation with Rob and Katrina. "You can't keep them as slaves. That would make us no better than Kraxx."

"Hey," Hutton said, "lighten up. I know they'll have to be released into society sooner or later. But we have to thoroughly pick their brains first, and they'll need to sign strict non-disclosure agreements and take secrecy oaths with severe penalties. But I suspect they'll get government jobs they can keep for a long time. They'll be well-treated, I promise you."

"I feel sure Karen and Tim Lassiter will marry," said Alyssa. "I don't know about Elena Alvarez. She'd been damaged. They all have really. I know all of them will want to see their families. They'll all need counseling."

"They'll get it," Hutton promised.

"And Fred," Alyssa said, "you need to keep them. Give them DIA jobs. Don't let those crazy bastards at the Company have them."

Hutton laughed. "Well," he said, "I'm sure that CIA, NSA, and FBI will want, and get, access. But DIA got them first. We'll keep them. I promise."

Alyssa hoped he was telling the truth.

"What about the aliens?" Mitch asked. "They're pitiful. They can't really breathe the air here without filtration. They'll die if a habitat can't be built for them."

"That will be a priority," Hutton said. "They are valuable assets, and we have to make them as comfortable as possible. That's another reason we need our three new friends with them. Now," he continued, his tone sharper, "what about Monica Gilbert?"

Monica was seated on a stool by herself, sipping coffee and staring at the conversation going on outside. Mitch turned to look at her, and she saw him doing it. Her return stare was, well, pleading. No one was talking with her. Diana and Ben had turned their backs to her, and were talking earnestly, it appeared. But not to Monica.

Alyssa told Hutton she believed Monica had willingly helped the Kraxx's human agents abduct Diana, and why she thought so.

"Can you prove that?" Hutton asked.

She sighed. "Well, no. But I'm convinced of it."

Hutton had been jotting notes on a pad, and tapped the pad with his pen. "Look, you two. She doesn't work for me. She's Bureau. As long as she could have been mind-controlled, I have to let Springfield have her back. You say she helped at the end?"

"She did," Alyssa admitted. "I think she was really remorseful, and probably still is. I'm not sure how long that will last."

"Okay," Hutton said, "I'll do a confidential memo to my boss and ask her to send it to the DNI. But that's all I can do."

Mitch was sneaking glances at his watch. He wanted to end the meeting and get away. He wanted to go home.

"Well," Hutton said, "That's about it." He paused and smiled at them. "You two are becoming super-stars. I feel sure I can find a bonus for you. Maybe even a goose for your base contracts, too.

"But I'll tell you one thing. We're going to have to accelerate your training program on these advanced Portal spells, in light of what we know, now. We need more people who can use them."

Both Mitch and Alyssa nodded. They hadn't even discussed the subject, but they had known this was coming.

They were going to have to un-hex the grimoires and teach the spells in earnest. The Kraxx threat was real.

"All I want to do is teach English," Mitch sighed.

"And you can," Hutton promised. "You're just going to have to teach other things, too. And soon."

"I want to train military personnel," Mitch said.

Hutton didn't answer. He knew that other agencies would want to get in on it, and would.

"You know," Hutton mused aloud, "contrary to all those wild conspiracy theories, we never had a captured alien spacecraft. And now – now we still don't."

"Yeah," Mitch said, "but you have real, working – I think – alien artifacts, real aliens, and humans who lived among aliens. What do you want – salt in your beer?"

Hutton chuckled, but his smile faded. "We don't have any Kraxx officers," he said. "I would have loved to have at least one."

Mitch and Alyssa exchanged a look. Someone had to explain. Alyssa nodded at Mitch to go ahead.

"I, uh, we, were going to take prisoners, as I told you. But Miller and Alvarez wouldn't have it." He shook his head. "I shudder to think about what they must have gone through the past eight years to make them hate like that."

"I'm sure they'll tell us," Hutton said, and changed the subject. "What about those mind-control boxes? I didn't see any of those in the inventory Sergeant D'Antonio gave me."

"We were moving fast," Mitch said. "The ship was going to implode at any minute. We grabbed what was easy to grab. Sorry."

"What about the ones those three" – he nodded toward Lassiter, Miller, and Alvarez sat conversing among themselves – "were carrying?"

"They discarded those as soon as we hit the deck on the ship," said Alyssa. "You can blame me for that; I asked them to do it. I was afraid the aliens could reactivate them and track us, maybe even take back control over them. They didn't argue, so it must have been possible."

There was silence as Hutton gave them a long, shrewd look. Clearly, he didn't completely buy that story. But he didn't argue, and his expression didn't imply disapproval.

"Well, that will be in your report, I'm sure," was all he said.

"It will," Alyssa said.

"And maybe it's just as well," Hutton went on. "I don't know who can be trusted with that kind of power."

"That's easy," Mitch said. "Nobody. I don't care who it is. I mean, if you put those devices in the hands of a political party, do you think they wouldn't use it?"

Neither Hutton nor Alyssa answered. They didn't need to.

But Alyssa put in, "Don't be sure someone isn't trying it now. I doubt this is the first or only attempt at Kraxx infiltration."

Hutton fidgeted. "Did your new friends tell you that?"

"No, and they may not know. The Kraxx didn't share much with them. But you ought to ask."

"Oh, I will," Hutton said. "You can be sure of that...Anything else, for now?"

There wasn't.

They had agreed that Mitch and Alyssa would take everyone to the Tompkins mansion first. From there, Alyssa would Portal Monica back to the resort, and then meet Mitch and Diana at their home. Mitch would Portal Diana and Ben back home, collect Samantha, Megan, and Sally, take them back to the Tompkins place, and then would return home himself.

Minutes later, farewells having been said, Mitch and Alyssa gathered a group of people to travel, for the third time that day. They caught each other's eyes and exchanged smiles.

The mission had been accomplished.

They would be home for Christmas.

EPILOGUE

Rob and Samantha

Big Jim had offered them another suite, in case they didn't want to go back to the one where the shooting had occurred. Rob, who had just wolfed down two bowls of soup, and then downed a generous serving of Tompkins' single malt, had said he was too exhausted to move tonight.

Sam hated the thought of another minute in the sitting room where she had almost been taken by Sorrelli, and where, truth be told, she had so desperately wanted to be taken until the hold on her was released. But she went along with her husband, who had just gone through a harrowing experience in an alien ship, in an effort to rescue friends and keep everyone safe.

When they went upstairs, Samantha refused to look at the couch, the wall with a bullet hole, or the sheet covering the blood-stained carpet. They had gone directly to the bedroom and shut the connecting door. She was pretty tired herself. She had not gone through anything like what Rob had experienced, but she had traveled twice through a magic Portal and had spent the whole time at the McCaffrey home worried sick about her husband.

Rob suggested they shower together before bed. Samantha agreed, and they hugged and washed each other, not amorously, but affectionately, hugging frequently and talking quietly.

"What were you and Christina whispering about?" Rob asked while they were drying.

That was a question Samantha did not mind answering.

"Oh, she got a text from her boyfriend," she replied. He found a dealer in Boone that will open up in the morning to rent him a snowmobile. He figures the road will be good enough to tow it to the road up here. She expects him to be here for Christmas dinner. She's real excited. I think they're serious."

Binding her hair with a towel turban, she asked her own question. "Tell me what you and Mitch McCaffrey were whispering about."

Rob hesitated while he pulled on boxer shorts. Seeing her continued expectant stare, he finally said, "Sam, he said he needs me to meet with him and Alyssa McCormick soon. He says they need to arrange for my training. Actually, for both of us."

Samantha's brow furrowed. "Training in what?"

Everyone had been told to expect a visit from somebody in the government who would interview each of them and extract secrecy oaths, but this was different, something more. She wanted to know what it was.

Rob actually blushed. "Well, uh, he said Alyssa and he believe I can, and maybe you can, uh, do, you know..."

Samantha gasped. Her right hand flew to her mouth.

"You mean...you have paranormal abilities? You're some kind of wizard? You mean I'm a witch?"

There was fear in her voice. It made Rob miserable.

"That's what they say," he said, his tone anything but happy. "McCaffrey said we have the Talent."

Samantha pulled on a fluffy white bathrobe.

"Rob, I don't know what to say."

That actually made him laugh. "Do you think that I do?"

She moved closer and looked into his eyes. Christina had said she had the Witch Sight. After a moment, she stepped back.

"I can believe it," she said, wonder in her voice this time. "I can sense it, I think. I never could before. Rob, this trip has changed both of us."

That made Rob feel better. "Hey," he said, "he didn't say I'm a powerful magician or anything, just that I have Talent they can train, whatever that means."

"I guess we'll find out," Samantha said.

They left the bathroom for the bedroom, where Rob pulled on a plain tee-shirt and Samantha a cotton night-shirt with drawings of sleeping sheep and the lettering "Carolina girls, best in the world." Rob turned down the bed. They climbed in and turned out the light.

But they were both too wound to sleep right away. The adrenalin had not fully drained from Rob. Feeling Samantha tense beside him, he sat up and flipped on the bedside lamp.

"What is it, honey?" he whispered. "Is it me?"

He watched her tears begin to flow.

"No," she said, "it's me. I feel so dirty. And so ashamed."

"About what?" he asked. But he thought he could guess.

Samantha sat up, too. She continued to cry.

"Rob, what's happened the last few days. Not just today, but before." The dam burst inside her, and her words poured out. "That awful jealousy. And that awful lust. And it was coming from me. From me.

"Oh, I know we were being used. But you heard Mc-Caffrey outside. It worked on us because we were vulnerable. Susceptible. It was in you, too. In both of us. I can handle the idea of aliens better than I can handle this.

"Don't you feel it, too?"

The sobs took over. Rob held her and listened. Eventually, the sobs subsided. He drew back, and placing a palm beneath her chin, lifted it so he could look into her eyes.

"Sweetheart," he said, "listen to me. Yes, I feel it. But honey, you need to give yourself a break. We need to give ourselves a break. We need to forgive ourselves."

Her eyes opened wider, and she waited, knowing there was more.

"You know," he said, "we're both pretty young. I'm just barely past 30. You're three years younger. We're only four years into our jobs. We've only been married three years.

"Of course, we're going to be tempted. It will happen again. It's nuts to think our bodies, including our eyes and ears, won't respond to someone else. Our hormones don't think, don't even feel except at one level.

"But we have control of our hearts, our minds, our spirits. Drew and Elena never had those. They never would have.

"You...you have my heart. I hope I have yours."

She started sobbing again, but came to his arms. Eventually, they slept.

In the morning, they made love, and it was good. Better than good, actually.

It was going to be a lovely Christmas after all.

THE END

AFTERWORD AND ACKNOWLEDGEMENTS

All of my novels are designed to entertain. If the story in this one doesn't carry the reader along, if the reader doesn't like the likeable characters, and disapprove of the ones that are not likeable, I have missed the target. And only the readers can judge that.

But I also always have some other things in mind in writing, and *A Snowstorm of Magic* is no exception. In its case, the first thing on my mind was that if there really are people with paranormal abilities, whether one calls them "witches" or "psychics," they exist in the same universe with more mundane and accepted things like automobiles, cellular phones, airplanes, and vaccines.

And yes, if "UFOs are real," the paranormal exists in the same universe as alien visitors. So, from that standpoint, a novel that features ghosts, witches, and aliens in the same story is not so unexpected. I am not the first writer to tumble to this concept. You can find it the late Poul Anderson's works.

The mention of aliens brings me to the second thing that was on my mind in writing this novel. It appears more and more likely that we really are being visited by someone or somethings from other solar systems. As yet, we know nothing about them, or why they are here. Some folks are frightened of the prospect of alien visitors, who may be up to no good. Others seem convinced they are completely benign and are here to help us. I see no reason to assume either is true. Or false.

I suspect that, whoever they are, they take only an academic interest in humanity. I also suspect there is more than one group or race involved, and that their motivations may vary from race to race, or group to group. But in any case, it is not unreasonable to suppose that aliens from an evolutionary path that is at least somewhat similar to our own are subject to vices as well as virtues similar to our own.

The totalitarian impulse has been the bane of the past century, and has led to much tyranny, misery, and death. Socialism, whether of the "national" or "international" stripe, has always led to oppression, and frequently to poverty, for those societies that have tried it in its undiluted forms, as opposed to simply enacting policies that are socialistic.

But a look at human history shows us other roads to tyranny, too. In Rome, the populism of the Gracchi brothers led to the brutal reaction of Sulla, which in turn led to the dictatorship of Julius Caesar and the military dictatorship of his nephew, Octavian. The Roman Empire, at first, continued to follow, at least nominally, the forms of the Republic.

In the novel you hold in your hands, we really never learn how the Kraxx movement began. We don't know whether they marched, if they marched at all in the human sense, under banners that proclaimed "take back our planet," "equity," or "power to the people." We only know that they have ended in a repressive society, but one that manages to appeal to humans who yearn to control others. Whether those humans think of themselves as "left-wing" or "right-wing" hardly matters.

We know humans are not immune to the mass politics of slogans or to the temptations of trying to control the speech, or even the thoughts, of others, all in the interest of the common good. In that respect, Americans are as human as Germans, Russians, or Chinese. And that is the serious message of this Christmas fable: Beware the temptations.

I would be remiss if I did not acknowledge that I am indebted to those who have written of alien invasion or incursion through mind control before me. There is, of course, Heinlein's *The Puppet Masters*. I am especially indebted to Joan Hunter Holly's classic, *Encounter*. I do not pretend this novel is their equal, or anywhere close. In film, there is 1954's *Invaders from Mars*. The story is not equal to Heinlein's or Holly's works, but the film scared me when as a child I watched it on television in 1961; and it is still chilling.

As always, I want to thank my beta readers and copy editors, including Lisa Fuller; Danna Smith; Roseanna Rigdon; Kelly Long; Rod and Mary O'Mara; Anita Hughes; Sam B. Miller II; and my sister, Margaret Arrington Studenc, and her husband, Bill Studenc. Their input, critique, and willingness to help has been invaluable. I am especially indebted to Sam, Anita, and Bill. Again, I commend Sam's novels to you.

I am happy for readers to contact me at r_arrington@chartertn.net, and more than happy for them to post reviews of this novel online. All authors need customer reviews!

Robert L. Arrington

October, 2021

ABOUT THE AUTHOR

ROBERT L. ARRINGTON practices law with the King-sport, Tennessee firm of WILSON WORLEY, P.C. He holds A.B. and J.D. Degrees from the University of North Carolina, where he was admitted to Phi Beta Kappa. He is a member of the Tennessee Academy of Arbitrators and Mediators.

But his first love has always been writing.

He and his wife Deborah live with their three cats, Pyewacket, Miss Katie, and BJ. You can find him on Facebook and LinkedIn.

www.ingramcontent.com/pod-product-compliance
Lightning Source LLC
Chambersburg PA
CBHW022140170626
46807CB00005B/2016